THE ASSOCIATES

THE ASSOCIATES

A NOVEL

JOHN JAY OSBORN, JR.

BOSTON

Houghton Mifflin Company

1979

Library of Congress Cataloging in Publication Data

Osborn, John Jay.
  The associates.

  I. Title.
PZ4.O7694As [PS3565.S38] 813'.5'4   78-25672
ISBN 0-395-27097-9

Printed in the United States of America

To
A.M.M.K.O.

Author's Note   This is a work of fiction. The characters in this book do not have counterparts in real life. Any references to real jurisprudential scholars, including Mr. Oliver Wendell Holmes, are purely fictional. Finally, I've taken the liberty of altering the names and locations of some Wall Street landmarks.

TO ALL EMPLOYEES:

It has been brought to our attention that an associate lawyer mentioned the firm in an elevator.

All employees are reminded that the firm, and its clients, should never be discussed.

Bass and Marshall

Contents

Prologue

"There are four great principles of contract law, gentlemen, and they serve not only to assess the guilt but to measure the damage of our shattered illusions concerning the trustworthiness of our brothers. The principles? EXPECTATIONS OF THE PARTIES INVOLVED. Shall they be honored by the court? Expectations are constantly destroyed. When shall we play the good fairy and take Cinderella to the ball? The second principle: RELIANCE. We rely on other people, accept their word. We cause other people to rely upon us. And when we do, their detriment becomes our detriment, their injury our injury. We are all interconnected, gentlemen, by the great principle of reliance. The third principle, gentlemen? RESTITUTION. One man has unjustly enriched himself at the expense of another. Shall we restore the injured party to his prior position, forcing the wrongdoer to disgorge his ill-gotten spoils? The fourth principle is SPECIFIC PERFORMANCE. Here, gentlemen, we take the lives of others directly into our own hands. You have promised to perform? Then you shall perform. You have promised to walk the tightrope? You shall walk it without a net.

"If there are but four simple principles in the entire realm of contract law, then why do the courts have such difficulty in reaching decisions? Why is it necessary for me to lecture, to teach? Why do treatises and law review articles multiply and muddle the striking simplicity of the law of contracts? Why do the courts bulge with cases, why are our problems not resolved?

"The reason, gentlemen: All four principles are interconnected, each the mirror image of the other. Just when we seem to have a principle in reach, it changes like a chameleon into one of its brothers."

From the *Lawson Prize Lectures*, delivered by
PROFESSOR CHARLES W. KINGSFIELD
June 13, 1934

BASS AND MARSHALL

MAIN FLOOR OFFICE PLAN

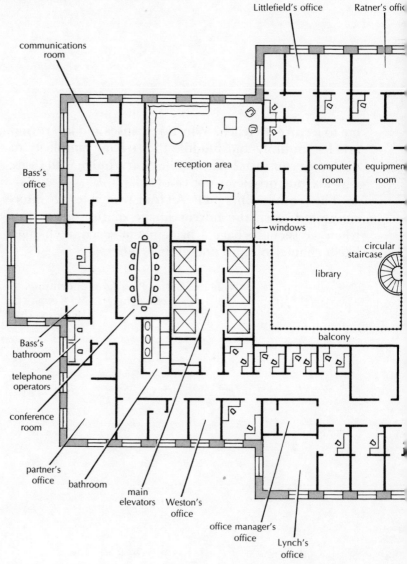

Littlefield's office

Ratner's offic

communications room

Bass's office

reception area

computer room

equipment room

windows

circular staircase

library

Bass's bathroom

telephone operators

balcony

conference room

partner's office

bathroom

main elevators

Weston's office

office manager's office

Lynch's office

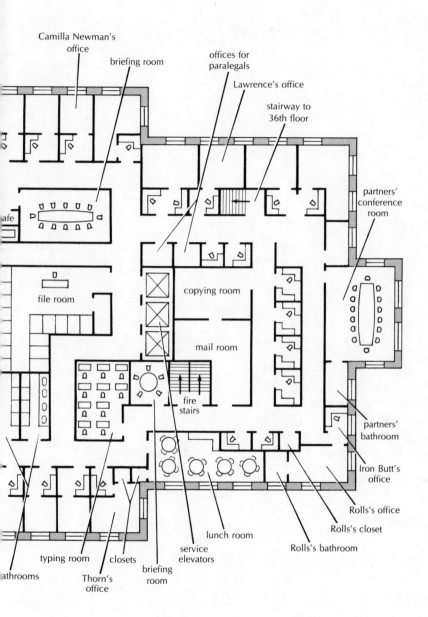

Camilla Newman's
office

briefing room

offices for
paralegals

Lawrence's office

stairway to
36th floor

partners'
conference
room

afe

file room

copying room

mail room

fire
stairs

partners'
bathroom

Iron Butt's
office

Rolls's office

Rolls's closet

Rolls's bathroom

lunch room

service
elevators

briefing
room

typing room

closets

Thorn's
office

athrooms

Part One
Expectations

1

"Mr. Weston, you didn't sign out," Debbie said.

I walked back to the receptionist's desk, and its recessed telephone, blinking lights and vase of roses.

"Mr. Weston, what's your problem? You never sign out. What if someone important wants you?"

Not likely, I thought.

"What if there's an emergency? How would I find you? What would I tell them?"

While she lectured me, I stared down through the three thin churchlike windows cut into the foyer wall. Through them, I could see into the library, the heart of the firm. At the far end of the room, a circular bronze staircase led to bookcases that ran along the upper wall. Soft light descended from hidden holes in the ceiling.

There were maybe twenty young associate lawyers spread around the big library, working through lunch. Some of them sat at the teak tables, scribbling citations on long yellow legal pads. Others snatched reporters from the bookcases, searching for the perfect case, the perfect holding. In a dark corner, a solitary associate in a black suit working with the tax digests pulled at his hair as if a legal problem had unhinged him.

Then they froze. For an instant, the associate lawyers looked like manikins — the view from the windows a diorama in the Museum of Natural History. A frozen picture called "law firm — nineteen hundred and seventy-seven."

"Mr. Weston."

"Hold it."

Cosmo Bass came into my field of vision. The associates in the library had seen him first, felt his presence. Bass was over eighty, but easily outdistancing the two senior associates who trailed behind him. He was not wearing the required suit jacket, but then he made the rules and had special ones for himself. His face was gray granite, his red suspenders surged with his chest — he could wear suspenders, they were like the lines of climbers on a white mountain, looked nailed to his snowy shirt with pitons. His hair was silvery and I thought: My God, he doesn't even wear glasses and look at him move.

One of the senior associates placed a volume of Federal cases on the table in front of him. Then both of the associates stepped back. Bass snapped through the pages of the book, looking for a case. The associates stared at each other.

Christ, I thought, there are two associates and one of them is wrong. There's been an argument about the meaning of a case, and Cosmo Bass will certainly murder someone.

Bass slammed the book shut. He strutted out of the library, the associates racing to keep up with him.

"Mr. Weston," Debbie said, "will you promise to always sign out for lunch?"

"What?"

"Mr. Weston," she pleaded, "will you reform?"

*   *   *

I got a hero with turkey and cheese at the deli behind the Manhattan Trust Building. Manhattan is number

One Wall Street, United States Warranty is number Two. I figured the deli was one and an eighth but they hadn't given it a street number. I thought they ought to call it Deli Plaza — every new, second-rate office building got called a plaza something. I yelled my order in over the suited shoulders of my colleagues at the bar, screamed it out in the sparse Italian my college roommate Valenti had taught me. Italian in the deli put me ahead of senior associates, bankers, trust officers. It put me ahead of partners too, but they wouldn't be here, just their secretaries, whose bare arms, seemingly unconnected to any body, stuck up through the crowd. Bare arms, the backs of heads and suited shoulders. My hero passed from hand to hand to me, my money bobbed back in the other direction.

*   *   *

Having eaten my sandwich and drunk two cups of coffee, I pushed aside some of my books to do an afternoon's work. I had hundreds of books piled around, all part of a project I called *In re Newman.* I'd even taken out Dodd's *Treatise on Burial Codes,* Franklin's *Essays on Timber Regulations.* Camilla Newman had an office near the library, and picking up books gave me an excuse to visit her. But I'd have to clear them out soon, or the mean law firm librarian would come searching for his books. How would I explain *In re Newman?* As a holding action, I piled the books in a neat column behind the door of my office. Then I spread out the correspondence file on my clean desk top.

*   *   *

I was searching for an old letter relating to a forgotten patent application. A job like this should have been given to a paralegal to cut costs, but the client wanted a lawyer to do the job and was willing to pay the extra. I didn't mind. The work was fun, and I was wasting hours on it. I'd combed all the letters written in the fifties, and had moved back into the forties.

The letters told a history of this Wall Street firm. Today the name Cosmo Bass tottered on top of a list of forty partners. But in the fifties there were only twenty partners below him on the letterhead, in the thirties only ten. I was watching a slow-motion backward film of how the firm got built. Slowly the names under Cosmo dropped away, as if the bricks, the structure of the firm, were being dismantled. Now it was a huge skyscraper. Then it had been a room. I was reaching toward the beginning, toward plain white stationery, just one name: Bass, Esquire.

I found no letter about the patent. I got to the end of the file, two names: Cosmo Bass, Wyatt Marshall. The first letter, the first contact with the client: 1920. At the bottom, in bold strong script, the signature: Cosmo Bass. The way he wrote it, the name was like the stamp on a coin.

*   *   *

At eight o'clock that night, Camilla Newman came into my office to say good night. She looked serious, small, blond and snappy. Her coat was in her lap. The tan purse from Bottega Veneta on the floor beside her attaché case.

"What's the rule, the holding, laid down by Judge Gwerkin in the *Tallox Imperial Salt* case?" she asked.

Lawyers always talk about the law. It's as if the law is a script with too many lines, requiring constant rehearsal.

"Didn't Gwerkin hold that insider trading in publicly held stock is prohibited?" I said.

"That holding is too broad, way too broad," Camilla

Newman said. "It's also probably incorrect. What's the specific rule Judge Gwerkin developed?"

Imperial Salt was an important case that had gone up to the Supreme Court. It had something to do with insider trading. I'd studied it briefly for my exam in corporate law at Harvard.

"Failure to disclose insider trading in stocks listed on the New York Stock Exchange is a violation of rule ten-b five? And you're an insider if you own more than ten percent of a company's stock?"

I stared at Camilla Newman's eyes. They looked fine, intelligent.

"Is rule ten-b five part of the securities act of 'thirty-three or 'thirty-four?"

"I forget," I said. *Her eyes.*

"'Thirty-four."

"If you know, why ask?"

"A background check on your general knowledge of securities regulation."

Camilla Newman got up. She started for the door, then turned back. "I think I will go out with you Friday night," she said. She gave me a final curt Miss Newman look. Her eyes blew me away.

2

At nine the next morning, I was in the crowd, moving down Broadway. Now and then a sprinter took off from the pack, swinging his attaché case for balance, coat trailing behind him, diving for an open space in the crowd, clearly out of control, brain disease taking over. What makes them sprint to work, tie back over their shoulders, hair blown back in the wind, bug-eyed, kicking, shoving? And some of them are old men, clawing like boys, pushing with their cases. Maybe it's the clean air of fall. Sometimes they push off the sidewalk into the street itself, spring between the cars, dodging hood emblems. The cab drivers honk at them, threaten them with the jerking forward movement of the cab's hard front end. Sometimes a cab will push one along, give him a slight pat in the rear. I keep wondering when one of them will get pinioned between two cars, squeezed, put in the Iron Maiden, the way they did in the Inquisition.

I took my time. I was not involved in some million-dollar deal. I did not figure Cosmo Bass would fire me if I was five minutes late. It was a nice crisp day and the subway had run all right. I moved with the flow around the corner, and down into Wall Street, the street sloping gently, rolling toward my tower.

Inside it, green and red lights flashed around the

walls of the cavern announcing the arrival and departure of the cages. Thick perfume blended with cigarette smoke, I was pushed into the right elevator by a pigskin attaché case that fit nicely into my rib cage. We went up staring at the tiny cracks between heads.

*   *   *

Instead of cutting through the library, I took the long dangerous way to my office, following the law firm's twisting white corridors around the perimeter of the thirty-seventh floor. The route took me past Camilla Newman's office and as usual she was already at work, her head down over her books, pushing at the pages of a case reporter with her small fingers. Her blue eyes, inches from the page, snapped from word to word. Her curly blond hair, held back by combs, swung in the airstream of the moving pages. She pressed in close to her work — hair, hands, eyes all moving, ashes from her cigarette falling into the crevices of the big legal volume.

*   *   *

Why was the long way dangerous? It increased the chance of meeting a partner in the hall and getting grabbed for an assignment. When there was a lot of work, the partners competed to snatch associates. They seemed to jump from doors, from corners, wild-eyed, heads coiled back, white teeth locked.

I turned a corner: Mr. Lynch blocked off the narrow passage. His arms were spread, his suit coat hanging from them like a wide cape, darkening the tunnel. He slid toward me, mouth moving, no words coming out. He didn't need them. I could read the message in his jiggling eyes. Without taking off my topcoat, I followed him into his big corner office.

Delivery boys were stacking it with cardboard boxes.

Lynch dodged between them and fell into the chair behind his desk.

"This is an important case," Lynch snapped.

"There are a lot of boxes here," I said. "Do they hold evidence?"

"You realize this is important?"

"Yes," I said. I could not believe the number of cardboard boxes. I didn't know if it was a big case or not. But if all the boxes held paper, it was certainly going to be a long one.

"This is the big one," Lynch said again, looking tall, thin and frayed, and his left eye twitched like a bug hanging from the side of his nose. Then his eye stopped moving, rounded out, and he stared at me like a big soft-eyed child.

"I'll need help on this one," he said. "Are you going to give it to me?"

Lynch didn't seem like a partner anymore, just a big scared self-centered kid. I bought it all. I believed I had a moral obligation to help this poor man who made two hundred thousand dollars a year and was going to work me through the night.

"Jesus," Lynch moaned. "This one is too big."

3

From Lynch's corner office, I saw the towers of the World Trade Center, and between them, some of the river. His office furniture was old, big chairs covered with dark leather, the desk so thick and mottled it looked like marble. Photographs and paintings lined the walls, all of them dark and closely packed together. Most of the stuff had belonged to Lynch's famous father and grandfather, and there were paintings of each of them, in their black judicial robes, gavels in hand, red books as a background setting off the dark figures. The office was a kind of legal museum, taking you back in time through a family of lawyers who had made it very big in the New York bar.

Under the portraits, at the desk, was their frayed fifty-year-old namesake. Descendant of a United States Supreme Court Justice. Keeper of the museum. He had the physical stuff all right, but he looked so jittery I wondered if the mental stuff was in place as well.

"Do you understand the case?" he said.

"I think so." It seemed straightforward. Even ordinary. "This California company bought some of its own stock at prices higher than the market price. The officers in the company bought some of the stock too. Then the company began to make a lot of money. The stock's price went way up."

"The price went way up," Lynch said. He began raising his hand toward the ceiling. "Doubled, tripled." He held his hand above his head and jiggled it.

"So the former shareholders want their stock back," I said. "They claim the officers didn't tell them how well the company was going to do. They want damages. There are law suits all over the country."

"They want damages," Lynch muttered. "Oh, they want them, but they won't get a penny." He looked up at the dark portrait of his grandfather.

"Right," I said. "Now the company's chief counsel is a Los Angeles firm. It's farming out the cases to law firms all around the country. We've got one."

"Got one? Just one?" Lynch boomed, coming around the side of the desk and leaning over me. "This is *the* big one. The Government's suit against the officers for securities-law violations. The Stock Exchange is in New York. So are some of the Government's best attorneys. We must get the case away from New York. Do you understand?"

"It's a venue question," I said. "We move to transfer the case to California under the Federal Rules of Criminal Procedure."

Lynch muttered and shook his head.

"That's what they want you to think," he hissed. "Venue lays where any part of a crime has been committed. It lays where the crime was hatched, facilitated. In a securities fraud case, it lays wherever the Government wants it to lay, because the stock is traded on the New York Stock Exchange by people who live all over the country. It's not a venue case. They could have brought the case anywhere. It's a moral question. Only a bastard would bring a case three thousand miles away from the defendant's home."

Lynch was known as one of the more eccentric

partners at the firm, and this was the first time I was really seeing him in action. When he said "bastard" there was a strange popping around his eyes — they flared, snapped, and the wrinkles around them expanded and flattened out. Sure, it was an ordinary textbook case, but Lynch's eyes scared me. He glanced suspiciously at the portrait of his grandfather. Were they communing? Lynch was up to something or crazy. Either way, I was sure it wasn't going to do me any good.

Suddenly, he pulled the top off one of the big cardboard boxes. He reached down and grabbed a fistful of paper in both hands.

"See this stuff," he boomed. "See it."

I nodded.

"These are papers prepared by chief counsel, that California law firm. See it?"

I nodded again. He was rattling the paper in the air.

"It's all bad," he said. "We can't use any of it in our brief."

Lynch let the papers flutter to the floor. He went to his desk and grabbed a Federal Reporter, handed the book to me.

"There's a case here. The *Swanson* case. Research it. Write it up. Shepherdize it. Run it down. Work all night."

*   *   *

Working through the night, I became tuned in to the internal law firm sounds: the elevators rattling at four A.M., the night typists plinking slowly away, probably drunk, the wooshing constant sound of the air conditioning system, the slow sighing of the high building as it swayed gently in the wind, rivets creaking. My ears were pitched to the soft padding sound of other nighttime ghost associates bouncing off the walls as they steered the twisting law firm corridors, and to the thudding, rolling wave sound of the copying machines as drafts of registration statements were run off.

Then the sun came up. It seemed to creep around the edges of my office window, an oozing foreign substance, coming at my back. You've seen *The Blob*? The teen-agers are making out in a car while the Blob sneaks up on them? The sun seemed to be doing that to me. I was getting paranoid, and what was happening inside the firm was becoming more important than what hap-pened outside.

At nine-thirty I took all my notes about the *Swanson* case to Lynch's office. My research proved conclusively that *Swanson* was completely irrelevant, and seemed to have been written by a moron judge. No other court had ever followed its holding. I had prepared a little speech to go along with my presentation of this fact. A small talk questioning why we weren't going to use any of the material prepared by the California firm.

"He does not wish to be disturbed," Lynch's secretary, Mrs. Guardo, said.

"I've got some news for him."

"He knows that, Mr. Weston. He said specifically that he did not wish to be disturbed by *any* associates. He is working on a new idea for the case you are assisting him with."

"I've been up all night doing this stuff for him," I said.

Maybe I looked fiendish. I was certainly angry. Guardo watched me carefully as I made a retreat around the bend in the corridor. Too tired and angry to think clearly, I sneaked out of the firm and retreated all the way back to my apartment.

*   *   *

When I got to my apartment, I did not have the energy to take off my suit. I lay on the bed, staring at a plain white ceiling. Thank God I was in a normal bed that did not have a ceiling mirror. I did not need to be reminded that I looked like a laid-out, all-dressed-up-for-burial, dead-from-exhaustion, lonely, coffinized stiff.

I shut my eyes. All over New York there are organizations set up to prey on newly arrived, newly monied, lonely associate lawyers. Take the bed for example. They try to sell you the environmental, sexual bed, the one with mirrors in the canopy and stereo speakers and hot water in the mattress. The environmental bed makes the implicit promise that someone will come to help you fill it. It all falls together, the ads for the bed and the secret box numbers in the personal columns of the Village newspapers. What you see when you finally look up at your new mirror is your own dead loneliness.

Why feel sorry for yourself, I thought. Why not, I answered, reading the answer in the cracks of my white ceiling. I was susceptible during transitions like the one from law school to law firm. Unsettled, unstable, easy prey. I wanted to be liked, needed rewards. I'd even have taken a grade. That was how low I felt. A full night's work. No kind words. Nobody to even look at it.

I could not get my mind to turn off. As I say, I was susceptible. I wanted Scotch to take me off to sleep. I would have taken Valium. My mind just kept driving. I hoped it would take a wrong turn and smash itself against a concrete divider. I was going someplace fast, weaving toward it.

Finally my mind swung through a turn and hit the brakes. My body rolled with the lurching stop. I grabbed the pillow, swung it under me. I was hopeless: as I warmed the pillow, my mind parked the two of us quietly on a beach. Her hair, her arms, her breasts. Warm. Camilla Newman. Friday night.

4

At Camilla Newman's apartment house, a doorman stood between a double set of glass doors. He wore a brown suit with square black buttons. I asked him for apartment 38F. He let me go through without calling up.

There were three elevators and no people on the marble floor. I got in the middle elevator and turned to face the doors. I was in an ordinary box. Miss Newman was upstairs in another one. The doorman was in his. We were all tidily packaged. My box flew up thirty-eight floors and opened to face nine doors. There were just doors next to each other, no wall between them. I rang the bell of 38F.

I wondered how they got all the doors so close together. The design innovation seemed to be the corridor. Half of Miss Newman's floor space was tunnel. It twisted along the other side of the walls of rooms in larger apartments, and emptied into a square one-room studio like my own. I walked across it to the window.

"How much do you pay for this?"

"Four-fifty."

"They give you a hell of an entrance," I said.

She said, "I've got to change," and went into the bathroom.

There was a divider separating the stove and sink

from the living area. The icebox was part of the divider. I leaned over it and looked at pots and pans. I sat on the couch. The sheets of the fold-out sofa bed were squeezing up between the cushion cracks. There were a table and four chairs in the corner near the windows. From the windows, I saw the East River. In the night, the river had an evil blackness that refused to reflect the thousand lighted windows lining it.

I sort of sniffed around the room, looking for secrets. There was a fine record player, and four huge speakers in the corners. A direct drive turntable on top of a hundred-watt receiver. If I turned that up it would evaporate the building. I knocked on the bathroom door.

"Camilla, could I play a record?" I yelled over the shower sound.

"Sure," she answered. I went to the record player. Underneath it, like slabs of slate, the records lay on top of a multicolored nest of record jackets. I sat down on the white rug and put on "Layla," my favorite record in the world. It brought back memories of college.

I went into the kitchen and found the sink full. There were sure to be submerged wrecks in the gray water. I got a glass between the surface and the chrome spigot. I put the three remaining ice cubes in the glass and covered the mess with Scotch, which I drank while looking down into the drive.

There were the usual wrecks. The building swayed in the night wind. What use was this expensive cube? It was really just a dressing room and a window. The architectural thesis that related these two features had to be defenestration. I was not yet ready to jump, so I turned back to the cube.

All and all it was a mess, the opposite of her office. Dirty clothes leaked out of a closet. A bra lay on the

record pile. The place reminded me of a wren's nest.
Everything thrown in and patted down.

She came out of the bathroom wearing a dark blue
dress. Her blond hair shone. The hell with the room.
She looked put together and perfect even if it wasn't.
We got out fast.

*   *   *

I was lying on my back, thinking about the economics
of associate lawyers in large New York firms. You make
about thirty thousand a year, but in the end all you can
afford is a one-room apartment on the East Side. You
live there as if it was another office. You're moving,
going and it's too late to worry about the decor when
you get home. You've got the view. So you turn off the
lights and look at it. Forget the room. Turn off the
lights, stumble over the records into bed. That was
where I was now. With Camilla Newman, who had
asked me up for a last drink.

Do the associate lawyers in Wall Street law firms sleep
with each other? The answer seems to be that they try
to.

*   *   *

We were half-clothed in her nest of a room. Square
chips of light were suspended outside, the windows of
Midtown like square insects flashing up in the night, a
swarm from the black, breeding river.

My pants were gone but my damn tie was still knotted
and caught on some part of the metal fold-out bed. Her
pantyhose were gone, her underpants a knotted ball
between my legs, but a few buttons kept her dress
hunched around her waist. Her bra had somehow
reclipped around my arm.

My hands were folded over my stomach. It had

definitely not worked. I felt dumb. It is probably never going to work. I wanted to say something, but what could I say? Tell a joke? A joke would probably get me punched out.

This had been doomsday dumb making love, good people screwing when they didn't want to, realizing it too late, but not stopping because somehow they felt committed. Committed to what, I wondered. We had fought with the clothes, rubbed each other, smiled at each other, kissed, but it was not right. So we tried harder. It still was not right. So of course we made love. That would make it work. We finally and definitely crashed, ended on our backs, still half-dressed, arms folded, not touching or talking, thinking there is a part to all of this that we will never understand. Hoping that we did not hurt each other. That we would still be friends. Bullshit like that.

"Fuck these goddamned clothes," Camilla Newman said.

"Look," I said, "Camilla."

"Fuck you," she added.

Miss Newman sprang violently out of bed. She snapped on the lights and pulled off what was left of her clothes. She looked a lot more reasonable standing nude than I did when she pulled the sheets off. She looked down at my prick. She looked at my socks. She bent down and ripped her bra off my arm, threw it in the corner. The underpants went after it. I sat up for respectability.

"Camilla," I said, "listen."

"Don't talk about it."

"Baby."

"Don't say it." She pointed at me. It was not her usual emphasize a statement point. It was a loaded finger, a threat aimed at my head. "Don't call me baby. Get up."

"Fine," I said. I got up. "O.K." I looked around for my pants, found them, began to put them on.

"Don't," she told me.

"Right," I said. "Just socks and tie?"

"Take them off."

She was moving fast around the room now, straightening it out. My clothes got thrown on top of hers in the corner. The bed got made. A record was turned on. Pillows were arranged. We leaned back against them. She picked up the alarm clock.

"It's three A.M.," she said, "is eight all right with you?"

"Nine?"

"Eight-thirty." That was where she set it. She snuggled down in the bed, turned away from me. I sat for about fifteen minutes, leaning against the sofa back.

Then she pulled me down under the covers.

"Listen," she whispered, "listen. Go to sleep."

"You can't tell someone to sleep."

"Sleep," she said.

"Sure," I said, "sleep. Camilla Newman says sleep."

I couldn't sleep. I lay there pretending.

"Listen," she whispered. "Actually." She paused. "Actually." She stopped.

"Actually?" I said.

"Actually," she added, "I like you."

We turned on the lamp beside the bed, slid up some, and leaned against the back of the sofa bed. Camilla Newman tried to smoke. She wasn't good at it. The cigarette swayed around, nearly singeing my shoulder.

"What do you make of this place?" she said.

"What place?"

"The law firm. Is the story making partner, driving toward that goal? Is the story really an Auchincloss thing, old-line, the history of the firm, power, control? Is it the lawyer as hired gun, working for anyone, big money? Is it Cosmo Bass and how he got to be a great lawyer and the head of the damn place?"

"I don't know what the story is," I said. The story of this Wall Street law firm was a lot of things, many of them insane. It was the girl who served coffee at the denlike cubbyhole shop on Broadway, near Wall—the girl with six fingers.

"Come on," Camilla Newman said, "what do you think of when you think about the firm?"

"Right now I'm thinking of the commuting," I said. "I'm thinking about the hunchback who rides his little trike up and down the subway cars, playing tape-recorded music from that box he's got strapped to his shoulders. Do you give him money?"

"No. I don't give him money." Camilla Newman put out her half-smoked cigarette, turned off the light and snuggled dangerously close to me. "Sam, you really think about the hunchback on the subway when I ask you about the firm?"

"It's what I thought about," I said. "And the preachers on the corners. Standing there yelling and trying to pass out God-Save-You pamphlets, and all the black-coated lawyers and business guys sweeping by. And the preachers yelling that you're going to hell, it doesn't matter how high your building is, even if you're on the top of the World Trade Center, you're going to hell."

"That's what you really think about?"

"I don't know what the story is at the firm," I said, sliding down next to her, turning off the light. "I just get impressions."

I reached out for her. She let my arm go around her, but that was all.

"The story," she said. "The firm. What does this place do to people? Like if they fall in love? How does it warp them? Why can't they get it together here?"

"So you'd like to fall in love with someone at the firm," I said.

Camilla Newman rolled away from me.

"Your holding is too broad," she said. "And probably incorrect. Now, Sam, sleep."

5

Camilla Newman got up before I did. I was dimly aware of her moving around the room. Finally, I sat up in bed, pulling the sheet up around me. She had dressed. She looked fine, businesslike but pretty. She handed me a cup of coffee.

"You look pert," I said.

"Pert?"

"Bright-eyed. Nice."

She said thank you. She stood out in the messy room like a picture in a magazine. I was part of the mess: unshaved, sheet coiled around my chest, eyes sticky. So we weren't going to spend that nice part of the morning together, when you wake up slowly, realizing there is someone next to you, rub each other awake. It was good coffee. A picture in a magazine is going to tell you something. Look at me, it says. Look at yourself. See the difference? Now, won't you do what I say?

"I don't think we should sleep together anymore," she said.

"Have we ever?"

"I don't think we should try."

"Come here," I said. She shook her head. "We're not going to sleep together," I repeated. "What are we going to do?"

"Hug."

"Great," I said. "Hug."

"Maybe hold hands," she said. "Go out to dinner."

"Christ," I said. I had a sick feeling in my stomach.

"Why bother to hug?" I added.

"We're friends."

I was getting sicker. Someone had thrown me off a ledge. I had vertigo up here on the thirty-eighth floor. I definitely had caught a disease. It would take me months to shake it, maybe years.

"Come on," she said. "We're friends."

"Sure," I said. "Fine."

"Hey," she said. She took my hand, then let it go to drink her coffee.

"It's a great idea," I said. "Hugging. Fine."

"Your choice. Hugging, no hugging. Friends. Whatever you say."

I wanted to say I loved her. I put my coffee cup down. I reached out and took hers away from her. I put it down too. I grabbed her around the waist, pulled her next to me on the bed. I began to hug the hell out of her. It was a hugging rape. The victim was limp, and had a disgusted look on her face. The hard fact was that she could control me by a look. She didn't have to fight me off.

"You're through?"

"Yes," I said.

"I'm glad."

"I'm glad you're glad."

"You're not going to pull off my clothes?"

"No," I said.

"Rip the buttons down the front? Pull up the bra? Pull down the pants?"

"No."

"Bang it in?"

"No."

"It's safe to get up?"

"Yes."

She got up, went around the partition and began to make more coffee. I gathered up my clothes and went into the bathroom. I used the least scented stuff of hers I could find, but I still smelled like a fruit when I came out dressed and showered.

"You look great," she said. "You blow-dried your hair."

She had her attaché case in hand. It was one of those nice ones they make for women: brown leather, with soft square handles. I looked around the room. I loved it all. I loved the fact it was a mess. I felt like taking a pillow case with me, anything for a souvenir, something to bury my head in when I got home. There was only one way to get out of here, knowing she'd probably never let me back in. I'd have to run through the door, the way you run into water when it's cold. I started for the door. She held it open. It was cold and lonely out in the hall.

"Wait a minute," she said. "You forgot something."

I felt for my tie. It was on. She put down the attaché case, put her arms around me, and gave me a nice long hug. It felt good, but why couldn't, why didn't, she love me?

"Hugging's good for you, Sam," she said. "It drives away the dangers of the work. It's good for whatever ails you. A patent remedy."

6

I became deeply involved in Lynch's litigation matter. Because I was helping him on his "big one," he arranged to get me pulled off my other assignments. I stopped doing the normal steady gray work of the firm, the preparation of corporate charters, the drafting of corporate minutes, the small moneymaking questions that were answered by letters from "outside counsel." I was no longer called by the white-shirted, balding competent partners who had pictures of their babies and wives on their walls, who wanted a small question answered, a case rechecked, a statute looked up and explained.

Then Lynch became convinced I had not found him enough cases. He was not interested in ideas, just cases, he explained. The ideas would come later. Since I was not finding him enough cases, he brought in another associate, Craig Littlefield.

I was glad. Littlefield had the quality of making me not feel lonely. He was small, just my age, with blond hair and an oval face. He dressed precisely and handled his relationships with the same careful regard he gave his clothing. That is to say he was considerate and kind, and helped to balance off Lynch.

I began reading hundreds of cases and giving copies of them to Lynch. Littlefield was doing the same thing.

Meanwhile, Lynch stuck to his office, thinking about the coming moment when our brief would have to be submitted.

Sometimes Lynch would read the Xerox copy of a case I'd given him and call me into his office. It would be dark and musty and he would say:

"This case you've given me talks about another case, one called *Swatz versus Johnson.* You didn't give me the *Swatz* case. Why?"

"It isn't relevant to our case."

"Let's see, shall we," he'd murmur.

I would not remember the *Swatz* case, just that I'd read it, and that it was not on point. Littlefield would watch me race to get the case from the library and bring it to Lynch. Lynch would read it quickly and say:

"All right. That's all right. It doesn't have anything much to do with our case, but copy it for me anyway and put the copy in a box."

Maybe he thought Littlefield and I were stupid and not reading the cases correctly. Maybe someday he'd discover that we'd missed something. He was going to have to submit a brief to the court, and maybe our opponent's brief would cite a case we had missed. I did not see how that was possible, but Lynch thought it was. The other side were bastards and might cite anything.

*   *   *

I'd been working for Lynch for so long I was immune to all this intense activity that seemed to go nowhere, but Littlefield was new to Lynch's pattern of irrationality. We'd been up for two days straight. It was the night before our brief was supposed to be filed with the court. Littlefield cracked.

I went to get some cases for Lynch and found Littlefield bouncing around the library like a wasp looking for a window. I was puzzled by his gymnastic approach to legal work: rather than walking calmly down the circular bronze stairway, he jumped the last six steps, vaulting the rail, dropping three books. Then he buzzed off into the maze of mahogany bookcases at the far end of the big room. I caught him in an aisle behind the black volumes of the C.C.H. tax manuals.

"What the hell are you doing?" I said.

"Working, of course."

He looked particularly elegant then and said 'working' the way a small child building a sand castle might say it.

"That kind of work won't make any sense in the morning, Littlefield." I pushed him against the bookcases. "Listen to me. It shows."

He stared at me so innocently, I began to feel guilty about holding him by his tie.

"Littlefield," I said. "Christ, are you all right?"

"I miscalculated," he said. "The lights have comet tails. Yes. A definite miscalculation. Sorry."

I'd been taking coffee to stay awake. Littlefield had taken speed.

"Chills," he said. "I need sleep. Perhaps right here. In this convenient corner, this thickly carpeted recess lined with such pleasant reading material."

He began to slide down the bookcase. I reached around his waist to hold him up.

"Hold on, Littlefield," I said.

But Littlefield was not holding on.

"I've got to get you out of here," I said. "What if Lynch comes searching for us?"

"You're a friend," he answered. "Yes. I definitely took too much. The reaction backfires. I must sleep. Just prop me up. It passes in time."

"I hope."

"It passes. You get a slight reprieve. Then you drop completely. How did it happen? This was an effective dose in law school."

"What do you mean — drop?"

But Littlefield didn't answer. He was staring walleyed around the library.

"Have you noticed how elegant this room really is?" he murmured. "The effect of the teak paneling, those perfect green lamps resting like turtles on the thick oak tables. Yes, I believe the rule that we must wear our suit coats in the library is quite correct from an interior decorating standpoint. Yes, and by the way is it true you are having an affair with Camilla Newman?"

"Littlefield," I said. "For Christ sake. Let's go."

"Excuse me. I am beginning to sway."

I was now the only thing between Littlefield and the carpet. He swayed over my arm, heavier than I thought. I didn't know how long I could hold him.

Then Lynch strode in — wild-eyed, frayed, steaming. I pushed Littlefield into the books. How could I present Lynch with a Littlefield on speed?

Lynch walked over to the corporate-law section. He peered down the rows of books. Then spun around. You could see how his mind was working. He was systematically searching the places we ought to be working. Was anything relevant in the tax section? I thought not. Maybe there was hope.

"You asshole, Littlefield," I hissed. "Lynch did come."

As if I'd stuck him with a cattle prod, Littlefield twitched wildly, and fell out of my arms onto the carpet. He was flat, spread-eagled on the rug. I must admit he looked better than I would have. The beautiful suits he wore seemed immune to wrinkles in any position. I'd lost track of Lynch.

"Stay put," I whispered redundantly to Littlefield, crept to the end of the bookcase, and was suddenly face to face with Lynch, his square, tufted head inching around the corner, his tie flapping.

"There you are for God's sake," he said. "And I hope working."

Lynch swung the rest of his body into the aisle. I could not block off Littlefield. Wildly, I thought of throwing my jacket over him. I turned, following Lynch's stare.

Littlefield had somehow gotten up on his hands and knees. He must have had immense reserves of strength. He pulled a book off the lowest shelf and stood up, wavered some, but the good-looking suit hid most of it.

"Tax," Lynch snapped. "What the hell are you doing in Tax?"

"Looking for cases, sir," Littlefield said.

"On your hands and knees?"

"The lower shelves."

"Tax cases?" Lynch snapped. "What's the matter with you?"

"We wanted to be thorough," I said, making my first moral decision as a Wall Street lawyer, putting myself definitively on Littlefield's side and probably getting myself fired.

"Tax cases," Lynch said to himself. "Tax. Yes. Perhaps. Certainly the bastards on the other side will not think of finding a relevant citation among the tax materials."

"That's what we thought," Littlefield said, his voice slurred. "Fool the bastards." I jabbed my elbow into his small stomach to shut him up.

"All right," Lynch snapped. "Get anything relevant you can but don't bother me until I call. I've got a new idea."

Then he spun on his heels and strutted out of the library, listing from side to side.

*   *   *

I got Littlefield back to his office, put him in his chair. His eyeballs rolled, and then he seemed to recover. He leaned forward and folded his arms on his desk top.

"Have you seen anything of Lynch?" he said.

"He's still locked in his office. I'm worried."

"I'm worried too," Littlefield said, "I think I may be losing my mind, and that perhaps Lynch has already lost his."

Through the high window I saw a basket of lights moving slowly up the Hudson River. Probably a freighter.

"Littlefield, a brief is supposed to go to court tomorrow. Parts of it are in my office, parts are right here on your desk. There are notes about relevant cases lying all over. The most important stuff is in Lynch's office, packed in boxes, and he's locked his door. It is now four in the morning. Do you have any ideas?"

Littlefield shut his eyes and leaned back in his chair. The air conditioning ducts hissed over the rolling wave sound of the far off Xerox machines.

"Should we write it ourselves?" I said.

His eyes snapped on. "Let us return to fundamental principles," he said slowly. "Who are we? Are you Cosmo Bass the Third, come to assume your rightful position as heir to your grandfather's great law firm? I think not. Cosmo Bass has no sons."

"Littlefield."

"What?"

I gave up, realizing that Littlefield was truly a different sort. And probably not long for this law firm.

"Go ahead," I added, "I'm sorry."

"I shall proceed. Are you Campbell Dix, former Presi-

dent of the *Harvard Law Review,* litigator before the
Supreme Court, counsel for a hundred corporations?
No. Dix is in jail. My friend, the bad news is that you are
merely Samuel Weston, one more Midwestern, middle
of your class, acceptable-looking graduate of the
Harvard Law School, and you have been at this great
firm a mere three months. You are, as they say at the
large firms, cannon fodder. One of thirteen young
gentlemen hired directly from law school this year to
slave at Bass and Marshall. Your function is to be
obsequious. To wait. To obey. We do nothing. If Lynch,
the scion of judges, has locked himself in his office at
this crucial moment, we must assume he has some
purpose."

Suicide, I thought. "Are you all right, Littlefield," I
said.

"The speed has entirely worn off. Too much, for too
long a period of time, produces an inverse reaction, a
coma. But it usually passes quickly."

"So you think Lynch is actually doing something in
there?"

"Something significant?" Littlefield said. "Something
like writing a brilliant brief? I rather doubt it. Of course
it is possible that the man has a hidden plan. He is
definitely doing something. I would guess he was preparing a motion asking for a two week postponement of
the filing time."

"On what ground?"

"That is an intriguing question. I have no idea. They
did not teach me these things at Yale Law School. We
are associates in a very large Wall Street law firm. We
are preparing a memorandum on an essentially simple
issue — venue. We have a huge staff, a superb library,
even a legal research computer. What possible grounds
could there be to argue that we deserve more time to
finish our work?"

"We ought to do something."

"Sleep," Littlefield said. He curled up in his chair, his feet tucked under him. He folded his hands in his lap. He looked young, innocent, and deceptively in control, except for his bulging, speed-laced eyes. "Lynch will inform us when we are needed. Have no fear of that."

I went back to my office, sat down, put my feet up on the desk and tried to sleep. It was hard because at the back of my mind, I kept thinking that the next word from Lynch would be a note firing Littlefield and me. In a couple of weeks, we'd run up hundreds of hours of work, all to be billed to the client. Maybe ten thousand dollars of legal time. What had been produced? Lots of small, seemingly unconnected memoranda, parts of a nonexistent brief. Lists of cases, Xeroxes of cases, abstracts of cases. Most of the stuff went into Lynch's office. It got piled in boxes. Lynch now had more material in there than a man could read in a year. As far as I could tell, none of it had been synthesized. The paper had started out as trees. Now it filled boxes in the big corner office, and the boxes formed a sort of stubby forest. But there was no brief. Of course, it wasn't my fault or Littlefield's. But if someone got fired because of this it was not going to be a partner.

At the back of my mind, I kept thinking: Do it yourself. Get into the library, write a good brief, hand it in in the morning. You can do it, there are still a couple of hours. Do it. Be a hero. Associate saves law firm. Cosmo Bass makes you new partner after three months on job. New partner written up in law journal. Profiled in *New York Times.*

It was a nice dream all right, but I couldn't have done it even if I'd wanted to. All the important documents I needed to write a brief were locked up in Lynch's office. So I tried to dream about Camilla Newman instead. That didn't put me to sleep either. Hugging,

she'd said, the patent remedy. I wanted more: the real
thing.

*   *   *

Around nine in the morning, Lynch bolted out of his
office, and had Mrs. Guardo type up some papers.
Guardo was a fast, precise typist, and a messenger
brought in a copy of Lynch's work within fifteen minutes. As Littlefield had guessed, Lynch had been working on a motion begging for more time.

Lynch's argument seemed to be that he was flooded
with work and could not get decent help. He did not
actually argue that Littlefield and I were incompetent —
he stated that the associates assisting him were inexperienced. Along with the motion, Lynch had prepared a
letter addressed directly to the judge. I was familiar
with depositions and briefs, pleadings and motions, but
it had never occurred to me that you could file letters.

"I believe Lynch is only warming up. Next he will
present his major arguments on post cards." Littlefield
was standing in my doorway, wearing a topcoat, and
holding his copy of Lynch's motion.

"He's going to file this?" I said.

"It is already on its way to the court."

"Littlefield," I moaned, "this is the first major project
we've worked on. It goes to the court. It becomes part of
a permanent record. And it's an argument that we're
incompetent."

"Yes, an indelicate argument perhaps, but based on
solid fact."

"Don't you care? We're a major law firm, arguing that
our associates are idiots."

"At least it will give opposing counsel a good laugh,"
Littlefield said, yawning. "The law should be fun. I'm
going home to sleep."

He started for the door, then decided to give me a few more titbits of wisdom.

"The shocking thing is that the motion will almost certainly be granted. One extension of time is almost never refused. This means two more weeks working with Lynch."

7

About a week before the extension of time to file our brief ran out, Littlefield and I discovered that we had transferred everything concerning venue to Lynch's office. We had Xeroxed, or abstracted, every case and law review article, collated the stuff, and packed it in the big cardboard boxes. There was nothing new left in the library.

"Amazing," Littlefield said. "Through the miracle of the Xerox machine, and our fine staff of office boys, we have managed to transfer an entire legal subject to the office of a partner. I wonder if it makes him feel more secure to have this immense body of knowledge in his office, rather than fifty feet away in the library?"

"I hope it makes him secure enough to begin writing the brief."

"Your mind is tortured but down to earth," Littlefield said. "However, if we must consider the practical side of things, let me ask you a more pressing question: what is our function now?"

*   *   *

Our function was to listen to Lynch talk. I sat with Littlefield on the couch in small holes we'd dug between the boxes of paper. Outside in the hall, two secretaries read Gothics and waited for us to give them something to type. They were special secretaries — hired to sit all night and all day, kept there because Lynch might spring into action at any time. I hoped he would spring soon. Could we win another delay?

Lynch talked about the bastards arguing the other side of the case. The Government was all right, Lynch thought. He looked at the paintings of his father and grandfather. Nothing wrong with the Government. But even though opposing counsel were Government attorneys, they were still bastards. Even the Government might hire the wrong people.

Bastards might do anything, Lynch said. Opposing counsel had very bad reputations. You only had your reputation, Lynch noted, that was how you won your cases. Lynch would never put his name on a dishonest brief. The courts knew that. That was why we would win this case. Lynch had heard stories about the other side at lunch. They wanted to get out of the Government and make a lot of money. The courts knew that. So we would win this case. I thought it might help if we began to assemble our brief — there were only a few days left.

Littlefield and I sat in this jungle cavelike office, in the night the boxes of papers like tree trunks, the faces in the portraits like beasts ready to spring, and Lynch told us his entire family history. We learned about his famous father and grandfather, and that Lynch had been a United States Attorney and had put racketeers in jail. We also heard more about the bastards arguing against us, and how they were truly evil, and how a great judge like Lynch's grandfather would have never let them into court.

We listened and listened to Lynch's voice in this office hung with his family mementos, listened to him repeating the facts of the case over and over, the stories about his family too. All this at maybe three o'clock in the morning. And sometimes I thought I was dreaming, and sometimes I actually was dreaming, having fallen asleep, dreaming about the World Trade Towers and thinking about walking out Lynch's office window to them, while Lynch's voice went on and on about how his grandfather had resigned as a senior partner in a Wall Street firm to become a Supreme Court Justice, and carry on the great family tradition, and how hard that had been on the children, and on the grandchildren. It was such a burden to be a Supreme Court Justice, and you took a cut in salary, but the children understood and helped their father, and you always had to help your country, and the people, and fight the bastards, and Lynch had always done that. We were doing it now. He'd always fought bastards and that was why he had clients and was a partner, and had a reputation — and he had gotten his reputation on his own, in spite of his great family name. That was actually a hindrance, he said.

Finally, all the stories seemed to blend together in my mind, I did not know what Lynch was talking about anymore, his own career or his grandfather's, or which bastards he was hating. Was I going crazy? Or was Lynch? His mind seemed to swerve backward and forward in time. This small motion was tied to a much larger case — the huge cases of the great family Lynch. And finally it seemed that Lynch had placed his motion like a brick in the tremendous wall of history he carried around and there was only your reputation to rely on, and the two judges in the paintings were watching us. Finally Lynch stood up behind his desk and announced it was time to "spring" at them. The brief was due the next day. It *was* time.

*   *   *

We worked all night, and it was eerie. I remember
that the library seemed otherworldly — Cosmo Bass
floated through it like a ghost. I was making a last-
minute check on a citation, sitting at one of the corner
tables.

"Turn on your light," Bass said.

It was a dream. I saw him but didn't answer.

"Your desk lamp," Bass said. "Save your eyes. They
are your tools."

He was real though, not a ghost. He reached down
and flicked on the light. Then he floated away, walking
out of the library reading a law review article as he went,
seeming to know the firm so well he did not need to
watch his step — these were his passages, his walls, his
mazes.

*   *   *

Littlefield took one section of the brief, Lynch another. I got a third part. Tripartite organization.

This was possible because of the nature of the material. There are two kinds of legal reasoning, two kinds of
memoranda. The first is where you track down a line of
cases. Back in the dusty pages of a volume from 1899,
you'll find an egg, ready to hatch, some judge with a
new idea. In 1900, you'll find a case where the idea has
broken out of its shell. It's sitting there, a sentence,
words, a definitive statement, a rule. You catch glimpses
of the rule as it flashes through the cases. A rule has a
descriptive aspect, and a prescriptive side. It describes
some sort of conduct. For example, cross where there
are white lines painted across the street. It also prescribes — cross only there, nowhere else, or the law will
cut off your head. Because it prescribes — tells you what
to do or else — you'll find most people crossing at the
white lines, that is, doing what the rule describes.

As it flashes through the cases, you see the rule grow
or diminish. Say it grows. The descriptive side enlarges.
More and more activity comes under the kind of
conduct it outlines. "Do not discriminate." All right,
what's discriminate, against whom, for what reasons?
You start maybe with blacks, and a hundred years later
everyone is included in the description — do not
discriminate against the handicapped, women, homo-
sexuals, children, the aged.

The other kind of legal reasoning involves factor
analysis. Take a venue case. Where should the case be
tried? There are a lot of factors influencing the decision: where the defendant lives, where the crime was
committed, where the attorneys reside. The list is endless. Different cases emphasize different factors. You
gather together all the cases you can find that emphasize
the factors in your favor. For example, if your defendant lives far away from where the Government has
brought the case, you emphasize that. At the same time,
the Government runs around getting together all its
own factors, its own cases. If the witnesses live where the
Government has brought the case they'll emphasize
that.

Things can get interesting: you counter with an
immovable object, say a witness in Alaska strapped in an
iron lung. Now, venue is one of the more boring issues
in the law, so you can imagine the fun you can have with
something really interesting.

Tracking down a line of cases is hard to divide up
among different lawyers because you have to know the
very beginning, the germination of the idea, and how it
grew. But with factor analysis, you can just parcel out
the various facts in your favor to anyone willing to write
them up.

*   *   *

Littlefield and I finished around nine in the morning and gave our sections to Lynch to study. He gave us his. While he reviewed our stuff, his was typed in final. There were notes and arrows and strange signs on every page of his section, but working with Lynch for a month had taught me what his shorthand editing signs meant. I sat beside a secretary and read the pages to her. Down the hall, I could hear Lynch doing the same thing with my stuff and Littlefield's.

By eleven, the brief was somehow Xeroxed, stapled, jacketed in jaunty blue embossed covers labeled "Bass and Marshall." A trio of messengers were dispatched to take the briefs to the court, one messenger to carry them, the other two as guards.

Then Littlefield and I sat in Lynch's office while he pranced as he told us what a great job we'd done. He seemed to have boundless energy. Littlefield and I were in comas. Lynch bounced up and down and called other lawyers, extolling our brief. We were sure to win the case. Littlefield looked at me. I knew what he was thinking. We were both hoping that our brief would at least confuse the judge enough so that he would have to take a good long time to reach any kind of decision. We were not ready to "spring" at the bastards on appeal.

*   *   *

While watching Lynch bounce around his office congratulating himself, I made a mental dialogue with myself:

— What if the judge orders oral argument?

— He won't, I answered. He can't.

— He might. He can do anything.

— I can't take oral argument, I answered. Not yet, not for months. I can't take Lynch again for months.

— What if there's an appeal? What if the judge decides the motion tomorrow, and the Government takes an immediate appeal? What if you have to work with Lynch for the next six months?

— They can't appeal, I answered.

— They can appeal.

— They can't. The case is just beginning. It would be an interlocutory appeal, and they're forbidden. You can't appeal a trial court's decision until after a final verdict is reached. Piecemeal appeal is forbidden. Otherwise trials would never end. So, if we win, it goes out to California and I'll never work with Lynch again. If we lose, and the case stays here, the trial won't start for months.

— They can appeal.

— They can't.

— *Mandamus,* fool. They can take an immediate appeal by way of *mandamus,* arguing that the judge has abused his discretion. You could win tomorrow, and the day after the Government could take a *mandamus* appeal.

"Christ," I said out loud.

"What?" Lynch said.

"Christ, you did a good job," I said emphatically.

Lynch walked over, looked down at me. He extended his hand. "Thank you," he said. "I hope we get a chance to work together again soon."

*   *   *

Finally it was five. The rain had stopped. You were supposed to work at the firm until five-thirty, but we figured we could make an escape. I stopped at the door of Camilla Newman's office. Littlefield was behind me.

"You two are a mess," she said. She was looking pert again. Littlefield was looking like an angel — the speed had given his eyes a faraway look. I had no idea how I looked, but I felt strong.

"Come drinking with us," I said.

"Drinking?"

"You like to drink," I said. "Please?"

Camilla Newman must have been working on an assignment that was no better than ours because she got up and put on her coat. The three of us sneaked out in the freight elevator.

8

We did our drinking that evening in the Clipper Bar,
only five blocks from the firm. We drank and talked. I
had never really heard Littlefield talk about himself.
The speed and the liquor seemed to loosen him up.

His parents had been divorced when he was five. He'd
lived alone with his mother in a little house in Venice,
California, with a view of the beach. There was a screen
door, he said, and it was always left open. It was funny
the way his mind worked. He talked a long time about
the screen door. In the afternoons, his mother watched
the television shows that were broadcast from Burbank,
up the road. Finally, she decided to go after the prizes.
Littlefield's mother dressed up her eleven-year-old only
son as Cupid, with diaper, bows and arrows, and
dressed herself up as a witch with a broom. They went
down to Burbank for a television game show similar to
"Let's Make a Deal," and stood in line along the sidewalk. Men with clipboards walked down the line decid-
ing who would get in. You were supposed to show
enthusiasm. His mother told Littlefield to jump up and
down and scream.

"She told you to scream?" I said.

"Then she hit me with the broom," Littlefield said.
He'd obviously had time to think this all over, because
he began to laugh. He laughed uproariously. I looked

over at Camilla Newman. She looked as horrified as I felt. Littlefield kept laughing.

"Diapered," he roared. "Getting hit with a broom, jumping up and down and crying. That was Los Angeles. Growing up." He roared so loud tears rolled down his face.

"Have another beer," I said.

"That's where I got my Cupid face," he roared, swinging his beer around. He rocked from side to side. "I put it on so I wouldn't get hit by a broom. Now I can't get it off."

If he could think it was funny, I decided it was all right if we did too. He did have a Cupid, innocent face. He was all right. I started to laugh, too. Camilla Newman laughed with us, till the tears rolled down her cheeks, too. We roared at the image of the diapered Littlefield, smiling like Cupid and crying at the same time, being whacked by his mother with a broom.

We were too drunk now to stop. After we'd laughed over the diaper episode, we roared about Camilla Newman's divorce. I never even knew she'd been married, and of course I was pissed as hell to think that she'd ever slept with someone else. But I was so drunk I laughed anyway. Tears poured from my eyes as she recounted the moving van, how she'd cleared out in one day. How her husband had chased her in his car. How stupid she'd been to marry at nineteen. We laughed at the fact that she'd wasted five years of her life, that she'd been divorced for over a year, but had slept with her husband three months ago. We laughed because it was just like *Scenes from a Marriage*.

"What?" I screamed. "You slept with him three months ago?"

"Sit down," Littlefield said sensibly.

Now they started laughing at me. But I didn't think it

was funny anymore. They began to tickle me. I still
didn't laugh. They made me drink three more beers
and blew the paper wrappers on their straws at me.
Finally, I began to laugh too. I laughed because Camilla
Newman was so stupid. That was something I could
really get into. I did not care how pert and controlled
she looked at the firm. She was stupid as hell.

Finally, Littlefield stood up and commanded us to
come to his apartment. Somehow we paid the waitress
and found a cab. We were somewhere in the Village,
facing three flights of stairs that Littlefield promised led
to his apartment. The stairs looked like a mountain wall.
I sat down on the first one.

"I can't do it," I said. Sitting down did not stop the
stairs from moving. "Is this an escalator?" I asked.

"Forward," Littlefield yelled. "Up."

I stood up then. I grabbed on to the banister and
started to pull myself along, one step at a time. My new
silk tie slid up with me, bouncing over each step. It
looked like a snake hopping up the stairs on its tail.

"It's a hard climb," I yelled. "An impossible granite
face. But we are roped together. We will fight our way
through the snow. We will grasp each other to keep
from falling from this evil mountain wall."

"Get your hands off me," Camilla Newman yelled. I
had her around the waist.

"They whispered encouragement to each other,
keeping alive the spirit of hope," I screamed.

"Move up," Littlefield commanded.

"Get your fingers off my belt," Camilla Newman
shouted at me.

"Unhand her, knave," Littlefield said. Miss Newman
unbuckled her belt. I fell backward on Littlefield. Luckily, his leg caught in the banister. Then Littlefield's head
was between my legs, and Camilla Newman's belt in my
hands. I kissed it.

"This token," I screamed, "this small trinket, this favor from my lady, this lovely belt. I would pre- fer . . ."

"Foul," Littlefield mumbled.

"Jerk," said Newman.

A bearded freak opened the door on the second-floor landing. "Shut the fuck up you farts," he screamed.

"Quiet, quiet," I said, "respect this gnome!" The bearded freak came down and helped me get untangled from Littlefield. Somehow, he got us to our feet. He shoved us upstairs after Miss Newman. He got Little- field's keys and opened the apartment door for us. We crawled in past his kneecaps.

* * *

"What a nice place," Camilla Newman was able to say, even though she had a finger in her mouth. "I like all this Indian stuff, all the hangings and blankets. And it doesn't look legal."

"I'm so glad you approve," Littlefield said. He lifted his glass. "This bohemian palace reveals my split per- sonality. At the firm I am one person: suited, perfectly turned out. Organized with an attaché case that includes a calculator, spare shirt, toothbrush, Minox camera, and a Knirps expanding umbrella."

"Pills too, I'm sure," I said.

"A supply for an emergency. I am ready for anything at the firm, any legal challenge. My gear includes an electric razor — I can fly out on some special case at a moment's notice, and arrive looking dapper. No one ever gives me a special case of course." Littlefield swung his arm around in a circle. "Here, here, my true personality is in . . ." He stopped. Put his hand on his hip. "Friends," he said, "I must stop this monologue. I have something to announce. I am physically incapable of drinking any more."

He staggered across the room. He got through the bedroom door and fell into the bed. The glass he'd been holding broke on the floor.

"Want to be tucked in, Littlefield," Miss Newman called. All I could see were his feet, the soles of his shoes, sticking over the footboard.

"Yes, I do think that would be nice," he whispered. "I think that would be nice indeed. Very good. In legal terms, I am the tuckee. I require a tuckor."

The tuckor went into Littlefield's bedroom. She took off his shoes. She didn't bother with the rest of his Wall Street outfit, but she loosened his tie. She pulled a blanket over him, tucking it around his chin. He looked particularly cherubic then.

"So that was all you could take," Miss Newman said. "We are standing and you are asleep. This is it?"

He blinked his eyes.

"I can imagine making love with you," he said. I could too. In fact, I could imagine making love with Camilla Newman very readily at that point. "Imagine it," Littlefield said, "we would engage. We would disassemble. You would look. 'This is it' you would say in your snappy tone."

She kissed him on the forehead. He shut his eyes.

When Miss Newman came out of Littlefield's room, she lay down on the sofa. She put one hand over her forehead. I sat down on the floor, leaning against the sofa back. Her other hand came down over my shoulder. It went under my tie, and into my shirt. It felt very good indeed.

"I can imagine making love with you," Camilla Newman said. I wanted to. But drinking does strange things to you. Camilla Newman had hurt my feelings.

"I don't love you," I said. "Hugging. That's the end of

it. Friends. Cohorts at the bar. Hugging. The patent remedy."

She took her hand away. I was sorry to feel it go. She folded her arms across her chest.

"Now you've made me sad," she said.

"I've made you sad." For Christ sake, I thought. "You said you didn't love me. You said we wouldn't sleep together."

"I thought."

"You thought."

"Like."

"Like?"

"Like I had an option on you."

I folded my arms, too. "Sure you had an option," I said, "it expired." Hugging, I thought, in my drunken way, that's what she'll get, hugging. Her hand came down again, over the shoulder, under the tie, into the shirt.

"Then we need to make a new contract," she said, "for when we're drunk?"

"No deals," I said.

"A deal . . ."

"No," I said.

"I don't think my option has expired," she said. "I think I've got a section ninety argument here. Reasonable reliance. I knew you loved me. You told me so. I relied on that statement. Reliance can make an option binding. That's contract law."

"You never relied on me," I said.

"Sure I did. I do."

"How?" I asked.

"I haven't fallen in love with anyone else."

"That's reliance?" I laughed. It was a stupid legal argument. But it felt nice to be rubbed on the chest. She leaned over my shoulder, so her head was cradled on my shoulder, her face against my neck.

"I could have fallen in love with someone else," she said. "I gave it up for you."

"Sure," I said. "You gave it up."

"I did. You said you loved me. I gave it up when you said you loved me. Reliance on a statement. Giving up a legal right. Makes a promise binding. You said you loved me."

"I don't," I said.

"You do."

"No."

"Come." She kissed my neck. "You do."

She was leaning over me now, both hands working, kissing my cheek. All I had to do was turn.

"Come on. You do."

"I do," I said, truthfully. I turned.

In the early morning, we made love a second time. Maybe it was the pressure of wanting to come, maybe she was thinking of someone else, or maybe it was kind of squeezed out of her. That's what I like to think. That it was there all the time and never left, that it was just buried deep because she had been hurt the first time around, and it took all the squeezing, pulling, that final hard time when she grabbed the small of my back to pull me down into her as far as I would go. In that final squeezing and pressing, it got pushed out, and she kind of low-murmured-gasped it, as if she was fighting it, not wanting to let it go.

*   *   *

She just said "I love you." I should have tape-recorded it. There were times that winter, after she had fucked me over — that was what I thought in the winter — when I wished I had taped it. I know that there are reasons for everything, logical explanations. I know she did not actually intentionally fuck me over, she just did not know what the hell she was doing — so there were times when I wished I had that gasp on tape, and could have sat in her office playing it over and over to prove it to her. In the winter she told me that she had not said it.

Part Two
The Reliance Interest

9

The rain turned to ice pellets in November and we slid to work.

There are certain things at a law firm that are passed on without anyone ever being told about them, that seem to have been stamped into your mind at birth. One is that you do not wear a sweater at the firm. In November I wanted one. I could have used a little plug-in electric heater, but I knew that was not proper either. So I took to wearing a vest. My first protection was my shirt, thick white cotton. Then a tie. A vest over it. My suit coat. And a scarf coiled around my neck. Finally, there was a huge blue wool topcoat I'd gotten on sale at Brooks Brothers.

Brooks Brothers, why the hell was I shopping there? Just because it was near the firm? Maybe I wanted to look like everyone else.

What I really wanted was a down suit. Why can't they make them? I mean a regular, regulation Wall Street gray suit with the lapels, the buttonholes, three-piece, normal. Just the kind you buy at Brooks Brothers. But quilted, filled with prime Northern goose down. Sure you might look round, puffy, the way you do in a good L. L. Bean down jacket. But was looking puffy any worse than looking square and flat? And, wouldn't it be hard to be convincingly pompous when puffy? If I could have persuaded Cosmo Bass to have a down suit made, everyone else in the firm would have gone along. All two hundred of us.

*   *   *

Cosmo Bass. He could turn up anywhere. I was washing my hands in the men's room. He bounded out of a stall, and took the basin next to me. He did not talk to me. His chin jutted forward. He seemed to be studying his mirror as if it were a picture at the Metropolitan. He held his newly washed hand up to his chin. Maybe he was aging, but he was still the force, the power. I washed my hands and kept standing there while he watched his reflection. Finally, he shook his head, muttered, turned away.

*   *   *

Toward the end of November, the rain sometimes turned to snow. The snow reminded me of home, of Christmas. I was going home for Christmas. I wanted to.

*   *   *

On a day when it was snowing, I came into the office in a good mood. Months before I'd discovered that there was a supply closet two doors down from the one outside my office. My closet was full of associates' coats, partners' coats, the coats and purses of secretaries. Two doors down there was a clean empty closet. It would hold all my new snow gear: the big coat, the oversized rubber boots, the six-foot-long scarf. I kept discovering little things like hidden closets. There were still a lot of things to learn at the firm.

I started unraveling on the long walk down the corridor. By the time I reached the closet, I was unbuttoned, had the scarf unwound, and was reaching down to unsnap one of the rubber boots. From behind me, I heard the voice of Command:

"May I ask what you are doing?"

It seemed perfectly obvious what I was doing, but this was the voice of Command, so I answered:

"Taking off my boots."

I looked up. I was bent over and looking up hurt my neck. I looked up at Wellington Rolls. That happens to be his real name. I don't think he invented it.

"And you've been putting them in my closet." Wellington Rolls snapped. I quickly looked up and down the hall. The nearest secretary suddenly began typing furiously. His closet, I thought. He's got a huge corner office, he's got a closet in there. His closet? It was a situation out of *The Caine Mutiny.* Wellington Rolls was crazy. But in Command. He had done, they said, eighty mergers over a six-month period, changing the lives of thousands of workers and the headings on millions of stock certificates. Every strand of his gray hair was in place, marching across his tan forehead.

(Who's that cat with Stacomb on his head? President Johnson is reported to have said after meeting Robert McNamara for the first time.)

"You have certainly been sneaky," Wellington Rolls said. "This has been going on for several months."

I stood up. For the first time, I noticed the grimacing face bouncing over Wellington Rolls' shoulder, the face of associate Robert Lawrence, Wellington Rolls' shadow. Lawrence belonged to Rolls, like the closet. The two of them looked utterly disgusted with me.

"What is your name?" Lawrence demanded.

The bastard knew my name. We'd been introduced. This was certainly the Christmas spirit.

I told them my name.

"You are not to put your coat in my closet," Rolls said. "Do you understand?"

"Yes, sir," I answered.

"You are not to put anything in my closet. Do you understand?"

"Yes," I said.

"You are not to sneak around my closet, put anything in it, open its door, look inside it."

"Yes," I said, backing off. "Yes."

I picked up the one boot I'd managed to get off and began limping back down the hall. Christmas. I tried to stuff my gear into the overflowing closet near my office.

I was steaming, not understanding which bothered me most: the fact that they'd been mean to me, or the fact that I didn't have the guts to hit one of them in the mouth, but instead, had said, "Yes, sir."

Yes, sir, I thought. Of course, sir, I understand, sir. Let me get my coat out of *your* closet, sir. Tiny Tim, that's me, sir, and I know it's Christmas, sir, and won't you please give me a little dumpling goosey on Christmas Eve, sir, if I'm a good boy, sir? You are so kind, sir, Mr. Wellington, sir.

I'd walked away from the two of them with a mental limp, a sort of Tiny Tim limp, and the only way to get rid of it was to say, Yes, sir, let me move my coat, sir. And sir? These five fingers, sir? The ones I'm making into a fist, sir? Would you like them now, sir? And then give Wellington Rolls and the shadow a little Christmas present early, one that took out their teeth.

10

The next morning, it was crowded on the subway, and in the building, as if the fact that we all wore winter clothes had added a small extra layer to everyone, and all those extra layers, multiplied by the millions trying to get to work, took the same space that a thousand more real people might have. In the elevator we were pinched together.

I looked at the elevator lights. Green lights blinking meant you were going up. Green was good: forward, get your ass to the office, get to work. Red lights signaled a car was going down. Red: stop. Don't go. Stay and work some more.

I was pushed into a car with Lawrence, Wellington Rolls' shadow, and Camilla Newman. When we'd reached the nineteenth floor, there was room to breathe again.

"Hello, Miss Newman," Lawrence said. He had his smile down perfectly, I thought. They'll make him a partner soon, I thought, look at those plastic lips. A good merger smile. Probably taught him by Rolls. Your first lesson, Lawrence, will be smiling.

"Hello," Miss Newman said, "how are you?"

She was being nice to the bastard; I would have to explain him to her.

"Hello, Weston," Lawrence said.

I kept staring straight ahead. Yes, it was close to Christmas, but I didn't feel like extending the Christmas spirit. Now he remembered my name, now that Rolls wasn't here and Newman was.

"Good morning, Weston," he said, as if I hadn't heard him.

I'd heard him. But he was still an associate, not a partner. I didn't have to take him. Camilla Newman gently stuck me with her attaché case.

"Good morning, Weston," Lawrence said again, and then, using a slightly higher more squeaking voice, said "Good morning, Mr. Lawrence, nice day."

I didn't think it was funny at all, but Camilla Newman laughed with Lawrence. Maybe I was acting like an asshole, but it felt good.

We got off at the next floor. On our way to our offices, Camilla asked me why I'd acted so dumb.

"I'll tell you sometime," I said.

"Tell me now."

"Some other time. You thought that little joke in the elevator was funny?"

"I thought you were stupid," she answered. We were at the door of my office. She had a way to go.

"Stupid," I said. "Thanks." And slammed the door.

*   *   *

After I'd gotten all my winter gear stored away — and not in Rolls' special closet, but thinking about the special closet and how I'd like to put Lawrence in there for the day, lock him in, with a little note pinned to his chest saying, Mr. Wellington Rolls' associate, and a note on the door saying, storage room for Mr. Wellington Rolls' associate — after that, I went into the washroom for the purpose of washing my hands.

I was having a fine time today, everything was going just right. Cosmo Bass was in there again, washing his hands, too. Why the hell didn't he use the bathroom in his office?

"Good morning," he said. His eyes sparkled. Here he was, the senior partner of the firm, looking as wise and tough as an ancient mountain. Except he could never get the names of his associates straight. So far he'd called me Walters, Winter and Wainscott. Maybe he was old, but at least he was creative. I was beginning to wonder if I should report him.

"Good morning, sir," I said.

He dried his hands carefully with one paper towel. He looked at himself once in the mirror.

"No," he said, deliberately. "It's Whistler, isn't it?"

Why lie? I thought.

"No," I said, "not Whistler."

"I am sorry," he said.

For some reason, that touched me. Here was a truly great man, law clerk to Oliver Wendell Holmes, king of a great firm he'd built himself. Scholar. Author.

"I must be getting old," he said.

A great man. "No," I said. "it's me. I've got a confusing face. Everyone has this trouble."

Then he smiled. "You do have a confusing face," he said. "All associates do. Not Whistler? Perhaps Wessler?"

"No," I said. He had finished with his hands. They were clean, hard, smooth. Blue veins ran across the top of them.

"You have a confusing face, but I misname many others, too."

"It's Weston," I said.

But by now Cosmo Bass had forgotten me and was staring in the mirror.

He left. I stood there for a while. You are doing better, I thought, you no longer shake when you talk with Cosmo Bass. And then I thought, why should I shake? What did I expect? The old man wasn't scary: he was charming, courteous, inviting. What the hell had I expected? Did someone with a bastard's personality build a huge law firm?

I thought of Wellington Rolls. Maybe sometimes they did, I thought, or at least took them over.

*   *   *

Back in my office, I went over the draft of a tax memorandum. It had been boring work, but the final product was the best thing I'd done at the firm so far. I hoped someone used it sometime for something. I would probably never know. Secretly, I hoped the partner I'd done it for, Mr. Flanders, would ask me to put it in the firm's memorandum file — the bound volumes that kept what were considered "great" work, the memorandums used as reference pieces by other lawyers in the firm.

My telephone rang.

"Weston," Lynch said.

"Yes, sir."

"Nothing to report. Nothing has come down from the court. Who knows when they'll reach a decision. What do you think?"

"I don't know, sir," I said.

"Weston?"

"Yes, sir."

"I hope it's soon. I've got a feeling we're going to give the bastards theirs."

"I hope it's soon, too," I said. We hung up. I hope it's never, I thought. And I will not think about people as

bastards, no matter how long I work with Lynch. I will
not let him influence my mind.

Rolls, I thought, Lawrence. Bastards.

I went to find Littlefield in order to get a cup of coffee
with some sanity mixed in.

11

The lunchroom looks more like an elaborate coffee shop than anything else. It's got a nice white-haired short lady, Mrs. Squibb, behind a stainless-steel counter. She gives you your coffee and you take it to any one of the twenty round Formica tables scattered through the room. Secretaries are allowed in, too, and so are paralegals. I suppose partners can get in too, but usually they have their coffee sent to their offices. It's a full kitchen setup, and meals are cooked here: lunches, for the Wednesday afternoon partnership meeting. Huge floor-to-ceiling windows give a good view of other office buildings and provide the one place in the firm where secretaries can go to see the outside world.

Because it was early in the morning, we had the shop to ourselves. We carried our mugs to a table next to the windows, and I described some of the things that had been happening to me, concentrating on my closet story, and how I'd repaid Lawrence in the elevator.

"Tribal," Littlefield said, and laughed.

"Are you stoned?" I asked. His eyes looked round.

"I went to Yale," he answered. "You went to Harvard. That explains the differences in our perceptions." He bent forward. "Frankly, I'm just slightly stoned. But I'm sure that no partner here could detect it."

"You ought to be in teaching," I said. "This isn't your game."

"Correct."

"Why don't you do it?"

"I will," he said. "Three years on Wall Street, then into teaching. That is the traditional path. They like to see practical experience on your résumé. And frankly, it's nice to get the money."

"You can't operate here stoned," I told him. Mrs. Squibb was polishing the shining stainless-steel counter tops. She had to do something. Everyone does. You can't just stand there. Heavy black clouds were suspended above the near buildings.

"In a sense you're operating here, stoned. Stoned *In re Newman,*" he said.

"True," I admitted.

"It's all tribal, typically tribal." He looked out the window at the descending clouds. "Tribal mystery: Lynch talking to pictures. Our walking icon, Cosmo. Cosmos. From what you've been telling me, he's becoming absent-minded. Wonderful. The more forgetful, the more mystical. Aging is getting stoned, too. Soon, everyone will be trying to unravel the mystery of the stoned, elusive Bass."

"You'll be a good teacher," I said. "I can't understand you."

"A mile-high tribe, suspended in space. Look at those clouds. The new tribal societies are all up here, isolated, but preserving all the traditional customs. A caste society: secretaries, the untouchables. Associates: preparing for the initiation rite into partnership. Warfare: our closed society descends out into the forest of buildings to fight with other closed societies. Law firm against law firm. We shake papers at each other the way primitive tribes shake spears. Nothing ever really happens, no one is killed. These are mock battles."

"You are stoned," I said.

"Look at those rebellious clouds."

"Ice rain," I said.

"For some reason, I do my best legal work stoned," Littlefield said. "I float the partners away." He leaned forward again. "Closed societies: Internecine warfare. Who gets which office? You refuse to talk to Lawrence, there will be retribution. You've violated the customs of the tribe. He is a senior associate, a probable partner. Now what will they do to you?"

"They can't do anything to me," I said.

"Send you to Kansas City on a corporate search? That would be good. Five months in Kansas City poring over ledgers."

"I come from Kansas," I reminded him.

"Alaska, then? Put you on an antitrust case that eats up five years of your life?"

"I'd quit. I'd teach."

"Look at those clouds," he said. They were much lower now, almost grazing the top of our window. Ice pellets began to batter the glass. "Family relationships are always the most vicious. Here we have family relationships in form but we lack the lubricating ingredient that softens, blunts, the essential malignancy. That ingredient, my friend, is love. Having lacked it early, I know full well the effect of family relationships without that lubrication. Now I've got to get some repulsive corporate minutes written. What time is it?"

"Ten-thirty," I told him.

"This work is grinding me down. And law school was so much fun."

"Because you went to Yale."

"Another family," he said, "another tribe. My God, why do they take us, put faith in us? Yale students are the most flaky, have the most suicides, are unused to being ordered around, do not even have grades. A smart firm would take graduates from Hofstra, Fordham. Preferably from the military academies. They'd get people who feel grateful for the chance to do this shit work. But they take people from Yale. What possible reason is there for it?"

"I don't know anything about Yale," I said.

"Imagine heaven." He stood up. Outside the weather looked like hell. It was hard to imagine any law school, or anything concerned with the law, as heaven.

"I exaggerate," he said. "But Yale was a pretty fine place." He swung around for a last look at the storm. "I don't know what to tell you," he said. "Forget about Lawrence. Forget about the firm. Float. To think about Lawrence is to allow your mind to be messed with. Take some dope."

He buttoned the middle button of his suit. In spite of the fact that he was stoned, he looked orderly, almost immaculate. His suit was a lovely tweed. His shirt was milky white. A blue tie with small yellow stripes was knotted perfectly under his starched collar.

"Some play this weekend?" he said.

"I don't know," I answered.

"*In re Newman*?"

"Yes."

"A better cause." He took his mug over to white-haired Mrs. Squibb. He made an elaborate presentation of it to her, complimenting her both on her looks and on the coffee she made. She blushed. I could see she felt like patting him on the cheek. He had a young, baby look that brought that out. He knew it, too.

12

Camilla Newman had invited me to a party given for her grandparents' fiftieth wedding anniversary. We drove out to Long Island in a rented car that skidded on the invisible ice that coated the narrow roads. My first impression of her parents' house was that it was excessively neat. Someone seemed to have cleaned the brick walk so that the two-inch-high snow on each side looked squared with a trowel.

"You're going to like my mother," Camilla said in the car. She didn't seem in any hurry to get out of the car though. "Then there's my father."

"Don't worry," I said. "We'll talk law."

"He's not exactly the Wall Street lawyer type."

"Listen," I asked, "are we just going to sit here?"

"Maybe."

"We're not," I said.

"You're going to pull me in?"

"They are." A stocky couple had come out of the house, the woman moving fast, and the man coming on determinedly behind her.

*   *   *

I was in a book-lined study. There were pictures of Camilla on the walls. They seemed to cover her entire career. The one of her in a wedding dress startled me.

Didn't you get rid of that stuff when your daughter got divorced?

"At this big law firm," the father said, "what do you specialize in?"

"Nothing yet," I told him.

"Tax," he said. "Go into tax."

"I don't know what I like yet," I answered. "I haven't been there long enough."

Camilla's father was a patent attorney. He'd started as a sole practitioner, doing a lot of work for free, taking a percentage of the royalties from the inventions brought in by nuts. Some of these nuts must have known what they were doing.

"You can do tax anywhere," he said. "If you aren't made a partner, it's a skill to sell."

Sure, I thought. And if you join the tax department, you don't have to work with people like Lynch. You get protection: a little office, and fierce, small round partners who protect you from the other departments in the firm. On the other hand, tax makes you bald, round, and shrinks you. It's the truth. Tax makes you bald and round, and litigation makes you tall and frayed.

"Consider tax," he said.

Maybe it was just the difference in our ages. I thought the law was supposed to give you choice. You poked around in it, searching for a part of it that lit you up. To me, the tax department was a long gray tunnel where all your life was planned in advance.

"You'll find something," he said.

"I hope so," I said.

"And I suppose Camilla will too," he added.

* * *

Then we were at the party. A lot of round tables circled a dance floor. We had dinner, the band began to play. Camilla's grandparents led people out onto the dance floor. The ones who weren't ready to dance lit up cigars. When the grandparents started to dance, everyone applauded, and had more to drink.

"I hope you've been citing Justice Cardozo in your work," Camilla's father said to her.

I jerked around. Cardozo at an anniversary party? We'd had too much champagne.

"Not really. I think Cardozo wasn't a very good judge," Camilla said. She was wearing a dress with pink bows down the back.

"Cardozo invented tort law," the father snapped.

"Anyone can invent fiction," she answered.

"What you are talking about is a mystery I don't understand," Camilla's mother said.

I didn't understand either. They weren't really talking about Justice Cardozo.

"Cardozo is a genius you should not ridicule," the father said and had more champagne.

"He's the Jacqueline Susann of the law," Camilla said. "A judge who never looked at the facts of any case he decided. All fiction."

"You say this kind of thing at this big law firm?" the father said.

Camilla leaned forward. "I don't like to argue with you," she said.

"You're wrong about Cardozo, so you don't like to argue."

I'd had as much to drink as anyone. Camilla looked beautiful. I loved the bows, and the front of the dress too, and her breasts. We'd have to straighten out this Cardozo stuff. I'd decided to marry her.

"Listen, Dad," she said, "Cardozo didn't know a damn thing about women. He never married. He spent his whole life at clubs that excluded women. But he wrote

hundreds of opinions about women, love and marriage.
How the hell did women come out in these gems? They
got screwed. Cardozo never wrote an opinion that made
any sense. He construed marriage contracts as if women
were serfs to their husbands."

"And you think you shouldn't obey your husband?"

I tried to think of something witty to break up this
conversation. Maybe a discussion of the Warren Court.

"I don't think that you ought to, necessarily, automat-
ically obey anyone," Camilla said, locking eyes with her
father.

"And maybe that is the reason for all your troubles,"
her father said. He didn't mention Camilla's divorce,
but you saw in her face that he didn't have to.

Camilla stood up. Yes . . . well . . . I looked around
the table and smiled at Camilla's mother. She seemed a
nice sort and smiled back. I drained my glass.

"That was lousy," Camilla hissed. "Really lousy, Dad."
She grabbed my hand, pulled me up, and pushed me
out on the dance floor, and we swung away from them.

*   *   *

More snow had fallen during the dance, covering the
lawn in front of the house.

"I can't find the driveway," I said.

"Go over the lawn."

"Your dad's going to love that." I hoped the snow
would keep falling and cover our tracks.

"Sam, I can't see the driveway either."

We swished over the lawn and nestled up close to a
tree in front of the house. There was no noise, so the
dent had to be small.

"Good," she said. "We made it."

"Thank God."

We staggered through the unlocked front door, up

the stairs. On the second-floor hall, there were two open bedroom doors, with light coming through them.

"Come on in for a while," she said.

"Your dad. Remember Cardozo."

"Asleep," she said. "Dead drunk."

"You've checked?"

"Intuition."

I felt like I was back in high school, sneaking around. I shut my eyes and tried to listen for sounds. When I shut them, I began to lose my balance.

"Sure," I said. "Into your room."

The room was Early American. A dull light came from electric candles hung on either side of the big four-poster bed. The light yellowed everything, and put sparkles in Camilla's hair. It made the bows on the back of her dress dance. I felt as if our formal clothes were a masquerade — the long dress and my tuxedo did not relate to us in any way. We were snakes who could shed our skins.

Camilla leaned back against the good high sturdy four-poster and pulled up her long dress. It trailed out behind her over the bed as if a strong wind had blown it up. The folds of the material bunched and swirled around her stomach.

She pulled down my zipper, put her hands inside and with both palms formed a squeezing vise. Her head went back. I almost came then. I believe she almost came. I pulled down her slick snake pantyhose. It tore some. It sounded like my zipper. Her back against the four-poster, her legs like the frame of a house, stout wall posts straight to the floor, knees for joints, the thigh roof beams curving up, ending in the dark eave. The bulge of material from her upswung dress kept my prick from getting farther than the thick lip joint of her thighs. I tried to reach it. I could not get in. I would never get in. I wanted to plant the roof beam in the joint, enter firmly in the proper place like a good carpenter, drive in the final peg, lift her splayed legs off the floor with it.

She took the root shaft in her hands, the tip in her bulging lips. It seemed as if the folds of the long dress were flowing behind her as if they floated on water. From the waist down, we seemed to be standing in some hot stream that pulled my balls and prick in its current. She swung her arms around me, catching me low and yanking me in. Her legs came up, the dress gave way, I sank in deeply, locked the dowel, was pulled, tickled, blew off. I felt as if the top of my head had been blown off too.

*   *   *

In the morning, everyone was on best behavior and there were no arguments about Cardozo. Camilla and I took a walk together in the woods behind the house.

"What about children?" I said. "Would you like to have them?"

"Let's hope we're not going to."

"What?"

"Don't worry," she said. "Be thankful I'm handling the contraception. What do you think of my parents?"

"I like them," I told her. "I like your mother."

"They're all right," she said. There were tall pine trees, and no underbrush. We walked easily on the soft shallow snow. The sun came down through the thistles.

"This is where I'm supposed to run, and you're supposed to chase me," she said. "Then you catch me. We laugh. And twirl around. My hair flies out and it's all in slow motion and we fuck."

"Would you like that?"

"No," she said. "We ought to get back. The work."

"What about kids?" I said. "Do you want them?"

"How do you know I haven't had them?"

Christ, I thought. "Have you?" I said.

"No."

"Abortions, kids given up for adoption, miscarriages?"

"Yes. No. And no," Camilla said. "What's the matter with you?"

"You want kids?"

"How would I know if I want kids? Maybe. Love and work. I like the work. I need the love."

"This isn't love?" I stopped her, pushed her against a tree, arms on either side of her.

"Who knows?"

"Affection?"

"It's certainly affection," she said. "It's affection, reliance, section ninety, binding affection. We agreed to screw each other and not to screw each other over. We finally got the fucking part of our relationship worked out. Who cares if it's love."

I kissed the top of her head.

"The hell with it," I said.

"What?"

"The hell with it. I love you. I don't care what you think."

I pulled my arms away, and we started back toward the house.

"I'm glad you liked my parents," she said, as we walked.

When we left, Camilla's mother blocked off my path to the car.

"You're not going to give me a kiss?" she said.

I leaned down and gave her a kiss on the cheek, and she gave me a kiss back, her lips against my ear, whispering: "You see that nothing happens to my daughter at this big law firm."

13

Robert Lawrence had developed a compulsion to get me to say hello to him. I think he was concerned that some time, in some elevator crowded with partners, I would refuse to acknowledge his presence. Maybe Lawrence could hurt me, get Rolls to send me on a corporate search or something, but he would have to explain the reason for it. Because I wouldn't say hello? Could you explain that one to Cosmo Bass? Even the meek and unpowerful have some weapons. Lawrence wasn't a partner yet. Maybe he'd become one soon. But as long as he wasn't a partner he had to explain his actions to people. I was always very careful to say hello to Wellington Rolls.

*   *   *

I passed Lawrence in the hall, his hands in his pockets. He said good morning, and did an about-face. I knew damn well he was going to try to talk to me. I could avoid it by going into the library, but I went into my office. He came through the open door and sat down in the chair across from me. He stretched his feet out. I began to sort the papers.

"You're pretty busy, aren't you?" he said finally.

I put the papers down. He was maybe six years older than I, tall, thin. He had brown hair that had a natural part and fell at an angle across his forehead. In general, he was an intelligent-looking person, sensibly dressed, lawyerlike, all in place, except for his eyes. They were deep-set, in black brown sockets. There were blue eyes at the end of the black tunnels. Like water in a deep well. And the well is drying up, slowly, and more of the black shaft is being exposed, and sometime, I thought, sometime, the black socket shaft will be so deep you'll have to drop a stone into it and listen to hear if there's water.

"I am busy," I said.

"You're pissed off at me or something, right?"

"Right," I said, "I'm pissed off."

"O.K.," he said, "I can understand it." He let out a deep breath, stuck his fingers together, looked at the ceiling, stretched. "O.K. I'm not a nice guy, but I'm not a bastard either. What's the matter with you? What's pissed you off?"

He really didn't know. Christ, I thought.

"Would you like some good work?" he asked. "I can get you off some of this shit. Rolls is doing some interesting securities work. Want to do a private placement, a public offering? Want to do a couple of ten-Ks?"

"No," I said, "I don't want to do securities work."

"What do you want? Litigation?"

"I have litigation work."

"That shit with Lynch?"

"Forget it," I said. "Listen."

"O.K." he said, "tell me. Goddamn tell me what I did to you."

It was the eye sockets that got to me. Is that how working eight years at the firm affected you?

"I was angry about the closet," I said, "Rolls' closet."

"The closet?"

"I get mad when people yell at me."

"They're going to yell at you," he said. "You're going

to make mistakes and they're going to yell. You drop a comma, and the client spots it when the prospectus is already printed. You ought to hear Rolls yell. That bothers you?"

"It bothers me," I said. "Do you think Cosmo Bass yells at people?"

"Bass is senile. He's over eighty. He can't remember anyone's name. He's forgotten how to yell."

We all joked about Bass's forgetfulness, but Lawrence actually meant it. "Bass is not senile. How can anyone remember the names of over a hundred associate lawyers? You expect him to be a god so when he performs like a normal person you call him senile." Lawrence would never understand. I gave up. "Forget it," I said, "it's not Bass. It's something else. There are partners and associates. There isn't any union, but a kind of contract, an implied contract, implied in fact."

"I've forgotten contract law," Lawrence said. "I do securities work."

"Everyone is in competition to be a partner, right?"

"Right," he said, "but in different years. My year is now. I'm not in competition with you."

I tried to get his eyes to focus on me. He was still staring at the ceiling. Why did I have to explain this? It seemed so simple.

"Maybe I'm stupid," I said. "I don't know much about the firm, all right? But if we're all in competition, how do we work together without trying to screw each other over? We develop a set of implied rules? Right? We don't embarrass each other in front of partners, right? I'm still embarrassed, even if I'm not in direct competition with you. I'm still made to feel stupid if you help Rolls out when he screams at me."

Lawrence was still gazing at the ceiling. I waited for some kind of response. Finally, he brought the tunnel eyes down and stared at me.

"I don't have to take this shit from you," he said slowly. "I'm a senior associate, for Christ sake. I can tell you what to do." He pointed his hand at me. I could see it was shaking. "You're nothing," he said. "You don't know anything."

Then he stopped pointing. He shook his head. Christ, he was all confused. He wanted to yell at me; he wanted to make friends with me. He tried to put himself into another category, removing himself from me. We both knew that was bullshit. We were both associates, and both expendable. It didn't matter how long he'd been at the firm. They were cranking out five hundred new Harvard lawyers every year. And there were five hundred lawyers working at the SEC. The firm could easily hire one of them away, make him a partner, fire Lawrence.

"I'm sorry," he said. "Listen, I've been up all night and I'm exhausted. Why don't we try to be friends. I can't stand another face around here that hates me."

I was willing to be friends with him because of his eyes. Maybe not friends exactly, but I didn't need to make his problems worse.

"Fine," I said, "good."

"We'll go out for lunch," he said. "There are a lot of things I could tell you about this place."

"Sure," I said, "we'll go out for lunch."

As I said this, Camilla Newman walked into the office. When she came in, Lawrence stood up. Now his eyes worked. He took a good long look at Camilla.

"Securities work," he said. "You'd be perfect in securities work." He said this as if he were a movie director — you're perfect for this role. I smiled. Camilla smiled. Lawrence left on that happy note, and Newman sat down.

"I think I like that guy," she said.

14

"Is Lawrence married?" I asked my spy. We were talking on the telephone. I was smart enough not to use the intercom.

"How the hell would I know," my spy said.

"Would you find out? Find out about him generally."

"Why?" my spy said. "To put it bluntly, who gives a shit?"

"I thought we were friends," I said.

"Are you stoned, too?" he asked.

"No," I said.

"You wish me to find out about Lawrence," the spy said. "See if he's married. Check out his life. Meanwhile you forget I have work. I'm supposed to run to the Law Registry for Wellington Rolls. And Lynch keeps calling me. To tell me there hasn't been any decision."

"Forget it," I told him.

"No. I love spying. I love sneaking into offices. I'll check it out with the paralegals. They know everything. I'll grease the palm of Lawrence's secretary. Maybe start an affair with her."

"All this is deep background," I said.

"Check. Right. Sure. Call me Deep Purple."

"What?"

"Code name: Deep Purple. Isn't that the name of a rock group? You could call me Acidhead, or Dope. I like Dope. Double meaning. Double agent. Would you believe they've put me on a real-estate assignment. Do you know what real-estate work is?"

"No," I said.

"A system designed to bore you to death, a Chinese water torture. They drip the words on your forehead. You don't mind the first couple of words, but the cumulative effect is devastating. 'Metes and bounds.' 'Heirs.' 'Successors.' 'Assigns.' 'Thence.' They use thence all the time in the deeds. Thence running. Thence turning. Thence jumping. 'Thence.' Real-Estate Law has a lisp. Is that torture?"

"I can see it," I said. "Yes. Torture."

"I mean there is a whole real-estate department here at the firm. I may be snatched into it. I feel as if I'm in quicksand, with my nose just above water. They never told me about this at Yale. I must develop a plan to save myself."

"You wouldn't fit into real-estate work," I said.

"Where will I fit in?"

"Teaching."

"I don't know if I can last that long. But perhaps I can develop a plan. I *am* ingenious."

"Make a plan fast," I said.

"Maybe I'll grab a fistful of deeds and jump. I'll wave them in the air. The first man to fly waving deeds. A new energy source. Jumping is so much faster than the elevator. What was my assignment again?"

"Lawrence," I said.

"May I inquire as to your motivation?"

"No," I said.

"I've been screamed at," my spy said. "Yesterday Rolls screamed at me. I hadn't completed an assignment in time. Frankly, I'd repressed the assignment, hadn't even started it."

"I've just been talking to Lawrence about screaming," I said. "What was the assignment?"

"A question involving foreign trusts. Do the securities actually have to leave the United States in order for the trust to be immune from United States taxation?"

"I don't know," I said.

"I refuse to work with tax journals," my spy said. "The print is too small. And the names they give to the weekly bulletins that record the latest doings of our friends at the Internal Revenue Service! Can you believe *Taxable Tidbits*? Can you stomach *Tax Tattles*? Who makes these things up? Can you believe I'm supposed to cross-reference from *Tidbits* to *Tattles,* both worthy legal periodicals, and report straight-faced to a partner? I do not think I will win out in the ultimate race for partnership. I do not think I care. I think our firm lacks a sense of humor. Have you ever seen anyone walking down the corridor balancing a law book on his head?"

"I wouldn't try it," I said.

"I'd try it, but I don't think I could do it."

"Don't practice."

"I look good, though. I'm wearing a new suit. I fool them all. They accept my memoranda because of my suit. When do you need to know about Lawrence?"

"On Friday I fly home to Kansas."

"Christmas. Yes. Thankfully, I am not flying home and Mother is not coming to visit."

"Littlefield, I've got to get some of this damn work done."

"Lunch?"

"Maybe," I said. "I'd like to. I'm not sure."

"*In re Newman?*"

"Perhaps."

"I will proceed with spying activities at once. I have a

premonition I will discover something sinister about Lawrence. I am a consummate gossip."

"You read *Tattles*," I said. "You should be a good spy."

"Maybe I should write for them."

We finally hung up. It was nice to know that Littlefield had Christmas fever, too. He was bright enough to work stoned. I wasn't. I envied him. And I hoped he thought up a plan before he jumped.

15

There was a surge of work at the firm. If we were a tribe, as Littlefield said, then this was one of our rituals. Cleaning up for January 1, IRS tax time. Polishing our clients for inspection.

I was given hundreds of one-shot, small assignments by partners I'd never met. I worked with associates who had offices on another floor. Associates seemed to be coming from everywhere, as if new ones had been hiding in bathrooms and broom closets and coat closets. I wanted to see Camilla Newman; I was going away for Christmas and I wanted to be with her. But there wasn't time.

Associates ran down the halls, the telephones rang, and the secretaries pounded out copy on the MTST machines. Small secretaries scurried around corners, papers flapping. Associates lined up outside partners' offices, waiting to get in for a five-minute conference, to review a short letter, to get a signature.

I went with some other lawyers to the office of one of our big clients. The general counsel of the company was expounding some legal doctrine, to explain why the company had filed a wrong tax report. Oh, the company wanted to file the right report. Its heart was in the right place. All the lawyers from our firm nodded. They wanted to file the right report. They just forgot. The

general counsel said: "We picked up the wrong fork."
And we all nodded at his superb legal reasoning.
Nothing wrong there. Just picking up the wrong fork.
Law as etiquette. It was a big client, so we nodded.

*   *   *

One afternoon I worked late in the library, and
overheard my secretary, Mrs. Moultrie, using one of the
library phones. She thought she was alone, missed me as
I sneaked in. She was talking to her husband, defensive-
ly, and said: "You don't have to worry, I'm still a good
secretary, you can be sure of that. I'm still a good
secretary, I can follow orders."

*   *   *

I had to work late every night in the weeks before
Christmas, and from my office I saw through the clear
winter air, into the lighted offices of the buildings next
door. The buildings climbed around me, transparent
skins. I looked into a million magnified windows. There
was no serenity in the landscape. Behind the windows, I
saw people moving, saw flickers of movement, saw
people standing at their windows, turning, moving, as if
they were outside and climbing.

*   *   *

One associate who had an office next to mine picked
up and left right before Christmas. Picked up isn't right.
Left is what I mean. He just did not come in one day.
Nor the next. They tried to reach him. He was working
on several things. They could not find him at his
apartment, they could not find him anywhere. He just
disappeared.

Sitting in the coffee room, talking with Littlefield, I
discovered that this was common: the vanishing associate. Saying, Fuck it at Christmas but not wanting to

admit failure, just walking out one day. Leaving everything behind.

How could you just leave everything, I wondered.

"What would you want to take?" Littlefield asked.

I thought about it: maybe the diploma on the wall, but
you could always order a replacement. A stapler?

"Tell me one thing you'd take," he said.

I didn't tell him, but there was one thing, and I think
he knew what it was.

*   *   *

I recall driving uptown in the Mercedes of one of the
energetic younger partners. I sat in the back. Next to
the younger partner was an older, red-faced partner
who specialized in litigation. The young guy zipped the
big expensive car through the traffic, dodging cabs,
honking, shaking his fist. We hit sixty on Second Avenue. We ignored red lights. The older guy tried to light
his pipe. His hands were shaking. I wasn't worried: I
figured I was in the back seat, I would live.

"What do you call this method of driving?" the older
partner finally said. And the young guy laughed.

"What do I call it?" he said. We scraped the side of a
bus, making a right turn under its bumper. "The son of
a bitch method. Driving into the point of resistance.
While all the cars are switching lanes to avoid some
obstruction, I head right for it, gather up speed, get
going so fast they have to let me into the good lane when
I get to the stalled car."

"Son of a bitch," the older partner said.

*   *   *

That week I did a simple tax assignment (I could only
do simple tax assignments) for a partner named Robinson who changed his shirt twice a day. I had to leave his
office while he did it, and was supposed to stand guard

outside his door. Mr. Robinson had a shoe-buffing machine, and told me all about them, about the one he had, and the kind they had at the Downtown Association, and at the Attorneys' Club. He had trained his secretaries to place papers in special "spots" on the glass top of his desk. Letters from important clients went in one spot, letters from others in other spots. He had also trained his secretaries not to talk. He did not seem to like ringing telephones, either: his had blinking red lights.

Mr. Robinson pointed out the lights to me, and explained how he'd installed a special kind of stereo equipment in his house — Bolton equipment, little master control boxes with blinking lights. Teak, he said, the size of cigar boxes. He said his wife was not smart enough to use the boxes. There was a big picture of his wife on the wall. He said he selected music for her each morning before he left for work.

For two days I worked for Robinson. He used a fine-pointed architect's pen and made very sensible corrections on the memorandum I wrote for him. I went to lunch with him on the second day, just as we were finishing up. Striding toward the restaurant, I heard him hiss the word "cunt." It did not seem to have any sexual meaning. Of course there were thousands of women walking around us, secretaries, women lawyers and bankers. But the meaning of the word did not seem related to them. He just seemed to be a strange partner, and "cunt" was his moving, walking, striding word, a word that just hissed out as we sprinted up Wall Street.

*   *   *

In the weeks before Christmas, partners roamed the halls like panthers, jungle creatures, on the prowl for associates. There were simply not enough of us to handle the work. You would be trying to get some of it done and a partner like Derek Bush would slowly push open your door. His oval face, polished like an apple, would swing around the door frame. He would be like a huge jungle insect coming to sting you: little core hairs sticking up, beady eyes hunched at the top of his forehead like insect eyes, his suit black, scaly and hard as iron. Bush would smile, and kind of whine, his voice was like an insect's, too, as if he were rubbing his teeth together, producing a humming rubber band sound. He would not ask if you were busy, but would say: "Come into my office, I have a little project for you." You would try to explain how busy you were. And he would repeat: "Come into my office, I have a little project."

I went on hundreds of these "little projects" for insect-man partners I had not known existed, and did things like running to the Law Registry — which is a downtown law library that the Wall Street law firms keep to store exotic materials. The Law Registry was dusty, the tiny halls stank and had no light, old lawyers lay at tables drunk. And I would frantically search for some volume, say something to do with West Virginia real-estate law, or the notarization of documents in Guatemala. And usually I would actually, surprisingly, find the book, sign it out with the comatose clerk and sprint back through the snow to get the book to the insect man. I would hand it to him, and he would not say anything, but keep his beady eyes trained down on his papers, rubbing his hind legs together and just squeaking a little.

*   *   *

Toward the end, in the final hard drive for Christmas, I was literally impressed, grabbed the way they used to grab sailors to fill up the British ships. At ten o'clock one night, as I was leaving for Camilla's apartment, I walked by one of the conference rooms and three frantic, older associates pulled me in and shut the door behind me.

"What the hell is this?" I asked.

"You've got to help us," the tallest one said.

"I can't."

"You can," he said.

"You will," another one said. Just then, a partner, Mr. Thorn, who was slumped down like a shadow in a big leather chair in the corner so I didn't see him jumped up, yelled: "You will."

I did. They were assembling appellate briefs, to be flown down to Washington for an appeal before the Court of Appeals for the District of Columbia. They were also assembling "supporting documents." These were copies of various materials that had been introduced into evidence in the court below.

They had a screw press — like those old-fashioned printing presses that appear in Western movies. The presses with the big screw that you tighten, wearing your white printer's smock, and then you untighten it and you pull out freshly printed paper and hold it up. It usually says something nasty about some cattle baron and while you're holding the paper up, five bad guys come in and break everything up. It was a press like that, only it was used for making holes in paper, so that they could clip their "supporting documents" together. The packets were too thick for the staples, even for the big industrial stapler the firm had in the mail room.

As I was tightening the press to punch one of the holes, I asked them why they hadn't copied the documents on paper that was prepunched.

Thorn jumped up from the chair again. "They forgot," he screamed. He sank down again. "Shut up and work," he mumbled. By this time it was four in the morning. We had an assembly line going. Copies had to go to all the parties involved, fifteen copies to the court, more copies to keep at the firm. I guess we'd done about fifty. There seemed to be ten or fifteen more to go. About this time, one of the associates glanced down and said, "I think I've caught a mistake."

Partner Thorn jumped up again.

"A mistake," he screamed. "Now you've caught a mistake?"

"Maybe it's not a mistake," the associate said.

There were messenger boys outside waiting for us to finish. There was a cab in the street to take the boys to the airport.

"You goddamned think you've caught a mistake. If there's a mistake, you're goddamned fired."

"I didn't write this section of the brief," the associate said.

"You're fired anyway." Then Thorn turned to me. "Did you write that section?" he yelled.

"I just punched the holes," I told him. "They seem all right."

Thorn bent down over the page, looking for the mistake. The associate bent down with him. Everything hinged on the word *principle*. Was it *pal* or *ple*? What had they intended?

The partner folded his arms. He put his hand on his chin. He thought it over. "P-L-E!" he screamed suddenly. "We're right."

The briefs went out. I went home. It was eight in the morning and I felt like a plane doing a turnaround: being washed, gassed, then told to get out, get up, fly into the air again.

16

I wasn't stoned, but moving toward Christmas, I began
to feel that I was. Suddenly, in the middle of Thursday
afternoon I just stopped working. I put down my pen,
put my elbows on my desk and held my chin in my
hands.

Everything I saw seemed otherworldly. Through the
open door I saw the corner of a secretary's desk, not my
own secretary, her desk was way down the hall, but
another's desk — and on it a box of Kleenex and a little
red plastic flower next to it in a teacup. There was a
cabinet hanging on the wall above the desk. It was
probably screwed into the wall, but in my stoned, spaced
state, its method of attachment fascinated me. The desk
itself was a putrid green color, with a Formica top. I saw
just the top of a purse, peeking from behind a file box.

The desk looked as if it were floating in air, maybe
because of the fact that the carpet was speckled with
brown and white droplets. The desk looked confining.
The secretary was surrounded on one side by her huge
typewriter, and on the other by the corridor. She
couldn't turn either way, she was forced into the crack
in the middle, focused straight ahead at the desk in
front. Why didn't they turn the desks around so that the
secretaries could look at each other, and not at each
other's backs? And those carpet colors: brown drops

spotted with white. They seemed the strangest colors in the world. What kind of associations were you supposed to get from them? Mud with white snails? Puke? Chaos? Was chaos disgusting, or disorganizing, or both?

Littlefield woke me from my stupor with a telephone call.

"Good morning," he said. "Spy here. Report to follow."

"Report?"

"Lawrence."

"Right," I said. "Is he married?"

"Yes," Littlefield said. "Married. One child. Wife teaching fellow at Columbia. Wife has money. They have big apartment on the East Side. He works almost exclusively for Wellington Rolls. Partnership? Up in the air. Maybe yes, maybe no. Rolls can be erratic. Decide that it is, quote, not in your best interest to be made a partner, unquote. Did that to a guy last year. Hates to make people partners. On other hand, Lawrence may have made himself indispensable. Who knows?" Littlefield coughed. I began to realize that I ought to get back to work. I was leaving the next day!

"There's more," he said. "The famous bow-wow scene."

"Bow-wow?" I said.

"Bow-wow. Lawrence can get dangerously drunk. At a party last year, he apparently engaged in a bow-wow. A sure sign that he's coming unhinged. I'll bet you'd like to know what a bow-wow is, wouldn't you?"

"Sure," I said.

"Am I getting paid for this?"

"Talk," I said.

"It was at a party given by a young acceptable associate for a departing female lawyer. Lawrence did his bow-wow there — getting down on all fours and

barking at an old partner for an hors d'oeuvre. Barking.
I do not think the bow-wow is a sign of mental health. I
think Lawrence's problems run deep. There appears to
be a double edge to his humor. He makes fun of other
associates, seems to reserve his pathetic fawning for
partners he thinks may help him. But it appears that
he's almost ashamed of his actions. Resents the fact that
other associates see him doing his thing with partners,
and therefore tends to slice up associates even more.
There is one more thing. Recall my premonition?"

"Yes," I said.

"Lawrence is trying to seduce Camilla Newman."

"Oh Christ," I said.

"That's it. Everything I know. How's your work
going?"

"Jesus," I said.

"Talk about your work. It will help to keep your mind
off this."

"I don't care how it's going," I said, "Thank God I'm
leaving. I'm going home for Christmas whether my
projects are finished or not."

"Good boy," Littlefield said. "Listen."

"What?"

"I'm in a new office, two doors down from my old one.
They moved me this morning. I'm sharing a secretary
with a monster associate named Ratner, two years older
than me and eight feet taller. Ratner felt it necessary to
come into my office and make the following statement:
'I will have to pre-empt your work whenever I feel it is
necessary. I am the senior associate and my work is
more important than yours, and when I need something typed or proofread, or require dictation, it is
always a rush job. Your work will have to wait.'"

"Jesus," I said, "what did you do?"

"I could not believe I'd heard this. I sat there stunned.

It was beyond anything I could imagine. Yet the giant seemed to be waiting for a reply. I said, simply, 'You're on a strange trip, Ratner. I don't know what to say to you.' I didn't know what to say to him. He stalked out."

"Maybe he'll mellow," I said. "You'll mellow him out."

"I think not," Littlefield said. "Listen, he looks as if he's wearing a permanent wig. His hair is shaped like a helmet and frozen in place. He's a monster locked in ice, a frozen Frankenstein waiting to thaw. Did you see that movie? I mean, he looks as if he's wearing a wig he can't get off. Helmet hair, ready for combat. He looks like Haldeman. Ready to kill. Scary. I mean, he forced me to the wall, and all my pretend, law-firm-vested-suit-starched-shirt, low-profile disguises slipped away. I reverted to my California, Yale origins. And instead of saying, 'We'll discuss this sensibly,' I said, 'You're on a strange trip, man.' Now he recognizes me for a dangerous hippy, something left over from the sixties. He scared me so much he penetrated my disguise."

"If you need help, call me," I said.

"I'll call the Mafia. I need enforcers."

"I need to work. Thanks, I'll see you," I said.

"Wait." He screamed it into the telephone. "Let me talk." I waited. I could tell he needed to talk. The way he screamed had scared me.

"Talk all day," I said. "I'll listen."

But he didn't talk. I could hear him breathing. We were connected by this telephone line, breathing together. Maybe that was what he needed. "Sorry," he said finally.

"Sorry?" I said. "For Christ sake."

"I shouldn't have screamed."

"Forget it," I said. "I've got another ear."

"Funny," he said.

"I thought a joke might cheer you up."

"Not your jokes. Listen: I want to say more than the firm lets me, more than the partners let me, more than the telephone lets me. I feel stifled here. Where is the mellow conversation? I am trapped. Like even the little things. I'm in the elevator, with my coat, ready to go to the Law Registry, and the doors are closing, and I'm inside and a partner comes out into the hall, and I don't have time to open the elevator door for him. I want to tell him where I'm going, what I'm doing. I want to tell him, Yes, I'm going out on a firm job, not running away. But I can't. The doors close on me. It would not happen this way if we had stairs. Why don't we have stairs? Where is the human equipment? Snap, the doors slam shut on me."

"Come down here and talk to me," I said.

"You're going away."

"Come down now."

"No," he said, "I'm going to work on my secret plan to save myself."

*   *   *

I went to work too, trying to clean up things before I left for home. I worked through dinner and into the night. My mind floated in the law. Working in my office seemed like a flight in deep space. There was blackness outside the windows on the ship and there was the hum of the ship inside. Every now and then, a thruster turned on and I heard the boom, boom, hum and then the winging spinning gears from deep inside the ship's service modules. I did not know exactly where the sounds came from: all of this great building/ship was remote-controlled, all of it taken care of by computers that were programed long ago when the flight started.

I was alone with the hum of the ship, my mind seemingly controlled by drugs that made me oblivious to time and insured that I did not go crazy during this endless flight across the night of giant galactic space.

Had the computerized thrusters made a slight correction in the deep space trajectory? I came back to some semblance of reality. The blast of air was from the air conditioning unit over my head. It was only eleven o'clock and I had finished. Out the window, I saw the lights of a plane going for La Guardia or Kennedy, but I could not hear any sound inside the building. I saw the blinking lights of Midtown, and Jersey and Staten Island — dots of light like far planet systems. It was time to leave and say good-bye to Littlefield.

The lights were on in Littlefield's office, but he wasn't in sight. I checked the library. The lights were on, the usual associates were there, slumped like mannequins over their books, but not Littlefield.

Maybe he was in someone's office, having a good nighttime conversation. Maybe he was having a heart-to-heart with Camilla, warning her about Lawrence. I hoped he was talking to someone. I hoped he realized that in my mind we had become friends. I do not mean workmates, or dinner companions. I mean that there was that deep connection where you will always think about the other person, and sometimes, even if you are working thousands of miles away, you will call him, on impulse, even in the middle of the night. We were friends the way you sometimes become friends with people in college.

I did not want to leave the firm without having seen him. I circled back to his office. He wasn't there. His overcoat lay on a chair; his presence was in the room. Maybe he'd just decided to take one of those late-night Wall Street strolls, left his coat so he'd get the full bracing effect of the cold winter wind. Hell, maybe he was in the bathroom. I went in there. Ratner, old helmet

hair, the giant, Littlefield's frozen "Frankie" was wash
ing his hands. I asked him where his partner was.
Ratner told me he didn't give a damn.

So Littlefield was probably out on a walk, or talking
with some friends. I sat down at his desk to leave a note.
I could not think of anything sensible to write. I could
not think of a joke. As Littlefield had noted, my jokes
weren't too good anyway. I sat there over a yellow legal
pad. I gave up on a big note. I'd try a small one. I
couldn't think of a small one. Maybe one word, damn it,
at least I could think of one word. Surprisingly, I could.
I wrote it in capital letters: TEACH.

In the morning, I got a response from Littlefield. It
came in the interoffice mail, delivered formally by one
of the gray-coated messengers. I tore it open, thinking it
was something from a partner. But it was Littlefield,
answering on the same scrap of paper I'd used. Next to
my one word, he'd written: "Or jump." Then below that
there were five more hopeful words: "Or make a
fiendish plan."

17

In honor of the fact that I was going home, that morning I decided to wear my cow tie tack. The tie tack was a small silver cow with tiny glass balls for eyes. Anyone with any sense knows that tie tacks are not acceptable at a Wall Street firm. They don't kick you out for it, but they are not going to make someone a partner unless they feel comfortable taking him to a lunch club. I guess if you've got a PT 109 tie clip it's all right, but one given you by Nixon or Johnson would be considered a political statement and might get you fired.

This morning I really didn't care. I thought the little cow looked kind of jaunty sitting in the green silk tie I'd picked up at Brooks Brothers. She looked ready to moo — as if she were sitting in the middle of delicious grass (not Littlefield's kind) having a fine time.

By four, my desk was clean. I was catching an eight o'clock plane from La Guardia. Things were nicely arranged. I had enough time to get back to my apartment and pack. I walked down the hall to Camilla's to say good-bye. I figured I'd walk in, shut her door, reach down, pull her up and kiss her before she had a chance to react. It was going to be a daring gesture all right. The first law firm kiss. It would give her something to think about while I was away. A kiss in the middle of business hours, a kiss on the same floor as Cosmo Bass.

Typing outside the door, kissing inside. Thinking of the kiss put me in a such a good mood that as I passed the offices, I thought of them as little houses, holding neighbors. There ought to be small flowerpots outside the doors, I thought, and we'd come out and water them, and talk to each other.

Camilla Newman was not in her house. I stopped at her secretary's desk.

"She's doing a project for Mr. Rolls," Camilla's secretary said.

"Is she in the office or working outside?"

"I believe she's working in Mr. Rolls' office," the secretary said.

I thanked her. I went back to my office. I sat there for fifteen minutes, and called Camilla. The phone rang the normal three times, and then, on cue, her secretary picked it up.

"She's still with Mr. Rolls." I was told. How long could I wait? I began refiguring my time, cutting down on packing. Rush hour ought to be all right. I'd be taking a taxi to the airport around six. Rush hour would be ending. I hoped. I could leave at six-thirty. Probably make it if I left at seven.

"She hasn't come back," I was told, "but your urgent message is on her desk."

"Thanks," I said. It was five o'clock. Anything could happen to the subways after five. They were like cattle cars, they broke down under the strain.

I called Wellington Rolls' office. The telephone did not ring the normal three times before Mrs. Lapido, his secretary, picked it up.

"Mr. Rolls' office," she said.

"I believe Miss Newman is in conference with Mr. Rolls," I said.

"May I ask your name?" Lapido said.

"My name?" Christ, I thought. "Weston," I said.
"Listen, I'm an associate here at the firm. I work here.
I'm calling from the office."

"Yes?"

"I wonder if you could pass a message in to Miss
Newman. I have to leave the office shortly, and need to
speak with her before I go."

"Mr. Rolls, Mr. Lawrence and Miss Newman are in
conference," she said. "And I believe a client is with
them as well. I can't disturb them."

"What if her mother is dying?" I said. "What if her
brother is dead?"

"I assume that neither is the case," the incredible,
hard-assed, steel-voiced Lapido told me. All this was
eating up time. And making me angry.

"I'm a lawyer here," I said. "Please buzz Miss Newman."

"I can't."

"So you won't do what I'm telling you to do?"

"No," she said, "of course not."

Why should she, I thought. I realized I should have
lied right at the beginning. Right now, I could think up
wonderful lies. Thousands of horrible disasters that had
happened to Camilla Newman's family suddenly occurred to me. Big lies, little lies. I thought of disguising
myself as a messenger and sneaking into the office. I
thought of insane excuses: delivering birth control pills,
Wellington Rolls' hernia support, lithium for Lawrence.

"Would you like to leave a message with me?" Iron
Butt Lapido said.

"Several," I answered.

"I am prepared to receive them."

You probably are, I thought, and give them back as
well. "Nothing," I told her and hung up.

But there was a way into that office, a way to say good-bye. The intercom. If I had the guts to use it. I could punch right through the door of that office with the intercom. My voice would flood their business meeting. May I interrupt you, gentlemen? Please stand at attention Mr. Rolls. Please squat Mr. Lawrence. Dear client, you may remain sitting. Now, all three of you will please place your fingers in your ears, as I wish to deliver a personal message to Miss Newman. I would have chosen a more normal method of delivery, but Iron Butt outside the door would not permit it. Ready? Fingers in ears? Good. Miss Newman, Camilla, I love you, I want you. Watch out for that bastard Lawrence, I don't care if he's married. Think of the long hug, Camilla, me giving it to you, and our talks, and lying in bed together. Think of that gasp. You damn well love me, Miss Newman. Good-bye. Oh, yes. Please signal to the gentlemen. They may remove their fingers from their ears.

I looked at the intercom. It challenged me. I wouldn't have to say a whole lot. I could just say good-bye, whisper it into their meeting. No one would know who'd said it. Except Camilla. I'd muffle my voice, put my tie over the receiver. One long, whispered good-bye. It would sound like the voice of God. They were probably writing an important loan agreement, or a securities registration. Good-bye. God has spoken.

Insanely, I pounded the button. The little red light lit up. I stuck my mouth down on the receiver. "Good-bye," I whispered.

Iron Butt Lapido, Rolls' secretary, answered: "Good-bye?" she said. "Is that the message you wish to leave?"

"I punched the wrong extension?"

"You punched right, Mr. Weston."

"I got you."

"While in conference, Mr. Rolls has his intercom switched over to me. Can't you do that with yours?"

"No," I said.

"Yes," she said. "Yes. Of course, you have an associate's intercom, don't you, Mr. Weston?" Oh, she said associate in a fine way, stressing the "ate." Snapping it out. Right, I had an associate, cannon-fodder, cheapie intercom. I could not stop the calls from coming in. I could not stop the partners from assaulting me.

"Is that the message you wish to leave? Good-bye?"

"Yes," I said.

I ran for the elevators, hoping the subways would run, the cab would not get stuck in traffic, the plane would not leave early.

* * *

I sprang into the elevator, coat flying behind me. The doors snapped closed behind me, and Cosmo Bass, standing rigidly at attention, his Chesterfield immaculate, each white hair in place, his chin slightly lifted, said good afternoon.

"Good afternoon, sir," I said, trying to button up, look halfway decent.

"I hope you have an enjoyable Christmas, Webster," he said. Webster. Why not? He was getting closer. Pretty soon he was sure to recognize me.

"Thank you. I hope you have an enjoyable Christmas." I sounded like a parrot, but I guess it was just like when he'd been looking in the mirror that time in the bathroom, staring at himself. I felt as if he'd made me into a mirror, too. I gave him back what he gave me.

Then he stared at my chest. There was something in the mirror he didn't understand.

"Wilson," he said, "is that a pig on your tie? Were you a member of the Porcelian Club?"

"It's not a pig," I said, looking down at the little silver cow.

Cosmo Bass squinted at my tie tack. "Not a pig? What is the nature of the beast?"

"It's a cow."

"A cow? What club is that?"

I wondered if the 4-H Club would be acceptable. It was Christmas, I refused to let anyone else make me feel bad, even Cosmo Bass, and told him the truth.

"It's a cow that my grandfather gave me," I said. "He's a farmer."

"What age?" said Bass.

"Eighty-seven," I said.

Bass straightened up. "Good," he said. "There is nothing like being alive."

We hit ground level. The elevator doors snapped open. The guard on duty elegantly pushed aside the crowd for Cosmo Bass. "Merry Christmas, Ralph," Cosmo Bass said, smiling to the guard, "and to all good cheer."

18

The pilot brought us in to Kansas City through a fierce snowstorm. I sat in my seat, waiting for the passengers to clear out. For some reason it's always the older people who want to get out first.

The plane interior seemed to connect me to the firm. It had that corridor feel, an elongated conference room. Finally I started on the long walk to my parents. They are just ordinary parents, not killers or murderers, but still I felt a certain dread. I got through the gate.

There was my mother bouncing up and down and my father standing behind her. Mom looked like a red beach ball in her quilted parka. It made her so fat she could barely get her arms around me. Dad was wearing a red quilted parka too, and one of those damn Mountie hats, with the flaps down over his ears.

"You're not going to carry it?" I said to my fourteen-year-old brother, putting my bag down on his toes.

"Nope." He was one of those guys who grow two feet in three months. He was now taller than Dad.

I carried the bag myself, although mother tried to snatch it away from me. The bag was thrown into the back of a G.M. Blazer. Our huge Newfoundland started going nuts. He jumped from the front seat to the middle to the back. He sniffed the bag. Then he jumped back into the middle seat. It was crowded sitting there with the one-hundred-and-fifty-pound dog and my giant kid brother, so I tried to lever the dog back with the bag. He started barking. The more I pushed, the more he barked. Dad yelled at the dog. The dog was certainly not going to obey my father, but the yelling distracted him. I took advantage of his momentary lapse of concentration and threw him back.

We took a left into Kansas. Dad put the car into four-wheel drive to get us through the snow. We were moving along at about thirty miles per hour, but the snow flying past the window made it seem as if we were going much faster.

"So we're not going to the house?" I said.

"Nope," my brother said.

"We're going to the ranch?"

"Yup."

"Why?"

"Grandpa's not feeling too well," my mother said.

The driving was serious now. Dad had slowed us down to about five miles and kept peering out trying to find the highway. As long as we kept heading west, we would eventually find the land. It was a big farm, five thousand acres. We'd find it sometime. And if we got into trouble, we could use the C.B. Someone from the farm would come and get us.

We passed a gas station. Lots of cars had pulled up at it to wait out the storm, but I knew my father was not about to stop. In New York a touch a snow and the subway ran two hours late. Dad was a farmer, and didn't stop for snow. When he was small, he worked at my grandfather's place during the summer. He met my mother. He married her. He just kept working at the place. The place became a corporation because of the taxes. Stock was given out. I got some of it. Even my brother did. Now Dad sat in an office in Kansas City and ran a corporation.

You tell people your father is a farmer, but it's always more complicated than that. How can you explain all of it to people? My older brother went to Stanford. My sister went to Wellesley. My parents were the kind who went nuts at college graduations, shooting hundreds of rolls of film. They kissed you in front of the college gateway and photographed that, too. Mentally, they operated very well in Kansas, but had trouble whenever they visited the coasts. They went to see my sister in Boston and lost their luggage. They stayed for a week with my brother in Los Angeles and destroyed two rental cars. Dad could drive through snow, but could not handle sun.

I could not explain my parents to people. My father was a farmer but we grew up in a regular middle-class suburb outside of Kansas City and went to local schools. Living around us were insurance salesmen, business-men, lawyers, doctors. My father went off to work like the rest of them, went to a big office building too, but dressed like a maintenance man. All of us, the chil-dren, were bound to be a little schizophrenic. We were newly rich in that we were in the suburbs. But my grand-father kept telling me how we were the oldest family in the area. His idea of the area seemed to come from a time when you drove a wagon into Kansas City for supplies.

"I'll shoot this dog," my brother said. "No, I mean it, I'll shoot him." The dog was slobbering my brother. The dog's head was on my brother's shoulder and the slobber was running down my brother's coat. New-foundlands were bred to slobber. They tell you New-foundlands were bred to pull sleds, but anyone who takes a good look at the dog can tell that it took hundreds of years of selective breeding to develop a dog who could slobber at the rate the water comes out of your kitchen faucet. They are slobber machines. If you

can stand that, they have a good side. They will let you
sleep on them.

"Do you mind if I shoot him?" my brother said.

"Let Dad drive," Mother said.

"I don't mean shoot him right now. I mean when we
get home."

"We should hit the gate right now," Dad said. He took
a blind faith turn to the left, and there was a big gate,
the snow whistling through the heavy wire.

"Is someone going to open it?" Dad said.

"I'll open it," I said. I got out into the snow. It was
snowing at an angle that seemed parallel to the ground.
I swam through the snow to the gate. Unlatched, the
gate flew back, knocking me to the ground. Dad went
through, leaving his son to die in the cold.

"I knew you couldn't do it yourself," my brother said.
He was out now, too, pushing the gate. I managed to get
up. Pushing and pulling, we got it closed. When we got
back into the car, the dog was sitting in our seat smiling
at us.

My brother decided he would sit in the back with the
bag. Dad was driving by the compass. Under the snow,
there was iron-hard ice. It did not matter if we were on
the road or not. Dad was using the compass to get us
near the lights. He'd told the manager to have the big
silo lights turned on. Sometime we were supposed to see
the three huge lighted blimps.

We saw them. They were spacey, fantastic through
the snow. Dad had built a farm that looked like Cape
Canaveral. Finally, to the left, I saw the lights of the
house.

"There," I said, leaning over my father's shoulder and
pointing.

"I know. Get back." I was twenty-seven, but acting like
a kid. Soon I'd be wondering what I was getting for

Christmas. We pulled in under the big front arch of the house and suddenly there was no more snow.

For some strange reason, none of us were jumping out of the car to get inside the big warm house.

"Is anyone getting out?" my brother said.

"We're all getting out," my mother told him. She buttoned up her coat, opened the door, and started up the steps. I looked up at the door. Mom opened it. Grandpa was sitting in his wheelchair, his arms folded across his chest; Mom bent over and kissed him on the cheek. His arms unfolded. He pressed something on the chair and went flying backward.

*   *   *

Grandpa had had a stroke in the fall. The upper part of his body was intact. Apparently, it was just his legs. After we all shook hands with him, he shot down the wide hall toward the dining room and we followed like the cars of a train. The big table was loaded with food. We sat down to eat it, Grandpa asking Dad questions about the drive, my brother saying nothing. Mother sometimes going into the kitchen to help.

Suddenly, I seemed to wake up, warm up. Look at these damn crazy people, I thought. Dad still wearing his Mountie's hat, Grandpa zooming around the table like a parking attendant, my big dumb younger brother attacking a chicken with both hands, stuffing away potatoes like popcorn. Christ, these dummies are my family. I cannot explain how suddenly warm and rich and mellow I felt.

19

I had two long talks at home, one with my mother, one with Dad. I tried to explain to Dad what it was like at the firm. I was not able to make him understand why, at times, I felt a driving desolation at the firm, a feeling of being caged in and of being very, very far away from home. I tried to explain that the thirty-seventh floor is a distant city and all these people rush around you, and you don't know what to make of them, you can't talk to them, there isn't time, and you can't slow them down. And you start conversations, and the partners look at their watches, wondering about the time sheets, and if the talk is to be charged to a client or not, and if it's not being charged then why are they having it? I tried to tell Dad that it was possible I might not stay at the firm; that got him to think it over.

It was all right to leave the firm, he said finally, but first it was important to be "trained." How did you learn to work the farm, he asked. You trained. Training was hard, you didn't understand what was going on, but in the end it was good for you. Dad did not feel that you could be "trained" in school, he was one for training in the field. I told him that the law firm talked about how they "trained" their associates. And that made Dad happy, and he said they weren't so stupid after all. I did not bother to explain to Dad that there were times when I thought the training was mental, and bad for your mind, and that once they'd fully trained you, whipped you .mentally into shape, it might be impossible to get untrained.

The other talk was with Mom. I'd been at the house two days. It was on the third evening, after dinner. I was up in my room, lying on the bed, staring at the ceiling. She came in, sat down at the foot, and said, "What's the girl situation?"

"Girl situation?" I said. "There isn't any girl situation."

"Sure there is."

"There isn't."

She shook her head.

"Come on," she said, "there's a girl situation here."

"You'd like there to be one," I told her.

"Maybe so," she said. "But I'm not the one staring at the ceiling."

"Resting," I said, "I'm resting."

"Staring it seems to me. Not talking. Or playing with your brother. Moaning."

"Playing with my brother," I said. "I'm supposed to play with my brother?"

"You're not even fighting with your brother. What's the situation?"

I looked down the bed at my mother. She looked something like Camilla. They both had blond hair and blue eyes. They were both small. They didn't talk the same way, though; my mother was simple and direct. And smart. Camilla was smart, too. Of course there was a goddamned girl situation.

"Now listen," she said, "are you in love?"

"Right. Yes. I'm in love."

"All right," my mother said. "Now who's the girl?"

"Who's the girl?"

"Right. Who's the girl."

"The girl?"

"The girl."

"She's a girl," I said. "You know, blue eyes."

"Older, younger?"

"My age. Nice. Pretty. Smart. Nice." I went back to staring at the ceiling. How could I explain? Screwed up? Divorced? Smart? I couldn't explain the firm. I couldn't explain Camilla. Mothers. Girls. Christ.

"One last thing," she said. "One thing."

"Right. One thing."

"Are you getting married?"

"No."

"Why?"

"Why?" Why? Why? I sat up again. I looked at my mother. "Because she doesn't love me," I said. "Understand. She likes me, but she doesn't love me." I sank back. God I thought, she doesn't love me. She doesn't love me. I'm screwed, I thought: SHE DOESN'T LOVE ME.

"Of course she loves you," my mother said.

"Right."

"Who wouldn't love you?" my mother said.

"Right." Lawrence, Rolls, Lynch. Who wouldn't love me? Right. I'm lovable. "Mom," I moaned, "goddamn it. Mom. Leave me alone." I rolled over to face the wall. My mother got off the bed, but I could feel her presence in the room.

"She loves you," my mother said. "Anyway, you can run her down, track her down. Make her love you." She leaned over and shook me. "You dummy," she said. And left. I resumed my ceiling stare.

Run her down, track her down, I thought, Good idea, Mother. Sure she loves me, Mother, sure. Dummy, I thought. Dummy.

20

The day before Christmas, at lunch, my father said he'd like to take a trip to New York.

"I'm not going to New York," my brother said. "No way. You get mugged there. I've read all about it."

"I'd like to meet this Cosmo Bass," my father said.

"Brass?" my grandfather said.

"Bass."

"Funny sort of name. Bass." My grandfather said, "You know Cosmo used to be a popular name. You don't see a lot of Cosmos anymore. There were some good names. Barnabas, that was a good name. Pemberton. A fine name. Ebenezer."

"They called people that?" my brother said.

"There isn't anything funny about Ebenezer," my grandfather said. "Eb. It's a damn good name. No one is named good anymore. Hezekiah. He used to work here. Good name. Augustus. Augustus Mandell. Killiam is a good name. No one uses it anymore. Josiah. Good name."

"Duane is a good one," my brother said. "Dick is all right."

"I met a lot of people with good names in the First World War," Grandpa said. "I remember sitting on a bench on the top of a hill, and there was Binker Sturgis dead in the grass beside me, and a dead German behind me. Binker Sturgis. Now wasn't that a good name? I almost stepped on the German before I saw him. In front of me there was a wide valley with the village all in ruins and our guns were spitting out death in venomous flashes.

"I remember thinking that there were just a few people who want war, or would say they approved of it, but they would say it was inevitable, fate. I sat there and thought the trouble was that people just didn't have the gumption to get together and settle questions in a rational manner. That's why so many people die young. But maybe it doesn't matter. Everyone dies. And it looks like I'll be going, too."

"You're not dying," my mother said.

"I know honey, I'm not dying," my grandfather said. Mother went out to the kitchen.

"I've got to make a telephone call," my brother said, excusing himself. He went out into the hall.

"You mention dying and everyone clears out," my grandpa said. "Jesus Christ. I can't even talk to my own family." He turned to my father. "I like what you've done to this place, I even like the goddamned blimps out there at the end of the field. But I can't understand anymore whether we're making money. I can't read the damn statements."

"We're making money," my father said.

"We'd better."

"We are."

"I like what you've done," my grandfather said. "All of it. Let's go into the study."

We followed Grandpa down the hall toward the study. He looked like a wise little old king in his big, moving, magic chair. I noticed that certain things were not getting done, the house was changing with Grandpa's age, getting a patina of dust. There were people to clean, of course, but they were old, too. Everything seemed to be winding down.

The study was at the end of the hall, through a passage under the wide wooden stairs. There was a chair on the stairs that ran along a metal rail. The chair had been put in for Grandma, but now that Grandpa was alone, the upstairs had been forgotten, and he slept in what had been a maid's room and now looked like a hospital room.

The study was probably the dustiest, worst room in the house. There were papers all over the desk and sofa, pictures all over the walls. A set of antlers over the small fireplace held old fishing poles and a single shot twenty-two. Dad moved some of the papers so that we could sit on the couch. Grandpa poured three very small glasses of bourbon. My glass looked as if it had been cleaned about the time the antlers had been mounted. Dust floated on the top of my drink.

"What do you do with these people that are so stupid all they do is kill each other?" My grandfather swung his chair toward me. "You're supposed to be a lawyer. Why can't these people make agreements? Are they just so stupid they can't avoid killing each other?"

I thought about my agreement with Camilla Newman: *We agree to screw each other and not screw each other over.* How well was that going to work?

"You've got to imagine a spectrum," I told him. "Now at one end, you've got intimate relationships, families, relations between children and parents, husbands and wives. Then you've got more formal relationships, like businessmen, or companies. Finally, at the far end of the spectrum there are hostile relationships. Like those between countries. At either end of the spectrum it's very hard to make agreements that stick. It's hard to make agreements at all."

"It's in their interest to make agreements. They're just too damn stupid."

"At one end of the spectrum, they know each other too well, at the other they don't know each other well enough," I said, giving him a good dose of basic Fuller contract-law theory, "Now, in the middle, which is mostly business relationships, you don't have those problems."

*   *   *

All kinds of strange things began coming out of Grandpa after Christmas. All kinds of memories. I began to realize that it had been very different in 1889, when Grandpa was born: he was talking about kerosene replacing candles, horses, mules, oxen, firewood, running water, plumbing. Children all born at home. Telegraph lines, but no telephones. And I saw why World War I had such a profound effect on him: that was when everything started to change, and suddenly, for him, the way he seemed to understand it, there were cars, and electricity, and planes. None of which he liked.

"My best friend in that damned big war was a mule." We were sitting on the glass enclosed porch watching a snowstorm. "I made a hat for him, cutting out holes for his ears. A damned good mule. A great one. Look at that snow. This is the best snow since nineteen eighteen. Look at those snow jets. This mule could walk through snow eight feet deep."

Then Grandpa went to sleep. The day nurse came out to take him off the porch. Just as she began to turn the chair, he jerked up.

"No you don't, goddamn it," he said. "This is exactly where I want to be, and I don't want you to touch anything in this goddamned house, not a thing."

Part Three
The Restitution Problem

Part Three

The Resolution Problem

21

Three days after Christmas, I powered out of the Midwest on a big jet whose engines ate the snow. Grandpa powered around in his wheelchair, and saw war troops marching in the snow clouds. I saw Camilla Newman. Run her down, track her down, good idea, Mother. I was flying through Newman clouds. Where the sun came through them, I saw the blond strands of her hair.

*　　*　　*

She was at her desk. In her window I saw the sun breaking up the snow clouds, lighting the ice along the windows of the buildings climbing around us. The river, filling in the gaps between the buildings, was bright blue and coated with sparkling ice.

"How was Christmas?" she said. "How are you?"

"I'm going to shut your door."

"No," she said, "you're not."

I shut it.

The phone rang. For a second, the thought of an interruption bothered me — I didn't realize the possibilities.

"Don't answer it," I said.

"You're nuts," she told me and picked it up.

I thought about using the scissors to cut its cord; I could decord the intercom, too.

"Yes," she said to her phone. "Yes, sir."

I walked around her desk, reached down for her, stood her up. She tried to keep up the conversation. I put my arms around her, and gave her a long hug. I began to lose control. I began to feel her small breasts. Then I went for her thighs, pulling up her dress. All the time, she kept trying to keep her end of the conversation going, and beat me off with her one free hand.

"Yes, Mr. Rolls," she said. "I've gone over the Red Herring."

So she was doing securities work. The Red Herring is the preliminary filing with the Securities and Exchange Commission. The one that says, in red letters, "This is not an offer," meaning, it's not approved, doesn't count.

Camilla Newman's thighs felt wonderful under her stockings. Run her down, I thought. Take her here right on her desk. With my new mental attitude it was fun to be back at the firm. Then she hung up and gave me a push that sent me flat against the wall.

"Don't," she said. "Don't do that."

"I'm just glad to see you."

"Don't. Stay there."

"I'm staying."

"I'm coming around the desk. Stay there." I stayed. She came around. I stuck to the wall. She opened the door. "Now," she said, "sit." I did. We looked at each other across her desk top.

"You're glad to see me?"

"That's my excuse."

"I'm glad to see you, too."

"Let's talk," I said. Marriage, I thought. Live together. Looking into her eyes, I knew I loved her. Drugged on her eyes, I was sure I could get her.

"We're going to live together," I said.

"We are?"

"Yes."

"We're going to talk." She was looking into my eyes, too. What she saw, she didn't like. "We're going to talk, but not now, not here."

"When?"

"Later."

"Where?"

"Maybe at my place. Maybe at yours. I don't know when."

"Tonight?"

"Maybe. See this stuff?"

I saw all the paper, the printed copies, the typescript.

"We're five days into this S-seven. I've got to finish it. The target date for the offering is twenty days off. Then we go to Hudson Street."

"Hudson Street?"

"You don't know anything," Camilla Newman said. "You don't do any real work."

Hudson Street sounded ominous the way she said it. I thought of Jack Nicholson in *Chinatown*. I thought of Faye Dunaway getting shot in the eye. Camilla Newman looked a little like Faye Dunaway. She had the same kind of body, just on a smaller scale. They kept saying "Chinatown" all through the movie, and you knew it would be bad news when they got there. That was the way Camilla Newman said Hudson Street. You could tell she was getting into her work. Red Herrings. Hudson Street. It all sounded ominous. Tombstone. That is what they call the announcement of an offering that is printed in the *New York Times* and the *Wall Street Journal*. I'd heard the corporate boys talking in the lunch room. I knew a little. Bear Hug, Iron Maiden. Those are the actual terms they use to describe corporate takeovers. I wondered about the kinds of minds corporate securities people like Lawrence had.

"I'd really like to see you tonight," I said. "I'm sorry I don't know about Hudson Street, but I'd like to see you. I'm doing some work too. Lynch's case could come down any time, and then when would I ever see you?"

"O.K.," she said. "My place, around ten tonight. If you get out of this office now. If you let me finish the damn work."

"Your place. It's binding?"

"Offer. Acceptance."

I started for the door.

"Sam," she said. "Do me a favor?"

"Sure," I told her. Flowers? Candy?

"This time. This time." She stopped. She shook her head. "This time would you get it together and buy some booze, Scotch, anything? Maybe dope from Little-field?"

"Dope, booze, Scotch," I said. "Candy. Flowers. Lots of flowers."

* * *

I brought all of it, including reams of flowers. Bunches of course, not reams, but I asked the flower man for reams. He understood me anyway. The shop catered to lawyers. I probably could have talked equity jurisdiction with him. Maybe he could have told me about Hudson Street.

I bought it, brought it and we used it, but it did not go well. After I'd told her how much I loved her, she got off the bed and stepped over to the window.

"You ought to get some curtains," I told her.

"You're in a homey mood," she said, not turning. "Curtains, kitchens, cooking. You got homey all right. What the hell happened to you?"

"I'm in love. At least turn out the lights."

"Why?"

There were a thousand windows out there. She was standing there nude, tits against the glass.

"Perverts," I said.

"Perverts. Christ you're protective." Now she turned, leaning against the thick glass, butt against it. "Perverts. If there's some pervert out there with a telescope, if I'm part of his world, that doesn't make him part of mine. The windows out there don't count, they're not real."

"Come here and talk," I said.

"No talk. No more talk with you."

"You love me."

"No."

"We're going to talk."

"No, that's not what we're going to do." She stumbled a little coming back to the bed. Littlefield's dope was very good. She fell into bed, rolled over, face up.

"Fuck me," she said. She had a stupid, silly smile on her face that made her look very young.

"Fuck me."

"No," I told her. We were not going to keep on just fucking our brains out. Making love and working. And no time to think about anything important. I was going to marry the bitch.

"Come on," she said, "fuck me." She reached for me. As if she could just rub me a little, turn me on, and I'd fuck her. She was probably right, so I sat, cross-legged on the bed, looking down at her.

"You were going to," she said.

"I was."

"Do it." She put her hands over her breasts, rubbed her nipples. "We finally got the fucking part of our relationship straightened out. Now you won't fuck. What's the matter with you? Fuck."

"No," I said.

"You're nuts," she told me.

"You're stoned."

"Come on. Do you want me to fuck myself?" She put her hands down and began to rub herself. "Is this what you want me to do? You know what I'm good at. Do you want that?"

She was good at it all right, but I didn't want it. She rolled over on her side and pointed her enormous blue eyes at me. They were wobbling, but finally she got me in her sights.

"Tie me up," she said. "Fuck my brains out."

Jesus, I thought, a tough securities lawyer, clear mind, cold steel, sees the heart of a problem. A twenty-six-year-old child who lied to herself. I was not going to kiss her and make it well.

"I'll fuck someone else," she mumbled, rolling back and staring at the ceiling.

"I'm sure you will."

"I will."

"I'm sure you have."

"I will," she mumbled. "You broke the contract."

"You're a mess," I said, angry now, jealous. Saying she was a mess suddenly brought her to life.

"No mess," she mumbled. She seemed to be searching for something, but the room was such a mess she couldn't find it. Then she got her hands on the attaché case and pulled it onto the bed with some difficulty. "No mess," she said. "Look." She snapped open the case. Her papers were organized logically in the leather files. Her Mont Blanc pen was in its holster. The silver Tiffany calculator was in its straps. It was clean, organized. "Is that a mess?" she asked. "Is it?"

It wasn't a mess. It was the clean, organized part of her mind. Good for her. She was so proud of it. She

leaned against the back of the sofa bed, her legs out
straight in a V pattern, the organized clean part of her
mind resting on her cunt. She was in fine shape all right.

"O.K.?" she said. "O.K.?"

"It's nice," I said.

"Shut it for me."

"You can't?"

"No," she whispered. I shut the case and put it down
carefully beside the bed. She slid down into the sheets,
pulling them around her. Heavy breathing.

She was out. I turned off the lights and went to the
window; there were a thousand windows out there.
Maybe she was right: this was too much of a city and you
could not let the perverts make you part of their world.
I went back to bed and tried to sleep. I couldn't. Maybe
it was the dope, or maybe it was Camilla. I needed to
sleep and couldn't. I went back to the window. There
were chains of lights and boards of light. Blinking and
flowing. It was poured, bottled nightlight, thick and
heavy, oozing all over the city, pockmarking the buildings, flowing over the bridges, light like a pockmarking
plague. I watched the plague fall back into the darkness
as the final cars left, and the perverts went to sleep. I
watched the morning come in. It was a victory for the
morning over the plague. I just wished I had not seen it.

Camilla woke up fresh for work. We took a fast
shower together. She was rolling, ready to go, and
pulled me out with her.

22

"Your story of your homecoming was superb," Little-field said, "I shall visit Kansas."

"Your dope was superb too."

"I maintain my connections with New Haven." Littlefield was disorganized, his mind an old attic. His Village apartment looked like something out of the *Arabian Nights.* But his office was immaculate. The pens neatly arranged, desk top uncluttered, a conservation photograph of redwood trees by Ansel Adams on the wall.

"But it does not go well *in re Newman?*"

"No," I said, "it doesn't go well."

"But you do not wish to talk to me about it?"

"No," I said, "I do not wish to." Fuck me. Fuck her.

"Well," Littlefield said. "Well. I will talk for you. You are depressed, disgusted. Clearly, you have begun to dream about being left alone, left in some city in the night, with a little suitcase, and not knowing anyone in the city, and it's probably raining in your lonely dream. And there's nothing for you to do but go to a motel, and sit there on a double bed. And watch television, and wish you had someone to telephone, but there isn't anyone, because when you lost Camilla you lost interest in all the rest, in your friends and family. In your dream, you probably cannot even remember their names anymore. Am I correct, is this the type of depressing scene that pops up in your lovesick, depressed, Midwestern mind? Is this the kind of alternative you dream about? Camilla, or The Motel in the Rain?"

"Something like that," I said. Littlefield looked so clean and proper, his office so immaculate, that I felt I was talking to a shrink.

"Remember this," he said, leaning forward.

"All right. Just tell me."

"I'm waiting to insure your attention. Remember you probably will end up alone in some hotel somewhere. However, there are all kinds of hotels, the kinds in Graham Greene novels, the kind of bar in *Casablanca,* Rick's Place. Dream of those places, dream that you can just go down to the bar, and while you're there you'll fall in love with someone and take her back to your room and you will not be lonely anymore. Got it?"

"Yes," I said.

His telephone rang. He pressed the intercom, and his secretary answered. "Could you inquire who is calling?" he asked.

"Mr. Lynch."

"Will you explain that I am in conference, and will be with him shortly?"

"Mr. Lynch," she said again.

"I will be with him shortly."

"You want me to tell him that?"

"Please. Hold my calls. All my calls. Understand?"

"Sure," she said, buzzing off.

"Lynch doesn't want anything," Littlefield said. "He just calls, or pops in suddenly to remind me that we have not heard from the court. 'A lazy court,' he screams. He tells me how different it would be if his father or grandfather were the judge. I tell him he is right; which is not exactly a lie. It would be different. We might win the case through nepotism."

"Calm down," I said. "Look, how are you? I haven't seen you for two weeks."

"Unhinged."

"What?"

"Outside the walls, looking in. I feel like I've lost psychic contact with this place. I feel as if I'm outside my window, looking in at the place. The flying sociologist. I do not feel part of it. Perhaps it was the water torture of real estate that did it to me. I see no friends. I see liars, self-deluders, masochists, bores. I see people like Rolls, as mean as any mugger in the park. I see silly men here too, who play with themselves and with their shoe-shining equipment. Am I wrong?"

"You're wrong," I said.

"Good. There must be a purpose. At least there is the work." He pulled out his memorandum file. Every associate, every partner keeps one. It contains all the stuff you've written at the firm. "Every now and then I slip something brilliant and sneaky into the work. Even into the deeds. I am saved by the fact that sometimes I can get off on the work. I hate the people, and tell myself I hate the work, but once in a while I find myself late at night looking over what I've done, and I think, Who the hell ever wrote a memorandum as perfect as this? I did this thing! And there is not a case left uncited or a single misplaced comma. Now we are not doctors, we have no connection with our clients. But there is some vital connection with the work. I am ashamed of myself, but the only way I keep any form of sanity, and I have little left, is to look at my work as if it were a mirror. I am a narcissist of the Xeroxed copy and MTST machine."

"We all are," I said. "Once in a while we all do something good."

"Sometimes, I do something brilliant," he said.

"Sometimes I'll bet you do."

"And no one ever notices. It never reaches Cosmo Bass."

His secretary's voice came over the intercom. "It's Mr. Lynch again," she said.

"I'm in conference."

"What if he calls a third time?"

"Then I'm here."

"Fine," she said. "What kind of conference are you in?"

He clicked her off the machine. It was magical the way he made her voice disappear. I wondered why Lynch didn't just use the intercom himself. Probably because what he had to say was too important. A secretary might overhear it.

"What's Hudson Street?" I asked.

"Hudson Street?" he said, leaning back in his chair, folding his hands behind his desk. "You do not over- hear, you do not listen? You do not keep proper track of the firm. Hudson Street. Yes. You will certainly learn of Hudson Street if my prognostications are correct. Recall I am a spy?"

"What news?" I asked.

"We are short-handed. Two bodies have departed. Having not been elevated, as they say, to partnership, they have joined the litigation department of one of our large corporation clients. It is a phenomenon I do not understand. Having worked here eight years, and been given progress reports every six months, which always said they were working splendidly, they are passed over, as they say. Now, would you not expect anger in that situation? No. Because the brainwashing is complete. So the firm has a departure lunch for them, and gives them speeches saying what fine lawyers they were, and the departees rise and say what a fine time they've had at the firm. They thank the firm for the splendid experience. Then take jobs with the firm's big clients, and continue to feed the firm business. I call that brainwashing."

"Was Lawrence one of them?" I asked.

"No such luck. His future still hangs in the balance."

"What about Hudson Street?"

"Listen," he said, leaning forward, "they need bodies on Hudson Street, they always need bodies."

This was definitely Faye Dunaway, Jack Nicholson, *Chinatown*. I almost didn't want to know any more about Hudson Street, but I asked anyway.

"It's the printers, you dummy," Littlefield told me. "It's where the prospectuses, the ten-Ks, the twenty-twos, the indentures and all the rest of the garbage gets printed. It is four o'clock in the morning. Why don't you know these things?"

Just then Lynch burst into the office.

"I'm glad to find the two of you together," he said. "There's still no word from the court. Nothing. Lazy court. Not a damn word. They won't tell us if we won or lost. Should we sue the bastards?"

"Which ones?"

"The court," he yelled. "Sue the court."

"Sir," Littlefield said. And he could be courteous, obsequious, a courtly little associate who gave the impression of complete competence. "May I suggest another of your excellent letters?"

23

In the lunchroom, I asked a few of the corporate/ securities boys about Hudson Street and the funny thing was that they didn't know where it was. No one who'd been there did. Maybe in the Village, perhaps in Little Italy. You went to Hudson Street in a cab, a lot of lawyers, bankers, and flunkies packed in together. You talked and joked about how cramped you were while the cab driver took some mysterious twisting journey through the secret roads of the city.

Littlefield was right: they needed bodies on Hudson Street. The corporate boys were exhausted. The firm was doing a lot of work for its investment banking client, work that Wellington Rolls supervised, that his shadow, Lawrence, nursed. Camilla Newman was doing some of it, too. The corporate boys were putting in eighty-hour weeks: older associates, already on the fringe of lunacy worrying about whether they would make partner, putting in a steady eighty billable hours, which is to say they were earning the law firm approximately six thousand dollars a week, almost three hundred thousand dollars a year.

You do not talk about salaries at the firm. You are told not to talk about salaries. Frankly, you're told not to talk about anything. But these boys were making a lot of money for the firm, for the partners, and were probably being paid something like forty-five thousand dollars a year.

This was a gang of tough boys. A misplaced comma and they told their secretaries to fuck themselves. That was the way they talked — unless Cosmo Bass was around. They powered down to Hudson Street, putting together deals, screaming at the printers, drinking, arguing, proofreading until six in the morning, then catching the first flight down to Washington to get final approval of the Registration Statement from the SEC. You got that approval around nine-thirty, unless some-one had made a mistake, and at ten, when the market opened, the securities, stock or debentures traded. The next day the tombstone appeared in the big papers. If there had not been a mistake. If there had been, heads rolled. That was how they talked: rolling heads.

They were shell-shocked infantry troops, veterans of the line. Their eyes had Lawrence's socket look. They were fighting it out for partnership, but they'd been at the front line so long they half expected to get shot down. They almost hoped for it.

Campers on Corporate Law does not convey to the law student what corporate work is like. It gives you nice little cases arguing the fine points of "due diligence," and rule 10(b)-5. It makes securities law seem like a logical exercise in mental gymnastics. These boys in the lunch room should have been teaching the course but they were not the kind to teach or write. Their conver-sation was on a "need to know" basis. I did not need to know anything except how to proofread. That made it hard to find out the background to Hudson Street. I got some of it, though, because they thought it was funny I was so stupid.

Suppose you're a large, well-known company. You want to issue a long-term debenture. Not a bond, that's for utilities. A debenture: You're going to borrow money by selling some kind of debt obligation on the New York Stock Exchange. You set up a target date, maybe twenty-five days away. There's a managing underwriter involved, an investment banker. They're going to buy the debentures and do the actual selling. There are other people involved, too: accounting firms, other underwriters, and dealers who will sell the bonds. You're putting together a deal, you've got a target date, and you're the lawyer for the investment banker. You file an S-7, which contains the Red Herring, with the Securities and Exchange Commission "SEC." It's a preliminary disclosure document, so that the public will have all the information it's supposed to have to insure it makes wise investments and doesn't get cheated.

The days click off. Other documents have been prepared: an agreement among underwriters, an underwriting agreement, a selling dealers' agreement. Maybe a legal investment memorandum and a blue-sky package. Meanwhile the SEC is arguing with you on changes in the S-7. The company and the investment banker argue over the price of the debentures, and watch the market. Papers fly, commas drop, sentences get misplaced. Everyone screams. Twenty days into the deal, the SEC comes back with changes. You work all night, trying to revise the Red Herring into a final, truthful/untruthful document on which the public will rely. You can't make it final without SEC approval. All the other agreements are being put into final form, but you're still haggling with the SEC. And you're only five days away from Tuesday night. Tuesday night is important because Wednesday is the day the market is most active. Tuesday is a good day too, but you'll never make it by then. Thursday is a possibility. But if you don't get the work out, you'll hit the market on Friday and the investment banker will be very angry with you. Anyone interested in buying debentures is already on the way to the country and won't get back until next Tuesday, when someone else with a better law firm will have a better debenture on the market.

It's Tuesday now, day twenty-four, and you think you've settled all the arguments with the SEC. You've got a few minor changes to make, but most of the Registration Statement is at the printer's. The company and the investment banker are still arguing about the price of the debentures. Some senior associates are already at the printer's, working on the statement. The market closes. The company and the investment banker agree on a price. Now it's into the taxi cabs, over to Hudson Street, everyone crowded together, lawyers and bankers, flunkies and senior associates, businessmen and accountants. You. Because you know how to proofread. They didn't teach you proofreading at Harvard Law School, but that is the only reason you're there, and someone is billing your proofreading skills at the rate of fifty dollars an hour.

24

Apparently, this was some debenture deal they were putting together in Wellington Rolls' office. I could hear him yelling something about the fact that it had a redemption feature. Certain of the debentures could be redeemed at a different premium in each of the following twenty years. Only, in the preliminary draft there were only nineteen spaces for the redemption prices. How could anyone make that kind of mistake, he screamed. I wondered how he could keep it up without having a heart attack.

Camilla came out of the office with red eyes, just keeping the tears in check. She passed without seeing me, heading for her office. Lawrence strutted out, too, nodding as he passed. Then Rolls came out. He stood on the other side of his secretary's desk, one foot in the hallway, legs spread, arms folded across his chest. He had a Captain Ahab look, even in his immaculate white shirt and striped tie. There was a certain instability around the eyes, combined with a power stare. You know that kind of stare: the eyes round, the head thrown back, so the balls bore into you. He looked at his secretary; he looked at me, and decided his secretary was the most essential.

"Why are you lurking in the corridor?" he yelled at me. "You invade my closet, you lurk at my office. Do you ever work?"

There must have been someone British in his family. He was manning the poop deck all right. This was his corridor. That was his closet. His secretary sat head bowed next to his knees. I was on his carpet, leaning against his wall. I wondered where his ship ended. Did it include the library and the bathroom? There wasn't much room to maneuver in the white corridor. I'd have to pass that foot stuck out into the hall. I started by keeping an eye on his eyes in case he decided to jump me. I didn't care how expensive his suit was, how tan and orderly he looked, how many bank presidents were his clients. He had the look of someone who could spring. I didn't actually think he'd try to grab me around the neck, but I could see him grabbing my arm, pinching it, while he yelled at me.

Going past, I managed to step on one of his carefully polished, black, shiny, wing tips.

"Clumsy idiot," he screamed. He was big on the territorial imperative, like a German shepherd, and for a moment, he *was* going to jump me.

Two things stopped him. First, I got by too fast. Second, his shoe. How could he plant a scuffed shoe on the poop deck? What would the officers think? What kind of example would he be setting for the crew? What if Cosmo Bass came by?

Over my shoulder, I saw him retreat into his office and heard his shoe-shining equipment turn on. I'll bet he's got clipper ship prints in there, I thought. I'll bet he's even got one of those expensive boat models in a glass case. His corner office did have the best view of the harbor. I'll bet he's got an oil painting of his father wearing a captain's hat and holding on to the wheel of a ship. He must, I thought. Look at what Lynch did to his office.

*   *   *

And I bet Lawrence isn't being obsequious when he calls Rolls "sir." He's just trying to save his life. For a second I felt sorry for Lawrence. That second was the time it took me to get around the turn in the corridor, past the mail room and the door to the typing pool, and into Camilla Newman's office. I wasn't trying to spy on her. We were friends. I thought she'd feel better when I told her about Captain Rolls.

"She's very upset," Lawrence said. "I don't think this is the time to burst into her office."

He had his arms around her. She was sobbing into his shoulder. I didn't think my talk with him had produced this sudden change in his attitude toward associates. I shut the door.

*   *   *

What about Lawrence's wife? I thought. What about her? She probably doesn't matter, I thought. She's not a part of the firm. She's just out there somewhere in the city. Those people out there don't count, none of them. They aren't real because they aren't here.

Don't imagine things, I thought, for Christ sake. Don't space out on things you're not sure have happened. Think about what Littlefield told you. There are other girls, different kinds of hotels. I told myself all that, but it didn't do any good. You get a sort of tingling Spiderman feeling about these things. My mind went its own way on instinct. I saw his arms around her, her face on his chest, her breasts on his chest, and the neat little words of the memorandum that sat on my desk top would not hold still. They bounced around the white page as if I'd stepped on an ant colony in a white desert.

25

It was some deal. They needed a lot of bodies on Hudson Street. I was a body, Littlefield was a body. There were a couple more, too. While the big boys argued over the premium on the redemption feature, which I did not understand at all, one of the young assistant accountants wandered into my office. He wore a shiny sharkskin suit, a colored shirt, and a huge garish tie. It was definitely not a law firm uniform, but then I supposed accountants lived in another world.

"It's a big one all right," he said. "Boxcar numbers."

"Boxcar numbers?" I said.

"Zeros. Boxcars. Lots and lots of zeros."

Accountants seemed to talk their own language, too. I asked him about Hudson Street. "It all depends on the printer," he said, "I don't know which one they're using. Some give you all the shit, Chivas, cigars, everything but women. Some take you out to Lutece while the pages clear. It's never the same. Some don't give you anything."

"I see," I said.

"You haven't met the salesman?"

"No," I said, "I haven't met anyone. I don't know the printer. What the hell is the salesman?"

"A good salesman gives you all the shit. But there are some printers who don't give you anything. They don't clean the rooms. They pretend all their money goes into doing a better job printing. That's bull. It all goes into profits. You don't know which printer?"

"I don't know anything," I said.

"I'll bet it's Maitland. They give you Chivas. And this is a biggie, so they'll probably give us a lot."

"Too bad I can't drink it," I said.

"Something wrong with your stomach?"

"I'm supposed to proofread."

"What the hell do you think everyone is supposed to do?" the accountant said. "How do you think they separate the men from the boys over on Hudson Street?"

"I can't proofread drunk."

"You'll learn," he told me. "For Christ sake, I've proofread stoned. And I'm the one on the numbers. A wrong number and you take the dive. We're up fifty floors. I mean they don't just take away your calculator. Do you have any problems with the SEC?"

"I keep trying to tell you," I said, very slowly, "that I don't know anything."

"If there are problems with the SEC this will probably be a late one. Are you flying or training it down to D.C.?"

"I don't know," I said.

"Have you ever done that?"

"No," I told him.

"Then you're not. You might get lost. This one is too big to let a . . ." He stopped. He was going to say something like dummy, and thought better of it. He strained for words. Since I was a lawyer, I supplied him with some.

"Capable but inexperienced?" I suggested.

"Just what I was going to say," he said. "You don't know when we pack it over to the Street?"

I shook my head.

"I think I'll find someone who does," he said. "I'll get back to you."

He wasn't going to get back to me, but that was all right. I hoped the next office he stumbled into was Littlefield's. Littlefield would be excited to know that official policy meant he could proofread stoned. The news might be enough to get him to specialize in securities law.

*   *   *

We packed it over to Hudson Street around five-thirty. We were a load of drone flunkies, with Lawrence and Camilla, who had both done a lot of work on the project, there to make sure the bodies arrived. There were six of us squeezed into the back of a cab, which is illegal, and explains why Lawrence gave the cab driver a huge tip. Lawrence was in a fine mood all right: all the way over, he had Camilla on his lap. I had Littlefield on mine. We were on different sides of the seat with a couple of drone accountants stuck between us. I could not see through the accountants, but my imagination went wild thinking about what Lawrence was doing with his hands. I could not see out the window either, because of Littlefield, so I still can't tell you where Hudson Street is, but the cab takes a lot of turns and goes over a lot of potholes to get there.

We spilled out into a warehouse district. It looked like a good place to kill someone. Maybe I'd kill Lawrence here. I wanted a dark night and the low black clouds suggested one was coming. Maybe I'd kill Rolls too and pretend they'd offed each other.

*   *   *

It was Maitland Printing, which must have made my accountant friend happy. There were lots of what they called reading rooms, and lots of people already in them, reading. The rooms were teak-paneled and had mahogany tables and thickly padded chairs. Rolls was in one of the biggest rooms with several distinguished-looking older men. They were smiling and laughing. Lawrence carefully placed Littlefield and me in a small room off to one side. He took another room with Camilla.

"Look what the fucker's done," I said.

"Calm yourself."

"He's separated us."

"It's traditional."

"Bullshit."

"Really," Littlefield said. "I'm not trying to console you or fool you. Usually, the big boys read for content. The senior associate on the job and his chief flunky read the important stuff word for word. I know these things."

"You know them," I said. "You've never been here before."

"I absorb information. I wonder when we get the Chivas?"

"I wonder when we get something to do," I said. We had no pages to proofread, just a bare table. Suddenly a man dressed like a cross between an accountant and a lawyer opened the door.

"Gentlemen," he said, "are you comfortable?"

"Fine," I said.

"Can I get you anything?"

My mind was not working right, thinking of Camilla in there with Lawrence, but Littlefield was on the job.

"What have you got?" he asked.

"Everything. Suppose you start with potato chips and a drink. Anything in particular?"

"Do you have Glenmorangie?" Littlefield asked.

"Morangie?"

"It's a Scotch, a single malt. Don't worry, not many people do have it."

The man looked hurt.

"We will have it," he said. "I promise you that. Glenlivet? Would that suit you?"

"Fine," Littlefield said.

"And you?"

I'm not drinking, I thought. For Christ sake, I can't proofread drunk. "Nothing," I said. Then I thought about Lawrence. I knew the bastard was telling Camilla to drink. I stopped our friend at the door.

"I'll have the same," I said.

"The same? And would you like anything else? Something special?"

"Just the booze."

He seemed to be very happy that I'd changed my mind. If he didn't make us feel at home, they'd fire him. Through the glass window in the door, I saw Rolls and his distinguished friends being helped into their coats by a better-dressed flunky than ours. Lutece, I thought. Boxcar numbers. Why not Lutece?

"Wonderful," Littlefield said. "Ritual. It is all ritual."

I wondered where they'd take us to dinner. Burger King? Lawrence came in. He handed us some pages. They were part of one of the minor documents making up the package.

"Clear these pages," he said. "There are a few changes."

I gave him a good look.

"I'm sorry we can't all go out to dinner together," he added. "But we've got to get the stuff out as it comes in. It's going to be a late one anyway. You're giving us a head start."

"Good-bye," Littlefield said. "Have a good time."

"They'll bring you food," Lawrence said. "Tell them what you want. Easy on the booze."

*   *   *

Now that we were alone, we actually began to work. There were other drones working, too, in the other reading rooms. I had no idea what they were proofing. I passed them on the breaks — when Littlefield and I went roaming the halls.

We actually found a few mistakes, places where the printer had dropped a word, left out a sentence. These mistakes usually appeared where he'd been asked to make some last-minute change. Finally we finished our little job. It went out. Then it came back so that we could clear the pages again. Every mistake brought back the page to be cleared.

*   *   *

The big boys came back from dinner around nine-thirty. Littlefield and I were eating our hamburgers. Rolls stuck his head in the door.

"Mush," he said. "Mush." Apparently he thought it was a joke we should appreciate. He seemed to expect us to laugh. Mush. His sled-dog command didn't seem funny to me. On cue, Littlefield made a small chuckle. "Mush, you huskies," Rolls said. I was glad that the big boys were reading for content and not for words.

There were maybe twenty people mushing in the reading rooms. Lawyers from the company, investment bankers and their assistants, a couple of accountants, and one or two more associates from our firm. Camilla and Lawrence got back from dinner at about ten, when the principal document, the Registration Statement came off the press and needed to be cleared. When they came back, I had another Scotch.

Now it was just work, clearing pages. Making sure the little changes that Wellington Rolls had made existed in the printed page, making sure all the lines that Lawrence had written were there, that the machines had not made some error. Around eleven, the big boys pulled out, leaving Lawrence in charge. He sat in there with Camilla going over all the stuff, clearing it all again. I didn't blame him. His ass was on the line, and the pages were finally ready to be run off.

"You stay while they run off the copies," Lawrence said. "When it's packaged, wake up the poor bastard in room four, and make sure he checks it. And do what the hell he says." Lawrence was riding high on the booze and the power he'd mustered to finally finish the deal. "If there's any question, wake him up and talk to him. Don't do anything yourself. He does it, understand."

"Then why do we stay?" I said.

"You'll love it, you'll see it out," he said. "They like to have a couple of lawyers to the end. It's traditional. When the work is done, get bombed. A hell of a deal, wasn't it?"

How would we know? Littlefield, already bombed, wiggled his fingers as a farewell gesture.

*   *   *

Booze and proofreading made me paranoid. While I worked, I'd seen mistakes that weren't there, heard ghostly voices. I was supposed to find mistakes, so I thought I saw them. Only Littlefield kept me sane. He really didn't care if we got all the mistakes or not.

The proofreading paranoia stayed with me until four in the morning and while Littlefield dozed, I saw images of Lawrence and Camilla at some hotel. Finally, just to settle down, I called her number. How the hell could they be in a hotel if he was married? I let the phone ring twenty-five times before I hung up. Then I called the firm. Some poor slob associate working on a tight deadline was nice enough to let me ring both Camilla's and Lawrence's extensions about fifty times. After that I called Camilla's apartment every fifteen minutes. I called until four-thirty in the morning when some guy in a white shirt and plaid pants walked in.

"You gotta clear the title page," he said.

"What happened?" I said, leaping up. The bastard had scared me out of my mind.

"I don't know what happened. Someone on the other shift screwed up. I don't know."

I woke Littlefield and we went to wake the senior associate.

"My God," Littlefield said at the door. "It's Ratner. We dare not wake him."

"What?" I said.

"Ratner. You know the last time they woke up Frankenstein. It is sure to lead to disaster. Look at that creep."

"We have to wake him up," I told Littlefield. "We don't have any choice." I went in by myself. Ratner was sleeping on his side, breathing heavily. His sleeping face was set in a grimace. There certainly did seem something Frankensteinian about him: he breathed in grunts.

"It's just one page?" Ratner asked the printer when I'd shaken him awake.

"One. The title page."

"O.K." He turned to us. "Can't you slobs clear the stinking page that is just a list of names. You got the master page?"

"Right here," the printer said.

"You slobs read it. I mean, it's just a list of names."

We started out the door.

"Remember to check that the company and the co-managing underwriters each have their own type-face, Littlebuns," he yelled. "They've all got their special typeface and we'll kick your butts if you get one wrong. You can do that can't you?"

"We'll look at the typefaces," I said.

"Good," he said.

"I ought to know the typefaces by now," the printer said.

"Sure," Ratner said. "You ought to know. I've seen your work."

"Nice guy," the printer said. Littlefield and I went into the fancy room the big boys had used. Why not? We sat down and checked out the page. The printer had been right: the company and each of the two investment firms had a special typeface. We checked everything over three times.

"I told you it was fine," the printer said. "I ought to know my work. Typefaces. I do these things all day, every day. We'll have the whole package out in twenty minutes for your nice friend to take to Washington."

I spent the twenty minutes calling Camilla's apartment. There wasn't any answer. In twenty minutes the packaged documents came out and we woke up Sourpuss.

"I can't believe you guys are too stupid to be sent to Washington. I've been here seven years, and I'm still making the trip. What's the matter with you? I ought to take you, Littlebuns, so you can do it the next time."

"You ought to, but you can't," Littlefield said. "My doctor says no trains or planes."

"Next week, I'll send you on a corporate search," the Frankie snapped. "You can walk to Montana."

He stalked out to a waiting cab.

"You guys got a cab, too," the printer said quietly. I wondered where the salesman had gone. The booze had dried up.

"You did an enviable job," Littlefield said. "We both express our appreciation and admiration."

"Thank you, Joes," the printer said. Joes. I liked that. It was a good Hudson Street term. We went out to the cab.

"Come over to my place," Littlefield said. "Come over and we'll finish the evening."

"No," I told him.

"*In re Newman?* But you're all right?"

"I'm fine," I said. And I wasn't. We cabbed for a while. It had started to rain. We hit Broadway. Broadway was still alive at six in the morning in the rain.

"I'll walk," I said.

"You're nuts," the cab driver said.

"Hold your tongue," Littlefield said. "Let him walk."

I got out.

"Good luck, my friend," my friend said, and he sped away.

The girl was gone. I was in the rain. Life was brutal. You flowed with it anyway. I matadored across Broadway, toward home.

26

When I left for work it was still raining. The subway was crowded with wet steaming bodies. Normally, I would have tried to squeeze away from riders who looked as if they were going to vomit, or from bums spilling booze down the coats of polished, scrubbed businessmen. Today I didn't care what happened to me, as long as I got to work.

I got to the office at exactly nine-thirty, made sure I put my coat in the crowded closet, and met my secretary, poor Mrs. Moultrie — white-faced eyeballs jiggling as if they were on strings.

"Mr. Rolls wants to see you," she said, "right now."

"Fine," I said.

"I mean right away. At this very moment. In his office."

"All right."

"Don't you understand?"

I understood. He wanted to see me. Right away.

"O.K.," I said, "calm down."

"Please go."

"I will." Rolls had obviously tied her to the mast and given her twenty lashes. He'd probably threatened to keelhaul her if I didn't show up.

Camilla wasn't in her office. Neither was her gear.

Rolls' secretary stood up, opened the door to his office keeping well back from me.

"I have been waiting for you," Wellington Rolls said. He was sitting at his desk. Lawrence was in a big chair in the corner.

I said, "Good morning." My God, there were ship pictures on his walls, and he did have a big oil painting of a snarling man, dressed in yachting clothes, holding sternly to the spokes of a wheel. There was a lot of rain outside the big windows of this big office, and a lot of spray in the painting. Since none of it was falling on the snarling man, I figured the painter hadn't known what he was doing.

"Please sit." Obediently, I sat. "Your compatriot, Littlefield, has not arrived; I suppose he didn't have the guts to show up."

"It was a long night," I said.

"It's going to be a long day."

Rolls sat stiffly at his desk. Lawrence had a hand up, covering most of his face.

"Please look at the page in front of you," Rolls said. I picked up the title page we'd cleared at four-thirty in the morning. "What is your explanation?"

It looked fine. I studied the comparison page, too. I couldn't find an error.

"You are very lucky that we didn't start the long run before we caught the error. You can thank Lawrence for that. If we'd started the long run, if we'd printed fifty thousand copies . . ." He paused. Apparently, even his lawyerly training hadn't supplied a word awful enough. "Luckily this soiled Registration Statement will reach only a few people." Soiled? What a mind. He stood up behind his desk, arms clasped behind his back. He was about to step onto the poop deck. The rain seemed to give him the proper frame of reference.

"Please study both pages," he said. "We will stay here until you find the mistake. I do not care if it takes three hours, three weeks."

I studied them again. Three weeks with Wellington Rolls?

"Don't you have eyes?"

"O.K.," I said finally. "On this copy the little 'and' sign is upside down. But in the cleared copy, the one we sent out, it's right side up."

"You are referring to the ampersand connecting the names of Snyder and Fox?"

"Right," I said.

"Do you realize that Snyder and Fox have been an investment banking firm for over one hundred years?" Rolls said.

"I didn't know that," I said. "They aren't one of our clients, are they?"

"It is our Registration Statement," he snapped. "They are one of the managing underwriters. It does not matter if they are one of our clients. We represent all the underwriters. It is the debentures they underwrote that are trading this very minute on the Exchange. If we had not been cautious enough to check this before the long run, you can bet that Snyder and Fox would never become one of our clients."

"I don't get it," I said. "I mean about the ampersand."

"You don't get it." Rolls turned to Lawrence. "He doesn't get it," he snapped. Lawrence twitched. "For one hundred years Snyder and Fox have had their ampersand upside down. You thought to correct a one-hundred-year-old history? You thought to alter the trademark of a distinguished firm? You?"

"Frankly, we didn't even notice the little ampersand," I said. "But we checked the typefaces the way the senior associate told us to."

"Ah, the senior associate, Mr. Ratner," Rolls said,

coming around the desk. "Yes. The senior associate. I am eagerly awaiting his return. We will deal with him. But I would have thought you'd have had the stomach, the manliness not to attempt to shift the blame to others."

He was standing right over me now. He was going all right, staring at the picture of the sailing snarler that hung over my head, drawing inspiration from it. His face was reddening. Let him do anything he wants, I thought. I was still detached. Maybe I wanted him to yell at me. If he yelled enough maybe I could get back in touch with myself. An ampersand. At least I'd learned something. I hadn't known what the symbol was called before. I would have to write Professor Campers and have him put in a chapter on it in his next edition. This was definitely something they ought to teach at Harvard Law School. A new course, perhaps. "Corporations, Securities and the Ampersand."

"What!" Rolls screamed.

"Nothing," I said.

"What!"

"I didn't mean to say anything."

"You do not take this seriously. You will take this seriously."

My mindless outburst sent him over the line. The harbor looked electric and alive. I saw the ferry heading for Staten Island. From the thirty-seventh floor Wall Street seemed beautiful and weird. Fish and skyscrapers. Old ferries and huge computers. Screaming evangelists and white-haired bankers. Those damn huge twin towers and beautiful, soot-black Trinity Church.

"You moron," Rolls screamed. "You do not deserve to call yourself a lawyer. You coward." Red blotches appeared on his face. "Blaming your mistakes on others. Lying. We will give you training you will not soon forget. We will remake your personality. I could give up on you, but that would be the coward's way out. I will train you until your feeble, pathetic, sniveling mind functions, until you've got some morals."

He leaned down over me. "Baboon," he screamed.

"That's it," I said. I wasn't detached anymore. I was back in touch with myself. I'd like to think it was his stuff about my morals, and lying, that did it. I don't think I minded being called a baboon.

"That is not it."

"It sure is." I stood up and headed for the door. Rolls came right after me.

"Get in here." He was yelling at the top of his voice, and followed me into the hall. "Get in there you coward. Get in my office." This was real screaming. You could hear it in the library.

I turned around to start for my office, and was face to face with Cosmo Bass.

"Excuse me," he said, in a very low polite voice. Rolls was still yelling. "Please stop it, Wellington," Bass said. There was an amazing change. Cosmo Bass must have been some "trainer" in his day.

"We do not yell at people in the firm, Wellington," Bass said quietly. His words were exact, low, polite, and sharp like bullets. Snapped off.

"Yes," Wellington Rolls said.

"Please go into your office."

"Yes." But Rolls didn't move. Bass seemed to have put him into shock.

Everything had happened so fast. Rolls stood like a dummy watching us. A partner who probably made three hundred thousand dollars a year stood like a messenger, waiting for an assignment.

"I asked you to go to your office, Wellington. Please retire." Why couldn't the bastard move, I wondered. Bass stared directly at Rolls. In a low, menacing quiet sigh, a sort of drawn-out sigh of resignation and power, like a long sword being pulled through a body, Cosmo Bass said, "Move." He did not raise his voice, but he said "move" so slowly and sharply that the word spread over a good twenty seconds.

Rolls backed away, turned, and jumped for his cabin.

"I imagine you have something to do in your office?" Bass said to me.

I imagined I did.

27

Camilla Newman and I had a talk the next night. We were all friends, she said. I was her friend, Lawrence was her friend. There are certain situations, she said. Then she decided not to describe them and launched into philosophy. It's not that life is bad, it's good, but it could be different, a different kind of good, if certain things had happened that hadn't happened. This was the sort of stuff she was talking. Just knowing that things could have been different blows your mind, she said, and you realize you can change your life, change anything. What did falling in love mean? she asked. I didn't know. Choice, she said. All of this came out in the Clipper Bar, at ten o'clock at night and none of it made any sense to me at all. Unless you understood that she was sleeping with Lawrence and didn't particularly care if he was married. We were friends, she told me, and held my hand.

I was very stoical, and didn't question her, didn't try to get her over to my apartment, or get into hers. I went back to the law firm.

I worked until two o'clock in the morning. At two o'clock I went into her office. What the hell. I turned on her desk light. Why not? I read her mail. I read her letter file. Fuck it. I did not care if anyone came in and saw me. Maybe I'd throw them out the window. I put my head down on her desk. I held on to the goddamned desk, quasi-crying.

*   *   *

Where do you go in a law firm when you need a change of scene — when you're too tired to face the elevator, or the street? I stumbled down the hall toward the small red emergency exit sign. The door was cut in the wall like a secret entrance. It looked like part of the concrete wall, but was made of heavy-gauge steel, and I had to push it hard with my shoulder. As it opened, hot air roared through the crack. I slipped through, and the blast of air knocked the door closed.

I was in the fire stairs, thirty-seven floors up. Hot air from the bowels of the building steamed up in long pounding blasts. I leaned over the railing, looking at the small yellow light bulbs that went down the stairs in a crazy spiral, disappearing as if they sunk down into water. The cracking sound of a deep-throated generator rode up with the wind. Good, I thought, the place is good. I sat down on a metal stair.

There were cigarette butts and beer cans lying on the stairs below. Nine or ten stairs down, I saw what looked like a court reporter book. The wind blew its pages back and forth. Some associate had probably given up here, I thought, thrown a book down the stairs, then walked back to his office, at, say, five in the morning, packed his things and left. Out the door, we were the smooth, rational lawyers, case-filled, book-filled. Our memoranda, our letters, smooth and clean.

There were initials smeared in lipstick on the walls. These stairs were a prison. The damn place was so depressing, I forgot Camilla Newman, got up, tried the door. It wouldn't budge.

Smart lawyer, Weston, I thought, why didn't you try

the door to see if it was self-locking? You could have kept it open with a matchbook. What's wrong with you? I began to pound on the door, and the image of Camilla Newman came back. SHE DID THIS TO ME.

After ten minutes, I sat down on the stairs again. I would probably starve here. In ten years, there might be a real fire — the lawyers trooping out would pass the skeleton of an associate. My suit flapping in the hot cyclone wind around my yellowed bones. Camilla Newman did this to me! I would leave a message. She would be a partner in ten years. Trooping out, she would see my skull, and behind it, on the wall the message: Camilla Newman murdered me.

Thank God, I had a felt-tipped pen, a good red marker. I wrote out the message, nice and big. In the yellow light, the letters seemed to dance away from the walls. I sat down again. Think, I told myself, think. She did this to me, I thought. And then: Use a credit card. That's what they do in the movies, for Christ sake, I thought. I got my American Express card out, and tried to shove it into the slot. Maybe I should have ordered Master Charge. AmEx cracked in two. In one desperate, last exhausted effort, I kicked at the door as hard as I could, screaming at the same time. Someone had to be walking by, someone had to be working late at the firm. Like a tomb door, it actually opened. I fell forward through it.

"You called?" Littlefield said.

28

Good smells were coming out of Littlefield's kitchen. He was making some sort of Indian dish. He wore his white shirt, striped tie and suit pants. Around his waist, there was a frilly blue apron. He had been working for more than an hour.

"What do you mean, 'What's the holdup?'" He snapped. He seemed genuinely angry. "I happen to be creating this fabulous dish in record time. What do you expect at three o'clock in the morning? Do you want it or not?"

"What fabulous dish?"

"Hindu marikimi with onion sauce. With my special flavoring."

Special flavoring? LSD? Quaaludes? I hoped it was just ordinary dope.

"Can I help to hurry it up?"

"You may not touch anything. Proceed to the living room and wait. I will be in shortly."

I proceeded to the living room. I'd put in so much time already what was the point of giving up on his fabulous dish now. Littlefield came in with a tray of bottles, and without his apron. Rather than let me make my own selection, he poured me something from an ominous red bottle.

"What is this, blood?"

"You really don't trust me, do you?"

"I trust you. It's just the cooking."

"You happen to be drinking a wine," he said, "nothing but wine. Nothing added. I am not the maniac I seem. And I find you very unappreciative. I'm attempting to put you into a different space, give you a new frame of reference. I'm losing patience with you."

He was losing patience. Sure he'd rescued me, but what good was that if I died of hunger?

"How long does dinner simmer?"

"It does not simmer," Littlefield said. "It grows. Think of this dinner as a living, growing organism. When it's ready, it will scream to be eaten."

"You're cooking a cat," I said.

He folded his arms across his chest, fixed me with an evil stare. I'm sure it was some kind of magic look he'd picked up on a trip to Tibet. Littlefield reminded me of Richard Burton, the explorer: culture absorption, specializing in the bizarre.

"I listened to you on the subject of *in re Newman* for many minutes," he said. "I've given you what consolation I can. I have my own needs. Are you ready for sensible conversation?"

"I'll try," I said.

"Good. Then I have an announcement. I have developed a plan!" He stood up, wine in hand. "The solution involved choosing a field of specialization. It is simply too chaotic to be grabbed for assignments right and left in different fields. Now, what sort of specialty do you think would suit me?"

"I've told you that you ought to teach."

"That is not a response."

"All right," I said, "you won't do tax, you won't do estates. Real-estate work drives you nuts. You hate corporate work. You didn't exactly thrive on litigation with Lynch. Securities is out: Rolls hates both of us. I can't guess. What's your specialty?"

"Jurisprudence, the philosophy of law," he announced.

"Great," I said, "you're going into jurisprudence at a Wall Street law firm. Very smart." Something cackled in the kitchen.

"Dinner calling?" I said.

"Merely a faint meow," he said. "You'll hear a screech. I realize that there is no such department at the firm. But I've decided that from now on all my memoranda will be jurisprudential in nature. Suppose I am asked a tax question? Will I go to the C.C.H. or Prentice-Hall manuals? Will I look up the cases? No. I will turn to Austin, H. L. A. Hart, Lon Fuller, Pollock, Gierke. I'll give them Cicero, St. Augustine, Clactus. Perhaps even Dworkin or Cohen. All the good philosophers."

"You'll be fired. Of course you know that."

"I doubt it. They probably don't even read my work. You know how our memorandum form works? First a brief statement of the issues, then the conclusion in one sentence. Followed by a long discussion, which the partner merely flips through. My theory is that if I return to basics, to fundamental principles, the answers I give them will be correct, and should correspond with whatever conclusion an associate would reach by reading the cases. Now, if my answer is technically wrong, there will be only two possibilities. Either my analysis from fundamental principles will be in error, or the current law is wrong. If current law is wrong, I will be a part of changing it."

"It doesn't make sense," I said.

"It makes perfect sense. Are you familiar with the work of Clactus the Short?"

I wasn't.

"Clactus was one of Cicero's disciples. May I quote him? 'The state shall not take those figs from the fig tree that are necessary to sustain both the growth of the tree and its owner's health.' This quote is, of course, directly related to bankruptcy law. Why go to the library and read dull cases when one can quote Clactus? Why do any research at all? All I shall need is about twenty books. Listen. What can your creditors take from you when you go bankrupt? How many figs? The answer is right there in Clactus: they can't take anything that is necessary for your health. Moreover, think of the subtle allusion to the health of the tree itself. That is food for thought."

I cut him off. "You don't really mean it. You'll be fired," I said. "They do glance through the discussion part of the memoranda. What are they going to do when they see you've cited Clactus or Cicero, and not the New York State Court of Appeals?"

"I'll disguise my work a bit," Littlefield said, "I'm not silly enough to say 'Cicero, the Roman legal philosopher states . . .' I will make up a citation such as *Cicero* versus *Union Carbide* and leave it at that."

"What if someone asks to see the case?"

"The book will conveniently disappear from the library until such time as my memorandum has been forgotten."

There was a big gurgle from the kitchen. I guessed the cat had drowned.

"Ignore that sound," Littlefield said. "Dinner is merely kicking up a bit, enjoying itself." He settled back down on the sofa. "Think of the time I'll save. No more trotting to the library. I'll only need about twenty books, which I can keep right in my office. Listen: I've got to keep my sanity. It's either back to basics, or I do my memoranda with the help of a Ouija board. I'm tired of all this research."

"Research is the trademark of Bass and Marshall, Littlefield."

"Yes, it certainly is, unfortunately. Bass created a law firm on the basis of analytic legal positivism, i.e., the law is whatever the judge says it is. Holmes, Bass's mentor and hero, was certainly not in the natural-law tradition. He refused to believe there was any a priori constant moral basis to the rules that men throughout history have made for themselves. The old man wanted to keep law and morals completely separate. Kant says that no man may be looked upon as a means, only as an end. Holmes, of course, took the other position. He combined the idea of scientific realism, which Coz carries to an extreme by demanding what might be termed ball-breaking research, with the idea that law is a one-way street, flowing from the rulers to the ruled. Exactly this same theory of law pervades the firm."

"I don't get it," I said.

"This scientific realism. We do not question what is right or wrong. We try to be detached and say exactly what the law is. We do not question tax policy. We merely research exhaustively to insure that our answers are correct. Am I right?"

"We do exhaustive research," I said. "I'm exhausted, dying of hunger."

"Listen, the other half of the theory. Our internal law of the firm. It is also a one-way street. There are intelligible rules, of course. You must wear a suit, not a sport coat. You must never, never talk about the firm with anyone, especially in the elevators. But there is only one direction to the flow of the rules that govern our little world: it is straight down, from Cozzie and the Wednesday partnership meeting. Now I am in the natural-law tradition myself. I find all that distasteful."

The boiling cat was screaming. Something was happening in the kitchen, but Littlefield just kept rolling.

"Moreover, I cannot accept the idea that the rules that

govern our basic life at the firm are simply maxims of efficiency designed to attain the aims of the partners," Littlefield said. "Need I remind you that Ludkin teaches at Harvard Law School? And that efficiency is his central jurisprudential thesis? Don't you think that an interesting coincidence? The philosophy taught at Harvard corresponds with the firm's? And where do they draw their workers from? I am amazed that you apparently are untouched by the Harvard experience. It must be your affection for contract law, the field that is certainly closest to the natural-law tradition."

"Can I interrupt?"

"Perhaps."

"Dinner is screaming."

He sniffed. "Yes," he said, "it cries to be eaten. And I have talked too long, given you no chance to express yourself. But now that I have disgorged my feelings and plans, I am an altogether different person. I will allow you to talk once again."

"O.K.," I said, "how the hell can it go on when Lawrence is married?"

"Let me answer that from a legal positivist point of view." He paused.

"How the hell can it go on when Lawrence is married," I moaned with the dinner. "Lawrence is married."

"So was Camilla Newman," Littlefield said.

29

I tried to use the work to forget all the things that were bothering me, and wangled an assignment involving the Uniform Commercial Code. It doesn't matter that you're working with the U.C.C., and that your case involves reviewing a provision of a million-dollar contract for computers. It doesn't matter that you're doing the work for a lawyer you don't like. The principles are still just contract law, no matter who you're working for. The principles are great, and fun, and using them makes you proud to be a lawyer.

There was a sociologist named Simmel, a German genius who wrote crazy stuff around 1900. His work came out of left field — little essays that got down to the basic issues in contract law.

Of course, he didn't know he was writing about contract law, he was just writing the rules of life, but he was writing contract law all the same.

That is the beauty of contract law: it reflects the problems people have with each other, and the ways they've tried to deal with those problems. In your own life you make contracts all the time, but you don't call them that, even though most of the time you use the same rules, and reach the same kinds of settlements as you would before a legal arbitrator. Contract law is kept down in your inner awareness, in the way your parents dealt with you when you wanted something, in the wars you had with your brothers and sisters.

That's something Simmel implied. He also felt that the rules of human relationships had evolved over such a long period of time, that people often forgot the reasons for them. But there were always reasons. Even for the rules at the law firm. Take care, Simmel said, before you change contract rules. The rules are interconnected, a hidden web, and an adjustment in one will affect another. Dig back until you understand the real reason for a rule.

That's the fun of contract law: digging down into it, finding the rule, finding the reasons for it, seeing how it relates to the other rules. You need to go back to the starting point and reason from there.

And there is a starting point to contract law, an implicit moral spike. Imagine contract law as a huge electric network, operating millions of machines, regulating all the companies in the United States, conducting the daily business of shipping goods, buying houses, making promises, flying airplanes. Now imagine that you're looking at a frozen picture. Nothing is moving. There's the airplane frozen in midair, and all the passengers on it are frozen too, each one holding his little ticket, his little contract, the pilot frozen at the controls is under contract, too. Nothing moves. There is no electricity in the grid. You're sitting at the master control. You've got to turn on the juice, essential energy, the basic stuff that makes the system run. You've got to light up the grid, make the people move.

What's the switch? What regulates the network of law? It has to be a rule. And what is the rule that channels all the energy, that directs all these people moving, that controls the tickets, the pilot's pension, the house you're selling, the million dollar deals? What's the rule? It's simple, fundamental: We are all connected. If you allow someone to rely on your promise to their detriment, their detriment becomes yours, too.

You throw the switch. All the other rules of contract law light up. The planes move, the trains run. Everything is derived from that basic assumption, that basic insight: their detriment becomes yours, we are connected.

I was dealing with a computer sale for a big conglomerate. And it was fun because I was dealing with a network of rules that went back thousands of years. In a sense, I was dealing with something sacred.

*   *   *

The telephone interrupted my quasi-religious escapade.

"Mr. Weston here," I said.

"Mr. Rolls would like to speak with you," Iron Butt Lapido said.

"Now, I suppose?"

"I can schedule your conference at your convenience."

"My convenience is now," I told Iron Butt.

"Fine," she said and hung up on me.

30

I did not look into Camilla Newman's office as I passed. There was no point in looking at her or talking to her. Nodding was what she'd get from me if I bumped into her in the corridor, but she was probably doing some big "deal" with Lawrence, tucked away in one of the small conference rooms.

Iron Butt stood up when I got to the desk. She went to Rolls' door and announced me. He was standing at the window, arms clasped behind his back, staring out. He did not turn. He needs the three steel balls the Captain had in *The Caine Mutiny,* I thought.

"Please sit," he said, not turning. I chose the sofa. If I was a "baboon" I should have tucked my legs up on the sofa and started chirping. I was thinking about it when he apologized.

"I should not have yelled at you in the corridor," he said.

I looked at the pictures of sailing ships, and at the small gold model cannon on his desk. Some of the most interesting contract-law cases come from the Britain-rules-the-waves era. The courts in the 1700s decided there were no contracts between sailors and captains. Maybe that was why England had ruled the waves. And why she didn't anymore.

"I would have discussed your error in my office, but

you felt it necessary to go to the corridor. Nevertheless, I should not have yelled at you. It is disturbing. Will you accept my apology?"

I wanted to see his face. How can you accept an apology when it's given by a back? But I'm a sucker. I accept almost anything.

"Of course," I said. "Forget it."

"Fine," he said, and now he turned around. Jesus, it had been hard for him. His face was dangerously red. I did not understand how he could control the tension generated by the work. You had to concede him something. He dealt all day with deadlines, boxcar numbers, and in the end, if there were errors, they all landed on his desk. Cosmo Bass had made him apologize. Cosmo was still training. Maybe the rules weren't any good for fundamental reasons, the way Littlefield argued, but at least Cosmo was a benevolent dictator.

"Are we finished?" I asked.

"No," he shouted, and then he calmed down. "No. We are not finished. There is one thing more."

"Fine," I said. The office really was nice and big. And well decorated, if you liked ships.

"I have an assignment for you," he said. Suddenly, I realized that there had to be a catch. Cozzie could make him apologize, but could not change his personality. I had been a part of embarrassing him in front of his chosen god. Something had to happen. He was not Captain Vere in *Billy Budd.* Well, maybe he was partly the captain, but he was also Claggart and he had to do something to me.

"It involves a trip to Washington," he said.

He was going to send me out on the milk run. Papers that could be delivered better by any messenger, but they send an attorney for form. Yes, we want to look good at Bass and Marshall. The hell with saving our clients money and mailing something. Send an attorney at fifty dollars an hour. I wondered if Lawrence had had anything to do with this scheme.

Rolls took a little trip of his own across his office to the shoe-shining console in the corner. It had three different-colored brushes at ground level, and a thin steel shaft growing out of them, rising to waist level, holding the control panel. There were lots of little lights and buttons on the control panel. Rolls selected the green brush, on what seemed to me slow speed. The shoe shiner operated as his captain's wheel. And pacifier.

"Confidentially," he said, "these are rather important papers. Ordinarily, we would send a messenger, but if any word of this leaked out, there would be tremendous implications. The papers must be delivered to the Washington counsel of our client. Confidentially, the slightest leakage . . ." He paused, turned away from the wheel, whispering now.

I could play that game, too. I leaned forward and whispered, "Yes?"

"What was that?" he snapped.

"Yes?"

"I see," he said. "Yes. Confidentially, the slightest leak could result in a certain stock's price rising dramatically. This is not a friendly takeover. We are applying the Iron Maiden. We come at them under the cover of fog, we are on them before they can respond, we blow them out of the water. Do you understand?"

"Yes," I said. "You're coming out with an offer to purchase all the stock of some company, and take them over, and fire all the management."

"We will murder them," Rolls said. "But we want no rumors." His hands were clasped together under his chin, squeezing each other hard. His face was red with excitement. His eyeballs bulged. "You see," he hissed, "any rumors and the Securities and Exchange Commission, or the New York Stock Exchange, might stop trading in the stock. Thus, we must ambush, attack with full disclosure and millions of dollars. Blast them. Send them down in an instant with all hands on board. These will be desperate men. They will try many things to foil our plans, but they will not succeed."

Now his arm swept out toward his bookcase. Captain Rolls had sunk a lot of ships. Each of the bound red volumes represented the indexed full documentation of some merger or takeover. They had leather bindings with the dates and names stamped in gold. His trophy case. His hand was clenched in a fist, his arm fully extended toward the red books. Frankly, I was a little impressed by all this. The man was a maniac, of course, but I was beginning to get into the whole thing. Attacking in the fog. Murdering them. I was forgetting that I was being punished. Sure, the trip was a punishment, to remind me that I was just a cabin boy. Yes, the fact that work could be used as punishment confirmed Littlefield's theory that the rules of the firm violated natural law. But Rolls had so much compressed energy, was so fully into his job of murdering the opposition, that the enthusiasm was contagious. I even forgot that Lawrence and Camilla had probably cemented their relationship, caught up in the same sort of enthusiasm.

"Seven-thirty, A.M., Friday. You arrive here. You receive the packet and instructions from my secretary. You depart on the shuttle from La Guardia. Keep the materials in your case: the name of our firm appears on the envelope. You may keep the instructions in your coat pocket. The instructions will be in a plain white envelope. But do not read them on the plane. Even white-haired grandmothers are stockholders. You do understand this, don't you?"

"Yes," I said, "I do understand it." I thought that had finished our conversation and stood up. "Seven-thirty A.M. Friday," I added.

"Good luck," Rolls hissed. Apparently some of his anger had gone too. He stared at me. What was I supposed to say?

"Good luck," I said. They happened to be the appropriate words: I had earned a snarl of appreciation from Wellington Rolls.

31

Thursday night I worked late, drowning myself. I was ignoring Camilla Newman, but working late so that she would have a chance to come to me. Many times I turned to stare at the big black buildings, light-pocked neighbors, shadows with random eyes.

"Do you mind if I come in?" Camilla Newman asked.

"Yes," I said. She could take a lot of work and still look awfully good.

"You're not talking to me anymore," she said.

"You're right."

"I'm coming in."

"Don't."

She came in anyway, sat down, her coat folded on her lap, her attaché case placed carefully on the carpet. The law firm was very quiet. Only masochists were here now. Only the people who were drawing something essential from the firm. I was one of them now. I didn't want to talk to her, but I was here because I hoped she would come to me.

"Let's talk."

"Don't talk to me," I said. "Don't say anything."

"There are some things I want to explain to you."

"Don't," I said. "Don't try."

"You don't understand anything."

"I do," I said. "I understand a lot. Good luck."

"You're not my friend? You won't let me explain?"

Friend got to me. "I may have to hit you," I said. It was very possible that I might hit her. I was beginning to see the reason I was here. "I don't want to," I said, "but I might do it. I'm just telling you."

"Go ahead," she said rationally, "hit me. That's going to make it good again?"

I got up, as angry as I've ever been, and started around the desk. She cracked. You saw it in her eyes. It stopped me cold. Then she slapped herself in the face. It looked crazy.

"Is this what you want?" she moaned. "Is it?" Slapping each time. What the hell do you do? I grabbed her hands, stopped her, gave her a long hug. She was crying now. When she stopped I went back to my chair.

"Why do I want to explain to you?"

"You love me a lot."

"I do love you a lot."

"And love Lawrence too?" I seemed to want to slap myself too.

"What gives you the right to be mad?"

"What stops me? Have you given any thought to the fact he's married?"

"I want you to be happy," she said. "That's why I'm talking to you."

She wanted me to be happy. I stared out the window. I wanted one of the big black buildings to fall over on its side like a tree, but they all kept standing. I wanted a lot of things but they were not going to happen. I kept looking and the buildings kept standing.

"You want me to be happy?" I could almost laugh at it.

"I need to talk to you."

"You need," I said. Here she was, the bright lawyer, refusing to make any logical connections. I wasn't really making any either. My mind was rambling. How had it happened? Were they working together in some small conference room? Had Lawrence suddenly sprung at her? How did it go? Camilla, I really like your work. I like your work too, Lawrence; I like your prick; I like these assignments you are giving me, give me more of them, give me more Lawrence, bigger, harder, fuck me. How did it go? Had Lawrence taken her to lunch and reached across the table for her hand? What was the first move in a law firm? Probably it was just rubbing up against each other. Excuse me, did I rub you? Yes, you actually did. Can I do it again? I was not feeling healthy, but I didn't lunge across my desk and grab her neck.

"I'm upset about you," she said. "I love you a lot."

"Don't slap yourself."

"Christ you're mean," she said and smoked. Her hand shook as she lit the cigarette. She was a lousy smoker anyway. It wasn't her game. She was not Bette Davis. No. She was too much the blonde with blue eyes. Too goddamned healthy looking.

"You're mean, and you always were." The hands were rattling now. "You made me feel bad. You didn't let me daydream about things."

"I didn't let you dream?" Crazy things went through my mind. *In rem sleep patterns. In rem jurisdiction.* "What the hell do you mean, I didn't let you daydream?"

She kind of raised her chin and squeaked. "Like about things like—"

"What?" I yelled.

"Things like being made a partner."

"Christ," I yelled.

"You made fun of it."

"Christ," I said. Lawrence, I thought. I'll bet they can dream a lot together. Being a partner must be the only thing on his mind right now. It's his whole future. So they dream together. He'll make it. She'll make it. Because he's made it. Deals. I could see them both getting off on it, talking at night, discussing the firm personalities. Taking Wellington Rolls seriously. They were both in love with the firm, but scared of being rejected, both wacked out lovers of corridors, books, memos, petitions, tax manuals, SEC forms, mergers, deals, power. I hadn't gone that far. I wasn't going to. These two were a fine pair all right. Lawrence needed to be told what a good partner he'd make. She did that for him. So they fell in love. Fuck the wife.

"You'll make partner all right," I said. "I can see your future perfectly. I have no doubt you'll make it. Maybe Lawrence won't because it's hard to imagine Cosmo tolerating a partner who sleeps with associates. But you were led into temptation by the older artful deal-maker. You'll make it. Maybe even Lawrence will make it. Who knows? Maybe the relationship can go on forever just the way it is? What does his wife matter? She's just out there somewhere, out in the city. That doesn't count. None of those people out there matter. She's just sitting in some goddamn apartment somewhere by herself thinking Lawrence is killing himself at the office. I'd like her to bust in here and beat some sense into you. It's real out there, not here. Take the law firm away, and you and Lawrence, you wouldn't give a shit about each other. Because he's not your type."

It was a long speech. All I was trying to tell her is that the damn buildings don't fall down when you want them to. You have to blow them up if you want them to fall. And when you do that, the people in them go, too.

"You really hate me."

"I don't," I said.

"You want to hurt me."

"It's better than crying." When I said the word, I felt

like it. I also felt like killing Lawrence. I also wanted to throw Camilla down on the desk and rape her. I wanted a lot of things but I was not going to do them. I would talk to her sometime. I would be her friend. She could probably talk me out the window, arguing it was the fastest way down. But my emotions were swinging too hard both ways to talk to her now.

"Is Lawrence here?" I asked.

"No," she said. "Why?"

"I'll walk you out." I put on my coat. She had her stuff right here. I looked at her attaché case. "I'll carry it," I said. We were at the elevator now. We had a good walk to the subway, and I was planning on maybe walking her all the way home.

"You don't have to carry the case," she said.

For Christ sake, I thought. "I want to," I said.

"I'll keep it," she told me.

For Christ sake, it's only work. What would happen if the case went out the window? My mood swung. "You won't keep it," I said. I grabbed at the case. It was amazing how strong she was. She kept her small fingers locked to that leather handle like someone dangling on a rope outside the window. I felt like I was raping her as I pulled it away. She tried to twist it back. I gave her a good push on the shoulder. Christ, I semi-slugged her. She fell down on the carpet. The attaché case was in my hand. She started to cry as the elevator doors opened. The cage was empty, thank God. I sat down next to her on the carpet. The goddamned elevator started blinking, telling us to hurry.

"You want to hurt me," she moaned.

"I don't. I'm sorry." I put the case down next to her. She snatched it, and told me she hated me. She told me to get out. She told me to get into the blinking elevator.

"Out of here," she screamed.

"I'm sorry."

"Get out." As if we were in her apartment, not in the law firm. She'd screamed "get out." And even a mild yell sounds bizarre in the law firm. Her scream went dancing all over the place, coming back at us from black corridors and offices. It was a very effective weapon and almost blew me into the elevator.

I looked down at her and said I was sorry. She was sitting on her butt on the carpet, her dress and coat hiked up to her underpants.

"Get out." Another good one.

"I'm going," I said, and got into the cage, and the doors slammed shut. It didn't stop anywhere else, just hurtled toward the floor in a free fall. Either that or it was all in my stomach from Camilla. Or were the buildings really falling down? Down I went, feeling I was falling from the window, and only snapped back to consciousness when the doors opened and I saw the security guard facing me, asking me to sign out, sign the book please. I went by him, did not sign, went by him like a thief, but he didn't shoot me.

3²

The next morning, I showed up at the office at seven-fifteen to pick up the packet from Lapido. The firm was deserted, and Iron Butt wasn't even there yet. I went to my office to wait, and found a square white envelope on my desk. I looked at it as if it were a letter bomb.

I was wondering what she would tell me and how much of it I could take. I probably deserved whatever was in it. I could feel remorse. She would be good at making me feel it. I knew I was going to open it, but I held it up to the light, fingered it, weighed it, developed a relationship with it, getting myself set for whatever was inside. Then I carefully used the letter opener, and extracted it still folded. Now I was ready to peek at it, and kind of turned down a small part to sample it and see if I could take it. I turned down more. All white, no words. I kept turning. For a second I thought the whole damn thing was blank, like my mind, but in the lower left-hand corner Camilla Newman had written in tiny pathetic little letters: "Don't hate me, I need you."

* * *

The plane bounced out of La Guardia. I had my attaché case sitting on the empty seat next to me. I had her note sitting on top of a yellow legal pad on my lap. "Don't hate me, I need you." Sure she needed me, I thought. I was going to bed alone at night. I could get off on needs, too. She needed me and a lot of other people. The plane thrashed around in rough air. The pilot apologized, sounding tired and spaced. Her need was the stopgap drug that told her she was loved. We all needed it.

The plane came down through the rough clouds and began to circle Washington. I was flying in my own rigid holding pattern of work. The captain tried to sweet-talk us. He told us about the scenic spots we could look out at, Virginia, Maryland. I wondered if we were waiting to run out of fuel?

I wanted someone to meet me at the airport. I wanted someone with breasts to give me a long hug. I dreamed. I would not care what she said as long as she added that she loved me. Goddamn it, I wanted HER. She was in New York. The airport was congested. Love was congested. There wasn't any room on the runways, the captain said. He gave up on the sweet talk. We might be up here all day. I didn't give a damn. Wellington Rolls could blame it on me. Sure I knew I ought to hijack the plane and make it land so I could get our papers delivered, so that we could murder them.

It would have been all right if I had not met her. But you always meet someone, I thought. We were still circling the city. I could get off on circling. That seemed to be my job. I was prone to circle until I ran out of fuel, then opt for the long dive. I was a stupid perfectionist: I wanted HER. And she wasn't perfect.

Now the captain told us to fasten our seat belts. We were finally coming down. He seemed to want to get there fast and put us into a crash dive. I enjoyed it. Go all the way, you fucker, I thought. Play out World War II. Give a hundred and twenty businessmen and lawyers a ride on the roller coaster. Let them start their day off right. Let them know this is the real world.

He leveled off. Since we were apparently going to make it, I began to wonder what kind of a tip you gave a cab driver in D.C. It was all on the firm anyway, but I certainly didn't want to embarrass anyone by messing up my important assignment. Just as we hit ground, a stewardess came by to untuck me. Nothing made sense. "Did I forget you, honey?" she asked.

Part Four
Specific Performance

33

Since Littlefield and I were working on a Saturday, we allowed ourselves the privilege of extending lunch. There are days on Wall Street when the harbor looks European and the sail boats fill it, and the clouds are clean and high. The wind blows strong and warm past the girls in Battery Park. Our lunch break had stretched to two hours, but we had another almond-covered ice-cream bar in the park and told ourselves we might come in on Sunday to make up for it. Who really cared anyway? It was not as if the president of General Motors was going to consult us. We were just grinding out the general run-of-the-mill law firm work, and there was too much of it.

"Another almond bar?" Littlefield asked.

I could not hold another one. "How many Cicero memoranda have you gotten away with?" I asked him.

"Three, I think. There have been no repercussions. Apparently, decisions interpreting section five-o-one(c) (three) of the Internal Revenue Code conform exactly with Rawls' theories of distributive justice, or the partners do not read my memorandum. You ought to toast my success with an almond bar."

"I ought to buy you flowers."

"How sweet," Littlefield said. He reached over the

green fence that lined the path and picked a daisy and put it in his buttonhole.

"Flowers for your funeral," I told him.

"You do not appreciate how inventive my memoranda really are," he said. "But I would accept flowers for any reason. I may even buy them myself. In fact, I will buy them. I am feeling very proud of myself today. I have been able to write exactly the kind of memoranda I like — really just the type of paper I enjoyed composing at Yale. I never have to go to the library. Moreover, the judge has yet to reach a decision in Lynch's case. It appears he may never reach one. We may never work for Lynch again. I'm feeling successful and lucky."

When we reached the flower cart, Littlefield asked for daisies.

"Take roses," the flower man said, "you can afford them." He was short and thick and wore a white apron.

"Roses are not appropriate for a funeral," Littlefield said. "Daisies it will be."

"Who died?"

"Interesting," Littlefield said, "he wants to know who died. He tells me what type of flowers I can afford."

"The flowers are for his own funeral," I said. "He's committing suicide."

"He's got an incurable disease?" the flower man asked.

"Yes," I said.

"I have no disease," Littlefield stated. "I am not committing suicide. But my friend and I conduct a very risky business. Someone may die at any time."

"Mafia?"

"Something like that. Do I get my daisies? Must I argue with you all day? Open shop."

"For you, three dollars," the flower man said, pulling out a bunch of daisies.

"For me, two dollars."

"Three dollars. You're wearing a suit."

"I am losing my enthusiasm for daisies," Littlefield said to me. "This man is ruining my afternoon."

"Three dollars. I throw in a rose."

"Is that an indication of a hidden sense of humor?" Littlefield asked me. I didn't bother to answer. There are children in Battery Park on Saturdays. They played on new grass. A ferry moved like a toy on the mirror-smooth bay. There was the water, and then the green, wet-looking grass, and farther back, the forest of buildings. You could imagine them as a black forest.

"I believe we have struck a deal," Littlefield said. "Do you have fifty cents?"

I gave it to him. He paid two-fifty and got the daisies.

"It's not quite as much fun when you buy them for yourself," he said. "I need someone who cares."

"Me, too," I said. We kept walking toward the black forest. It was as if I was walking against the wind. My emotions pushed me back toward the park, the water. I was like a kid in some story who does not want to go into the forest but has to. Usually there are two kids. They stop at the first tree, and peer into the blackness, knowing something bad has to happen in there.

"Why are we going back to work?" I said. "Why are we working on Saturday?"

"Why is Wellington Rolls making deals?" Littlefield said. "Why is Lynch bombarding the court with letters? Why do people die and make work for the estates department? Who knows the answers to all these things?"

"Let's get the hell into the forest," I said. "The sooner we finish, the sooner we can leave."

"The forest?" he said. "You have a touch of madness yourself. Well concealed, of course. A zany streak."

I may have a zany streak but I was the only rational person at the firm that afternoon. Maybe because we'd been talking about funerals, I was semiprepared.

There was the usual weekend skeleton crew at work. A few secretaries, a couple of the boys to run the copying machines. Of course, there wasn't anyone working in the estates department. They all got to go home every weekend. But various corporate deals were being run through. There were people from the tax department, and there are always litigation people at the firm on weekends. Even so, the office seemed still, motionless. Littlefield and I walked a corridor that was long, white and empty. Where the office doors had been left open, sunlight shot in, churchlike stabs of light. Littlefield, bow tie, dark immaculate coat, round shining baby face played the part of the altar boy, bringing flowers into the cathedral.

"I should be bringing these to Cosmo Bass," Littlefield said. He sensed it too. "I should place them carefully on his desk and kneel. Is the codger with us today?"

"I haven't checked."

"No need. He is always with us."

Then we heard the screaming, voices coming together, yelling, a choir out of tune, male and female voices, and something about a taxi.

"My God," Littlefield said, "have they discovered that I cited Cicero in one of my memoranda?"

"It's not that kind of yelling," I said, moving now, running down the corridor. It was the kind of yelling I had heard back home when someone fell into a bailer, or got a hand chopped off in a thresher. I forgot all about the fact I was wearing a suit, that this was a law firm corridor. I was running down the hall as if the carpet were grass and I was barefoot and had traction. I pushed off the wall making a turn, nearly bounced into the library, made another turn, and stopped.

"Get me a taxi," Wellington Rolls was saying. He had only one arm in his coat. His face was pale gray and there were beads of sweat on his forehead. One hand was on his secretary's table supporting him, the other was around his chest, clutching at his white shirt, pulling it sideways.

"Get him a taxi," Lawrence screamed at Rolls' Saturday secretary.

The secretary just screamed. Camilla Newman was standing like a statue against the wall.

"Get him a taxi," Lawrence screamed again at the secretary.

"Get an ambulance," I said to Newman. I turned around to look for Littlefield: Lawrence was obviously out of his mind. He'd been trained so long he didn't know when to stop obeying Wellington Rolls. Littlefield came chugging up.

"Can I assist?"

"Call the building people. They've probably got stretchers. I don't know," I yelled. Newman was still against her wall. "Get an ambulance," I screamed. "Move." Now she snapped. Maybe because my scream was louder than any Wellington Rolls had ever made. "Don't go to your office to call," I yelled at her back, "use Iron Butt's phone."

"Get me a taxi," Rolls shrieked. I grabbed him around the shoulders and got him on the floor, covered him with my coat. "Get me a taxi."

"Should we give him artificial respiration?" Lawrence said.

Christ, Lawrence was a fine one. Did he think that Rolls had drowned? Both hands moved under the coat. He was tearing at his chest. The pain must have been unbearable.

"Should we give him artificial respiration?" Lawrence yelled at me.

"We don't give him anything," I said. "He's having a heart attack. No more yelling. It probably makes it worse."

"What do we do?"

"Wait." I was down on my knees next to Rolls, ready to grab him if he started thrashing around. All this had taken maybe twenty seconds. Christ, I thought, it will probably be all right. There must be heart attacks all through this damn building every day. They'll be here in minutes. They've probably got all the gear to save Rolls' life. Maybe they've even got an ambulance of their own.

Rolls gasped: "It isn't fair."

"What can I do?" Lawrence said, finally coming to his senses. I thought about it. I told him to give me his coat for a pillow for Rolls.

"It isn't fair," Rolls gasped again. I loosed his tie, his shirt. He was breathing in gasps, but breathing. "Goddamn it." Gasping it out. "Goddamn it, goddamn it, damn it, Christ." Gasps between the words. "Goddamn it, it isn't fair, I'm not goddamned mad at any goddamned person. It isn't fair. I didn't. Lose. My. Goddamn temper."

"Don't talk," I told him. "People are coming for you. They'll be here in a second."

"They will arrive any moment," Littlefield said. I hadn't noticed he'd come back. He was still holding the daisies. More people from the firm came. I yelled them back. It didn't make sense to let them crowd Rolls now, even if they were partners.

"Daisies," Rolls gasped, "damned daisies. Why?"

These were weaker gasps. I wanted to do something for him, but I couldn't. If he went out, I'd pound on his chest, but it probably wouldn't do any good. We'd try artificial respiration, too. But if he went out, he was

probably gone. Where the hell were the building people?

"They're pounding me," Rolls gasped. "They're
pounding me apart." I could hear his shirt tear. He'd
ripped it open. He's still making sense, I thought, that's
got to be a good sign. What he says makes sense.

Cosmo Bass came around the corner. Littlefield was
right: he was always with us. When he came everyone
stepped back. And Cosmo didn't crowd Rolls. He stood
four feet away.

"I assume everything is under control," he said. "That
the building officials have been alerted?"

"Yes," Littlefield said.

"Then why are you standing here holding daisies?"
Bass snapped. "Why is anyone here except for Mr.
Weston, who can stand guard? The building men will
need room. Will you all retire to your offices?"

Bass was in his shirt sleeves, red suspenders. They
retired.

"It isn't fair, goddamn it, goddamn it. They're
pounding me. Didn't lose it."

"Of course it isn't fair," Cosmo Bass said. He got
down next to me. "It isn't fair, Wellington, but you are
going to be perfectly all right."

"No. The. Pounding."

Jesus, I thought, he's going to die right here. The
goddamned building people. Were they all at lunch?
Captain Rolls was drowning now all right. He gasped in
bubbles.

"Please conserve your energy, Wellington," Bass said
softly. "Do not talk. You are much too important to the
firm for me to let you die. Do you have your pills?"

Christ, good idea. Didn't they give them nitro? Did it
do any good? His pills! Christ, he'd had attacks before.

"No," Bass said. "Don't talk. Nod."

It was hard to tell if Rolls was shaking his head or just

thrashing, but it certainly wasn't a nod. I began to go through his pockets as best I could. Bass went into the office. He came back very soon. Empty-handed.

"Better," Rolls gasped. But he wasn't. He was kind of bubbling now. He's going to die, I thought. I was sure of it now. I could see the change in his face. It was going beyond gray into chalk. The sweat was rolling all over it. Bass mopped it with Kleenex from the box on Lapido's desk. He'd gotten up and down a lot of times for an old man.

"Of course you're better," Bass said. "You are not going to die." He said it with the conviction of a lawyer who was completely sure of his case. Coming that way from Cosmo Bass I actually believed it. I think Rolls did, too. As if Cosmo Bass had called them with the force of his argument, the building people swarmed around us. I think there were five of them, but it was hard to tell because they were all moving, doing something. They had some sort of machine, and the stretcher, and a mask was put on Rolls' face. Rolls went out in a hurry. I'm sure he would have appreciated the way they moved. He liked associates to scurry. These boys could do it: flying down the hallway, boxes, tubes, bottles, wires, all jiggling over and under the stretcher.

I looked at Cosmo. I could see he was tired. I felt like helping him back to his office, but you can't do that with Cosmo Bass.

"When Wellington recovers, I'm sure he will want to express his appreciation for your level head," Bass said. Damn it, Bass was tired. He meant to say Mr. Rolls, after all I was an associate, but he said Wellington. Bass was so tired he had broken a rule.

"I think I will go back to my office," he said.

I thought we both should go to our offices. With Rolls finally gone, I had a weakness in the legs, and shaking in my arms. I thought I should go home to bed.

34

"Cosmo Bass telephoned you at eight-thirty this morning," my secretary said. "Where were you?"

I threw my coat in the chair, dumped my attaché case on my desk.

"What do you mean where was I?" I said. "I was asleep."

"He also telephoned you at exactly nine-thirty," she said. "I had to take the messages. Do you have any idea how I felt?"

I had ignored this strange beast for over eight months but she had made some sort of identification with me anyway. Because I had been late to work on the one day when Cosmo Bass had telephoned she was ashamed of me.

My secretary was actually a nice woman of fifty-five, who had once been the secretary for Lynch. She'd been put out to pasture, handed down — her whole career was at the end of its parabolic curve. She'd started with associates, learned her trade, risen to be the secretary of a partner. Now she was back down with the associates again.

"I'm sorry I was late," I said. "Will you forgive me, Mrs. Moultrie?"

"Yes," she said.

"I'll call him right now."

"No," she said, "I will call his secretary."

It was all right with me to handle this with class.

"Mr. Weston?" Cosmo Bass said. He finally had my name right!

"Yes?"

"Your actions on Saturday were appreciated. I wondered if you would enjoy a luncheon?"

*   *   *

One of the taxi cabs from the company the firm employed was waiting outside the building. I opened the door for Cosmo Bass, holding an umbrella over his head. He entered carefully, steadying himself with a hand on the door. He was in good shape for a man over eighty, but he also knew his age. I went around the cab and got in the other door. When we were settled, the cab driver started slowly up Wall Street. He obviously knew who he had in the cab and how fast he was supposed to drive.

Cosmo Bass settled into his seat, carefully spreading his coat to avoid wrinkles. I sat still, wondering what the first thing he'd say to me would be.

"I'm afraid I'm not giving you a choice for lunch," he said. "When you reach my age, your habits are fixed. You do not alter them unless absolutely necessary. At least I do not. You once mentioned a grandfather. I imagine he is the same way?"

"Yes," I said.

"Good."

"He won't change anything," I said.

"Good," Cosmo Bass said. "Nor should he. I have no intention of changing anything at all. I shall never buy a new house, move to an apartment, change the decor of my office, ride the subway, conduct a corporate search, fly to California, or go to a wedding that does not involve my immediate family." He looked at me. "I have no intention of changing anything at all. Nor of retiring." It was a joke. He smiled to let me know it was a joke. It was all right to laugh with Cosmo Bass. Why had I been so scared, I wondered. It was logical to assume that someone who had built a big firm, wooed a lot of clients, would be charming. So I laughed. After I'd laughed, he laughed, too. There were rules to everything though. I saw that too, rules about talking about partners, and about laughing. He was a pretty old man and he'd built a lot of rules over the years.

He did not say anything else for quite a long time. I surprised myself by saying something about the weather. He looked over at me again.

"I am entirely uninterested in the weather," Cosmo Bass said. At least he smiled as he let me know. "I am also uninterested in how to raise children, schools in Westchester, LSAT scores, golf, tennis, the Mets, Nets, Sets and Bets, marriage, divorce, marijuana, modern fiction, interior decoration, new plays, the effects of television, the Bar Association, crime, or subways. I suppose I'm moderately interested in the bankruptcy of New York City. Have I left anything out?" He sat there and thought about it for a while. "My memory fails me," he said. "I'm sure I've left out numerous topics my friends and relatives try to bore me with."

I laughed. I was understanding the rules of the game pretty quickly. As long as he was running things, I didn't mind them so much. He laughed with me. Of course my laugh was a moderate one.

"How is your grandfather?" he said.

"He had a stroke, but he's pretty strong."

"Is he in a chair?"

"Yes," I said.

"Too bad. How is his memory?"

"Fine," I said.

"Good. That is what bothers one. The memory. I am interested in memory. I was born in a house lit by gas, saw horse-drawn streetcars replaced by trolleys on Fifth Avenue. Saw engines replace horses, too. I drove an ambulance in World War One and discussed the Civil War with Oliver Wendell Holmes. I've seen and talked with Woodrow Wilson at Princeton."

I understood the rules. I knew the subjects that were open for discussion. "I have no intention of writing an autobiography, for the firm or anyone else. I would only do so if I had an intention to retire," Cosmo Bass added.

I laughed. As I say, I knew the rules.

35

Cosmo Bass ate at the Downtown Association every day except Wednesday. On Wednesday, he ate at the Tortoise Club which is in Midtown on West 56th Street.

"We are little late," he said.

We slowly hurried through some unimposing doors, into a big marble hall. Someone took our coats. It wasn't a fancy place, but it was big. Big, and a little dirty. Like an old man building. I was a little nervous in the big hall, and got really nervous when Cosmo Bass signed me in, explaining that you were allowed only one guest at a time, and indicating that I ought to sign my name in a hurry. There was a big board near the book, with the members' names on it, and most of the names were the same as parks, buildings, streets or law firms, or they were very similar to the names of writers and artists I'd studied in college. Either it was a huge practical joke, or I was with the big boys. I was nervous, the way you're nervous when you're sure you'll trip even though there's nothing in your way. I was taller than Cosmo Bass, and regretted it. I wanted to be able to duck down behind him.

We had a choice of either big stairs or a small elevator. Since we were a little late, Bass took the elevator, although he told me he liked the stairs. The elevator was all right with me, but Bass explained that there was a exhibit in a room up the stairs and if we weren't a little late he'd show it to me.

"Hello, Julian," Bass said to a tall white-haired gentleman in the elevator with us, "I would like to introduce Samuel Weston, an associate of mine. This is Mr. Asher, Samuel."

"Hello, Coz," the gentleman said. "Hello, Mr. Weston."

This guy can handle himself, I thought. "An associate of mine." Rolls would have said something like a junior associate of the firm. Bass said "of mine." When you're going to lunch with an octogenarian who's built a big law firm, and you've taken a glance at the names on that big board, a little thing like that makes a difference to you. Bass made associate sound as if we were really colleagues together in some project. Rolls used the word associate to disassociate.

Even if you trip, I thought, Bass will bail you out. He's got rules for everything, and if you vomit at the table, he will know exactly how to handle the situation.

We separated from Julian and strutted toward lunch, Bass nodding to codgers as we went, and ignoring groups of younger men. Finally we arrived in a big dining room.

"My table?" Bass said.

"Unfortunately, you were a little late, Mr. Bass," the man in charge said.

"My secondary?"

"I'm sorry, Mr. Bass. Very sorry."

"The reserve?"

"Available."

"Good," Cosmo Bass said, and we headed for a smallish two-man table against a wood wall.

"Tio Pepe," Cosmo Bass said to a waiter.

"Tio Pepe," I said, as the man stared at me, waiting for something to come out of my mouth.

"Trust Schieffelin and Company," Cosmo Bass said, and smiled at me. "At least I have always trusted Schieffelin and Company. I trust them less since Blue Nun. Blue Nun baffles me. Hennessy. Teachers. Fine. Moët. Superb. But Blue Nun?"

I laughed. I was supposed to. Our Tio Pepe arrived. It turned out to be sherry. I got a quick glimpse at the label. Schieffelin and Co. Founded 1794.

Cosmo Bass explained that you were not allowed to discuss business at the Tortoise Club. That was fine with me. Just another rule. What business would we talk about anyway?

"How do you like the law?" he said.

"I like the law." That much was the truth.

"The concepts or the job?"

"You mean the concepts or the firm?"

Bass leaned forward a little, as if I had not been very smart. He did not want to embarrass me by having his reprimand overheard at another table.

"The concepts, the job, the firm are all the same," he said. "I mean research." We were off and running.

*   *   *

"My first memorandum for the Justice was unacceptable," Bass said. He was talking about Oliver Wendell Holmes. We were sipping our Tio Pepe. I had gotten past the point where I had to hold the small glass with two hands. "I tried too hard, perhaps, to impress him with my intellectual skills. I overlooked the necessary task of gathering information. I was, of course, reprimanded. I was to approach my job with no preconceived notions, to forget what I had learned at Harvard Law School, to do no thinking whatsoever. That was the command: no thinking. Work. I roamed the dark rooms of the huge library, finding facts or cases that related in any way to the cases at hand. I constructed no theories, performed no reasoning whatsoever."

Cosmo Bass ordered for both of us. We had a second glass of sherry.

"For my own good, as he said, the Justice allowed me to do no writing whatsoever. I was clearly a hopeless case. I became a farmer, gathering information and depositing it on his desk for inspection. I wanted to go home for my sister's wedding. The Justice refused permission. My father, in Vermont, was irate. He already had the misconception that the Justice was anti-God, and this confirmed his fears. He did not understand that if the Justice did not allow his clerks to marry, how could he allow them to attend a wedding in the middle of a particularly busy session? Frankly, I did not understand it either, I did not see the connections there. But I did not dwell on it. I was not supposed to be thinking in any case. I was doing research. Our relationship was not particularly cordial. I had been placed in some sort of lower station, and was angry that I was not allowed to display the skills that had gotten me the position in the first hand."

"I understand," I said.

"I am not sure you do," Cosmo Bass said testily. "It was true that I was editor-in-chief of the *Harvard Law Review*. But one of the skills that had particularly impressed the Justice was my ability to type, a very rare skill in those days. The skill had helped pay my way through law school. I had thought we would compose together. In that way, I would learn composition, legal writing, from the master himself. I had learned to type in order to pay my way through law school. Now I was merely a farmer, gathering field materials for inspection. Simply depositing them on his desk."

"I do understand now," I said.

"I remember the white mustache rising over piles of paper and the books organized like a topographical map on his desk. I remember clearly when I was elevated from my inferior position."

Now he stopped. He began to sip the white soup.

"What happened?" I asked. He ignored me completely until he had finished the entire bowl of vichyssoise.

"I sat across from him, handing him papers over the mountain of materials that separated us. 'Thank you, Mr. Bass,' the Justice would say, sending a book sliding back to me over the foothills. We came one time to Jay's Treaty. The Justice had the peculiar idea that Jay had, in fact, been the prime mover behind the American Revolution. He felt Jay had been unjustly ignored by the historians. 'Now for Jay's Treaty,' he said.

"I floated it up like a rain cloud.

" 'This is a filthy copy, Mr. Bass,' he said. 'I can barely make it out!'

" 'It isn't a copy,' I told him. 'Those are the effects of mildew, rot.'

" 'The original, Mr. Bass? On my library card? Do you think that was wise?'

"This was clearly a turning point in our relationship. I was angry, perhaps the way you are angry at times when you are assigned some point of law that you consider trivial, or asked to fetch some document. Naturally, you resent these tasks. Many of our young men do. They wish to write. They wish to compose. They wish to know the whole, and ignore the parts. I felt all those frustrations myself.

" 'Yes!' I sputtered, 'the original.'

" 'And are these letters the originals as well?'

" 'Yes,' I called over to him.

" 'Including the one I so blithely underlined?'

" 'Yes,' I said.

"The Justice leaned back in his seat, his head tilted toward the ceiling. His mustache tips were horizontal. The mustache looked like a white bird, its tail trapped in his teeth, its wings fluttering as it tried to free itself.

"'Bass,' the Justice said, 'I believe you have finally begun to learn research. Next week, we shall allow you to begin composing.'"

*　　*　　*

The fish was excellent.

*　　*　　*

"An associate never bores me with research," Bass went on. "He cannot do too much. There is only one way to complete a legal problem. That is to track down all of it. And charge for it as well. That is why clients come to Bass and Marshall. Research. But young men have the tendency to believe they are working with theory: That the law comes from principles traceable back to England, Rome, Greece, that it corresponds to some divine concept of fundamental moral belief. Holmes would have said, 'Blather, Bass,' had I tried to argue that position with him. The law is sometimes considered unchanging. Sometimes it seems unchanging. But that is only because lawyers are too lazy to uncover the reasons that explain why a rule was originally enacted. Once that work is done, it is usually quite clear that the original reasons for the rule bear no relationship to present life and work. Facts, not theory. More research. That is why we win cases. Sometimes there is no logic whatsoever to the law. Suppose a client comes to you with a problem and you discover that the problem has no logical answer. Do you create one?"

"Don't you have to come to some conclusion?" I said. "Don't you have to create some logical framework?"

"'Blather, Bass,' he would have said. You want the

law. Where there is no logic in the cases, you send your client the cases themselves. We are not law professors. We do not create law. We research and answer. If the answer is that each situation in some particular problem is treated differently, we send the client every example of how the problem has been treated. 'Blather, Bass,' he would have said: He said it quite a few times. Words amused him. Blather or balderdash."

We had moved to comfortable chairs facing a large window. There was a small table between us, and on it rested coffee cups. Mr. Bass had a cigar. Now I wanted one, too. I was angry at myself for having been afraid to say so.

"Are you sure you won't change your mind?" Cosmo Bass said, reading it.

"I will," I said defiantly. He produced one from some hidden recess of his vest.

*   *   *

"When I came to Wall Street," he said, "in the early twenties, a large firm contained twenty-five lawyers. Your salary approximated that number as well. In the firm I joined, Brewster and Cloud, there were five partners and twenty clerks. Seven of the clerks had already been told they would not become members of the firm but they remained on as seniors. Every lawyer in the firm had gone to Harvard Law School. I received a week's vacation a year, and never fainted at my desk, even on the hottest days, when we were allowed to retire at noon.

"I wore a black suit and wing collar and suspenders and vest and could never take my jacket off. I wore garters and silk socks. My shoes had twenty-four eyelets. Have you any idea of how hot it might get in the summer?"

"Pretty hot," I said.

"I wanted to complain too, I wanted to take my jacket off. Some of the other firms allowed it. I was a young bull wanting change. How can they ask for change now? Thirty thousand a year? Air conditioning? The chance to do research? There were no paper clips, no staples. Papers were held together with pins like the ones that ensnare a new shirt. There were no copying machines. Copies of documents were impressed into large books, stamped in and sealed, and the page signed by two lawyers as proof the copy was accurate and had been mailed. Typewriters, which would have ended some of the madness, were a sign of disrespect for a client, a sign of cheapness, of shoddy legal work. All important papers were typeset and bound. Ordinary wills were printed and bound. I wanted change, you can be sure of that. Perhaps most of all I wanted to eat.

"Railroads were the backbone of the firm. We were staying with railroads and people were learning to fly! For the railroads we condemned and bought property, created companies and trusts, drew contracts and made stock. There was a model railroad engine two feet long in the glass case outside the office of the scion of our firm, Raymond Brewster.

"These were the problems I perceived. It might take twenty years to become a partner; now we make them almost overnight. I might be forced into becoming a specialist in a dying field of the law; now our clients change with the times and a law firm is diverse. I wanted change. As I say, most of all I wanted to eat. Have you felt hungry in a starched wing-collar shirt? I recall feeling lightheaded and nervous, almost angry. I could not dress and live and work on twenty-five dollars a week.

"Most of the clerks lived with their families, waiting for advancement. I could not. I had no relations in New York. I ate well only when I could stay late and charge my dinner to a client. I had clerked for Oliver Wendell Holmes. I had fought in the trenches and marched the Mexican border. I was a young Turk. What do you have to complain of now? I was willing to take a raise in vegetables."

His cigar did a lot more to my head than the sherry had. I would have to tell Littlefield the brand. Cigars were certainly cheaper than dope.

"A young Turk, like your grandfather, I imagine," Cosmo Bass said to me, sitting at the window in the Tortoise Club. "Finally, in desperation I approached Mr. Brewster's office. I was not invited to sit down. I particularly remember the gold chain across Mr. Brewster's huge belly. From it hung small model railroad spikes. It was hypnotic. Tiny golden spikes. I recall thinking, clearly, Consider that chain, that stomach.

" 'Bass!' he said. 'Is there something of a problem?'

"I asked him humbly for a raise to thirty dollars a week. I explained that it was becoming impossible to live in this city on twenty-five dollars a week.

" 'Bass,' he said. 'Consider the training you are receiving. Bass, when I was young, lawyers paid to be trained. They paid good money to watch over an older lawyer's shoulder.'

"I explained that I had clerked for Justice Holmes, and been paid more for it than I was being paid at the present time.

" 'The Government is extravagant, Bass,' Brewster said. 'I do not understand the nature of your argument.' I saw his large stomach. I dreamed of the tomatoes that grew in the greenhouse at his estate. I had seen him consume an entire bird at lunch when I humbly delivered a message. Wine at lunch as well. I thought: If the pictures in the papers are to be believed, Mr. Brewster's stomach is bigger than the stomach of James J. Hill.

" 'Sir,' I said, 'I have to eat.'

"He put his thumbs in his vest pockets.

" 'Not necessarily,' he answered, little knowing he was founding our present firm."

*   *   *

I had a strong suspicion that our luncheon would be measured by the length of time it took to finish our cigars.

"It is good to meet with our younger associates at intervals," Bass said. "Do you have any complaints?"

"No," I said.

"You find twenty-seven thousand dollars a year adequate?"

"I can live on it," I said.

"I thought you could," he said. He laughed. I laughed, too. It was one of the rules. You did not make complaints to Cosmo Bass. His firm, his club, his cigar.

*   *   *

"Have you read *The Honorable Peter Sterling*? 'Bartelby'?"

I hadn't; I would.

"How will you learn anything?" he said. "Read the books. Peter Sterling had a small inheritance. My classmate Howard Marshall had a large inheritance, a huge estate. He was affectionate and ineffectual. We were friends. He ate at clubs. I worked as a typist to eat. We were friends in a loose way. I had never seriously considered a professional relationship with him. Now I was rapidly becoming more practical. The firm of Bass and Marshall was formed. Howard paid the bills for our small office. Unfortunately, he did not bring in clients. Have you ever thought about bringing in clients?"

"No," I said. How was I going to bring in a client? Call

up the president of some conglomerate and offer my services?

"You take for granted the mail room, typing rooms, copying rooms? I, in fact, regard each of them as a small jewel. I remember when none of them existed. The file room came in nineteen thirty. We did not have a safe of our own until nineteen thirty-five. Sixty years ago, what you found was an office, and two young men. One dusting, the other studying. Clients? Marshall did not bring them in. I did not bring them in. We sat. Do you have any idea how long we sat?"

Cosmo Bass leaned over and gave me a squinting frown. He puffed his lips. For a second he looked ancient. I thought: Cosmo Bass is not going to live forever, whether he knows it or not. He's going to die. When he dies, he'll be like White, Case, . Cravath, Cadwallader. A name. When he's not feeling powerful, he knows he's going to die, I thought. For Christ sake.

"I have no idea how long you sat, sir," I said.

"One month, two months?"

His eyes closed slightly.

"Two months?" I guessed.

"Two years," he said. "We sat for two years in a small office paid for by Marshall. Clients did not appear at the door. They did not fly in the window. We could not advertise. We became experts in the art of sitting. Now we send teams of recruiters to Harvard, Yale, Stanford, God knows where. I certainly do not recall."

He fell asleep. Maybe it was the soft sound of the rain. I was sitting alone with Cosmo Bass in this Tortoise Club and his cigar was falling. I could call an attendant, or take the cigar out of his hands. Could I touch Cosmo Bass? The damn thing was slipping out of his fingers. I got ready to catch it. Suddenly, just as it began to fall, he snapped awake, and caught the tip.

"Where was I?" he demanded.

"You were explaining how difficult it was to get clients," I said.

"Yes," he said, "sixty years ago, Air East was a one-man office in our building. It was a one-plane mail run to Albany. Sixty years ago a tall ugly man walked into our office because Bass was at the beginning of the alphabet. He had the nerve to ask if we would do his legal work for free. He had been turned down by the As. Bass and Marshall did not turn away clients. You do not lure away a large railroad from an established firm. You sit in your office for sixty years and your clients grow old. Suddenly you have a huge law firm. The secret to clients is living a long time."

"Yes," I said.

"Now only I know Air East's founder and still largest shareholder. Our junior associates confer with Air East's young men, our seniors with their vice presidents. Only I know the aged, bedridden founder, who lives in Florida and is wheeled four times a day out onto a sun porch to watch the sea gulls."

"That's too bad," I said.

He looked sharply at me. That floating graceful senile quality had disappeared.

"That will be some estate," Cosmo Bass said. "Some estate," he snapped. "And I certainly expect to live to enjoy the proceeds. We must return to the office."

*   *   *

I would like to give an accurate picture of how we got out of the Tortoise Club and back to the firm. Cosmo Bass was apparently in a very good mood, and stopped to speak to lots of old gentlemen. He introduced me, and then I took a step back, according to the rules. He totally ignored anyone under the age of fifty. I guess you might say we codgered out of his club. Codgering: two old codgers kind of rub against each other like white-haired shiny dolls. They even appear to use a special sort of handshake: first the normal shake, and then one or the other puts another hand on top of the shake, kind of sealing it.

*   *   *

I did not walk amicably through the corridors chatting with Cosmo Bass. We were in the firm now, and although he had graciously told me that it had been an enjoyable lunch, I was learning the rules so well that I knew instinctively not to try to walk around with him. I had to go the same way. So I stopped at the water fountain and drank until he'd rounded the corner.

36

I was in a haze the next few days, blown out by Camilla Newman, the lunch with Bass, and especially by the Rolls episode. I wanted to know if he would live. I suppose it would have been more sensible to hope that he died. ("Put him out of his misery, a burial at sea," Littlefield said.) But it was as if Rolls was one of my projects, as if he was an assignment, a memorandum I'd completed. I wanted him to live. He was not going to come back the same man, I told Littlefield, if he came back at all.

Two days later, we all received a memorandum:

Re: Mr. Rolls

Mr. Rolls suffered a heart attack of a serious nature within the last few days. His condition has stabilized but he will be unable to return to the firm for an indeterminate length of time. Flowers are not appropriate. Donations may be sent to the American Heart Associate.

Bass and Marshall

I took my memo in to Littlefield. He was reading his at his desk.

"Heads will roll," he said. "Have you studied this?"

I looked at it again, as I say, I was in a fog.

"This is a general memorandum, distributed throughout the firm, even to the messengers. Perhaps copies have been sent to important clients. I sincerely hope not. Unless Iron Butt typed this out."

"What's the problem?"

"Your problem is firm fatigue, which I have eliminated with my ingenious invention of the Cicero memorandum. You are now so acclimated that you are unable to see the distinction between Heart Association and Heart Associate. You see the word *associate* and think it is perfectly normal. There is no American Heart Associate. Perhaps an argument could be made abstractly of course, that there is some generalized associate, some generalized person who might stand for all associates, but I rather doubt that. We are all rather individualistic, even behind our drab uniforms. You may not have seen the error, but I am sure that Cosmo Bass will spot it at once. He will not be pleased, because it is a memorandum from Bass and Marshall. If it were signed by any particular partner, perhaps he would not be quite so upset. But it is not."

"Maybe Bass wrote it himself."

"Logically impossible," Littlefield said. "The brain may be old, but as it decays, the first fundamental skills, learned early in life, come to the fore. Proofreading for Oliver Wendell Holmes. Moreover, Cosmo is so much a deity that even if he were to admit that he had made the mistake, no one in the firm would believe it."

Littlefield was confusing me, and I could see his speech was just beginning, so I was glad when the phone rang. I hadn't gotten to argue my point, that I was glad Rolls had lived, and I could see I wasn't going to.

"Yes," Littlefield said. "Sir. Sir. Sir. Sir."

He hung up.

"You're not often that obsequious," I told him. "You're obsequious, but that was bad."

"So was Lynch," Littlefield said. "I think it might be advisable to scurry to his office. He wants the two of us."

*   *   *

I had had Rolls on the brain for two days, and now had to adjust to Lynch. They were both partners, both had big corner offices, but Rolls' had the feeling of openness, space, ruggedness, and the sea. With Lynch I was back in the dark cave, facing the skull-like judges in their big frames. Thank God the place was not stacked with papers. Apparently, we were not about to go into battle.

Lynch stood up behind his desk, tall, Lincoln-esque. He stood beside his grandfather and father.

"Gentlemen," he said to Littlefield and me. "Gentlemen."

I think he intended the term to include all four of us. His hands were clasped behind his back, his coat was neatly buttoned. "I have something to say. We won."

He blew out the last two words in an enormous gust.

"Oh, God," Littlefield said, spontaneously.

"We won," Lynch thundered. "Our case has been transferred to California. It was a slow court, to be sure, but a brilliant one. We won."

He fell into his chair in a state of bliss. He put his feet up on his desk.

"We won. I knew we would win. And we won. I'd like to see the smile on the bastards' faces now. Slimy faces. We won."

He had said "we won" so many times, I finally began to believe it. All the cases would be transferred to California. Out of the office. Littlefield and I would not have to work with Lynch.

"Congratulations," I said. "I think it's great."

"Thanks," Lynch said.

"May I add my own comment and tell you that I truly admire what you've pulled off," Littlefield said. It sounded obsequious, but it wasn't. Maybe it was all the letters to the court. Perhaps the judge simply wasn't

prepared to have the case stay around and be bombard-
ed with daily junk mail from Lynch. On the other hand,
maybe Lynch was a genius. How could you tell? He was
certainly into his work.

"Thank you," Lynch told Littlefield. "Thank you. I
accept your congratulations. I think I did a damn fine
job. I think you both did a good job, too. I think we
should all have a drink, but first I'm going to announce
the victory to the whole damn firm."

As I've said, when an idea got hold of Lynch, he ran
with it. He nearly vaulted his huge solid desk and
sprang out the door.

"What do we do?" I asked.

"Have a drink," Littlefield said, "at the Clipper Bar."

*   *   *

We had several over lunch. I'd never drunk at lunch.
I sort of rationalized it as being on a partner's orders.
When we got back, around three, Lynch's secretary said
he was still making the rounds, receiving congratulations. It was a big firm all right, a lot of offices. It was a
big ego and it needed to be fed.

At four Lynch walked into his office, where I was
waiting with Littlefield. I expected him to be elated.
Tired, maybe, but happy, satiated. Instead, he was
almost shaking, rattling. He walked across the office
very fast to the window and looked out. He took
another tour back. Back and forth. Finally he stopped at
his desk, leaned against it, folded his arms across his
chest.

"They've taken an immediate appeal," he hissed.

How could they appeal? It was an interlocutory
decision. They couldn't appeal until the end of the trial.

"They filed at three." His secretary scurried in with a
manila folder. She put it on Lynch's desk and got out as

fast as she could. Looking down at the folder, Lynch
said, "They *mandamused* the court. Asked for an expe-
dited hearing before the Second Circuit Court of Appeals. They question whether the judge exceeded his
authority. In effect they're saying that the judge is so
stupid his decision is a breach of his powers. At heart,
it's a question of his competence. Did he abuse his
discretion? That's not the issue. Is he sane? That's what
they're really saying. Bastards. A brilliant judge."

Three days. *Mandamus.* How could I have forgotten
good old *mandamus*? It was the drinking. At least I'd
had three happy hours. Now I was looking at three days
of hell. Maybe this time I'd take speed, too. I looked at
the paintings behind Lynch's head. Victory might be
snatched from Lynch. He would go very deep on this
one. Right into the center of the pictures.

37

We had three days. On the fourth, Lynch had to hand in a brief. On the same day, he had to present his argument before the Second Circuit Court of Appeals. The district court judge might have been lazy, maybe even crazy, but the Second Circuit Court of Appeals is not. It likes to think that it is the second court in the country, right after the Supreme Court, definitely better than the twelve other courts of appeal. At times, like when the Hand cousins sat on it, it has been better. Maybe it's the best right now. It was certainly fast: whenever the case has something to do with a judge, they always are. And that was our best point, although we could never mention it. The Government was arguing that the judge had "abused his discretionary power as defined in the Federal Rules of Criminal Procedures," but what they were really saying was that his decision was so incompetent, they had a right to have it overturned immediately instead of at the end of the trial. But if the decision was that incompetent, what about the judge? Could the Second Circuit reach a decision that implied a judge was an idiot? If they did it would be hot in the lunch room. Both the district court and the Second Circuit are in the same federal building.

We began work immediately, even though Littlefield and I were drunk. The time rush was so incredible that

I lost track of Littlefield. I was off doing my research on the points I'd been assigned. Lynch was off doing his work, and trying to think up some sort of special oral argument that would save the district court and kill the bastards. We got through the night. We got through the next day. We got down to midnight when the firm began to seem soft, spongy. It looked hazy. At midnight exactly Littlefield walked into my office.

"We are halfway through our alloted time," he said, "I have something to show you."

I had just the desk light on. His face was shining, but the rest of his body seemed to disappear into the blackness of the room.

"I'm pretty damn busy," I said. "I mean, I don't have a hell of a lot of time."

"Calm down," he said. Where the hell was his body?

"Calm down. Christ," I answered.

"It's not that serious, it's just work," he said. Finally he sat down. That relaxed me. I could see all of him. "Would you just look this over?" he asked. "I'm not asking for an in-depth study. A quick glance will give you the general approach I've taken. I'd like a simple evaluation."

"Lynch will give that to you," I said.

"I want your evaluation first. It's really more important to me."

He sounded too calm. Was he on something?

"O.K.," I said. I began to flip through the pages. It was clearly a brilliant paper. But it was a paper, not a brief. There wasn't a case cited for five pages. There were no cases cited from the Second Circuit at all. Sure, all the great jurisprudential scholars were there. Kant was there. Wittgenstein seemed to crop up on page four. I'm not sure if he's jurisprudential or not. After page five a couple of cases were cited as illustrations.

"It looks brilliant," I said. "It's also about the stupidest thing you've ever done. Lynch won't accept it. He might fire you. You've wasted almost two days, half our time. What went wrong? What are you on? It isn't speed. Valium? Dope?"

"I haven't taken anything," he said. "Moreover, I'm sober. You cannot create fictitious cases for the Court of Appeals. With small memoranda for the tax department, it doesn't matter. At least my ultimate results appear to have been fairly good. But you cannot take that approach in a brief before the Court of Appeals. Perhaps Lynch might not catch me, but surely the court would. And I do not want to be accused of misrepresentation. One can be disbarred."

"You'd rather be fired?"

"If my evaluation is correct, I won't be fired. I believe Lynch is capable of understanding this. The man has a few special qualities."

I hoped so. They would have to be very good strong ones. Lynch had been up for almost two days, talking with Dad and Gramps. Goddamn it. I wanted to strangle Littlefield.

"How the hell can you do this to me?" I said. "What if he fires you? What the hell am I going to do around here without you? You're walking out on me."

"One has to take an ultimate stand."

I sat down again. I couldn't let the bastard go. My sanity was at stake, too.

"What the hell will you do if you're fired? Listen, what kind of job will you get if you're fired? It's not good for your damned reputation, either." Then I got an idea of my own. "I'll do your section for you. You keep doing your thing just the way you want. I'll do your section, too. I'll do it." Maybe I could. Who knows? You can do amazing things on speed if you haven't taken too much of it, too long. I'd never been into speed. Maybe I could work twice as fast and stay relatively sane.

"You are a friend," he said.

"You're right."

"As to your first argument, I have a plan if fired. No, it does not involve jumping, the long dive. That I considered and rejected. It is slightly crazy, yes, but possible." He raised his hand, silenced me. "Don't argue, it's all thought through. And as to your gracious gesture, I will not give you any speed, and you do not know how to get any yourself, unless I am very much mistaken. Therefore, you cannot do my work. But it was a noble gesture."

I put my elbows on my desk. I put my head in my hands. You can't reason with Littlefield. He's just too smart and stupid at the same time. Moreover, he looks so rational and beatific that he continually throws you off guard. There isn't anything you can do with him.

"What's your plan if you're fired?" I said.

"I don't want to discuss it right now. You're in no shape."

"Thanks," I said.

"And in any case, I do not think I will have to use it." He receded back into the darkness. But a hand came out, as if through a curtain. "You are a true friend," he said, "probably the best I've ever had. Do not worry: there are options within options." Then he was gone.

Camilla Newman had talked about options, too. She'd told me once she thought she had an option on me. Option was not a word I trusted.

38

Three o'clock in the morning, the night before oral argument at the Court of Appeals, is not the best time for a conference about briefs. It's hard to be rational when your eyes burn and the coffee doesn't work anymore. Typewriters begin to look like big black clams, their mouths open, exposing a crazy row of clam teeth. Clams don't have teeth, of course, but who knows what kind of exotic weird clam-beast lives at the bottom of the deepest ocean rift? These are the kinds of thoughts you ask yourself. You're prepared to talk about weird clams, but Lynch expects a sensible discussion of the limits of *mandamus,* the breadth of a district court judge's discretion, and the Federal Rules of Criminal Procedure. Meanwhile, you feel as if you're under water, the blinking lights outside the black windows are shining fishes you pass as you sink. Telephones are manta rays with tails, pencils are eels. If Littlefield was going to present his weird brief, and drown, he had the perfect setting.

I stumbled into Lynch's office. His shirt sleeves were rolled up. There were four empty coffee cups on his desk. Books and papers covered the chairs and sofa. He didn't say anything to me. He winked. Littlefield came in, too, the only one of us who looked normal. He pushed aside some books and sat down next to me. Now that we were gathered, Lynch perked up.

"Here're copies of my stuff," he said. "Review it for me. I've got to start on my oral argument." His voice shook when he said oral argument. I felt a little for him. I was kind of glad I didn't have to stand up in the big courtroom. "Let's see what you've done."

What could I do? Grab Littlefield's brief and eat it? To give myself time to think, I pushed my brief at Lynch first. He seemed to interpret that as enthusiasm for the job, and nodded at me.

He was skimming, flicking the pages by quickly.

"All right," he said. "All right. I want Xeroxed copies of every case you've cited. Do it tonight. I want them on my desk. I want them arranged in the same order they're cited. Understand?"

"Sure," I said.

"Let's see what you've got," he said to Littlefield.

There wasn't anything I could do. Littlefield was enthusiastic himself and jumped up before I could grab his coat. Smiling, proud of himself, he dumped a pure, undiluted, unconcealed, fully and honestly documented Cicero memorandum on Lynch's desk. I hoped Lynch had inherited a sense of humor, but from the look on Gramps' face, that did not seem terribly likely.

Lynch began to flip through it, flicking the pages as he'd done with mine. He was obviously tired. I hoped he might just flip through it so fast he didn't notice anything, but he began to slow down. He turned back to the first page and started again. Littlefield was excited: leaning forward, hands clasped. He wanted Lynch to actually understand the brief.

I could not believe it. I looked out the window at the shining little fishes swimming in the dark. There were quite a lot of them. Maybe what was happening in here was happening in law offices all over town. Anyway, there were a lot of people up tonight. Or was it cleaning people? It was certainly taking Lynch a long time to realize exactly what he had hold of.

"I don't see the cases here," he said. "Is this the draft copy? I don't see the citations."

"There are a few case citations," Littlefield answered. "They're toward the end of the paper, small jewels adorning the central thesis."

"Central thesis?" Lynch said. He really didn't understand. He was trying to understand, but he didn't. He was damn tired.

Almost innocently, as if he really thought he was the one who was stupid, who didn't understand, Lynch said, "This isn't really a brief, is it?"

I shut my eyes. I wanted to put my hands over my ears, too. I wanted Littlefield to say something like, My God, sir, you've got my background notes, not brief. And I knew he wasn't going to.

"It's a somewhat enhanced, more elegant formulation of the traditional Wall Street law firm brief. It maintains some of the basic structural values, which I suppose originated with Cosmo Bass himself, and came down indirectly from Oliver W. Holmes, and which serve as the basic formulation, the underlying structure to the Wall Street brief. This brief, and indeed I think one might properly call it that, goes far beyond those tenets, however. Moreover, it compresses and yet expands our most solid arguments."

"Compresses, expands?" Lynch said. He swiveled in his chair, glanced at his dad and gramps, then leaned back and shut his eyes. "Compresses and expands?" he said again, this time to himself. "No cases?" he added like a dreamer. You could tell he was at least trying to come to grips with the problem. After all, he did have to argue the next morning before the Court of Appeals.

They would expect a few citations. There were a few other things on his mind. It was perhaps not the most sensible time to be hit with the Cicero memorandum.

"It's kind of like a paper?" he asked. Now his eyes were wide open.

"Not exactly," Littlefield said, "although I've tried to incorporate certain structural values reflecting my experience on the *Yale Law Journal*."

Unfortunately, he was talking to a Harvard-trained lawyer. I hoped when it finally hit him, Lynch would burst out laughing. You know how you can be at three A.M. when something comes at you completely out of the blue, ruining all your plans? Manic. If he laughed, maybe it would be all right. Wittgenstein at three o'clock in the morning might do it to a Wall Street litigator. Maybe if Littlefield got into the Wittgenstein concepts about certain problems being inherently unsolvable . . .

"I've got to get a hold of this," Lynch said. "Listen, is this some sort of sideline to the section I assigned you?"

"I've totally expended myself on this," Littlefield said. "I've given it all I've got. It's the best work I can do. I promise you, I would not have backed away from the problem and gone off on tangents. I consider it one of my major accomplishments."

"All your energies, all your time?"

"I've tried to write the perfect brief."

Lynch slumped in his chair. His hands went limp on his desk.

"This is it?" he said.

"Perhaps I could do slightly better," Littlefield added humbly. "I feel I may have slighted Austin. I've never had enough appreciation for his work."

"You're fired," Lynch said.

He snapped forward as he said it. At least he was

clean-cut, didn't use the normal law firm terminology of "separation" from the firm, or "has left us."

"Couldn't we go over the brief together once?" Littlefield asked politely.

Lynch's eyes were jiggling, both winking at once.

"Don't call this shit a brief," he growled.

Littlefield stood up immediately.

"In that case, sir," he said, "may I have the copy back? And may I add that I've enjoyed working with you." With dignity, he picked the Cicero memorandum up off the table and walked quietly out of the room. I sat there stunned. I sat there for about five minutes, maybe less, just looking at Lynch.

I noticed for the first time how ugly Lynch was physically. His neck and the sides of his face were pock-marked, like a concrete building, graying, spotted. His head was square. His pimples met each other in jagged straight lines at the corners of his face so that his head looked like a cube. On the cube's top, there was a tuft of grassy hair that seemed to float in the wind of the air conditioning. But there wasn't much hair on the sides of his head, so that the illusion was complete. His noggin looked like an old office building.

Behind Lynch, the top floors of the World Trade Center appeared in the window. It was as if there were not two World Trade towers but three, Lynch's head being the third, moved inside.

"Now it's just the two of us," Lynch boomed at me suddenly. "But we can do it. We'll have to do it."

It was just the one of us as far as I was concerned. I immediately ran out into the corridor. I made good time, but Littlefield had gone before I reached his office. It was spotlessly clean. Looked unused. Whatever his plan was, he'd already begun to put it into effect. I walked back to my own office. Littlefield had drowned me when he left. I could not face the work alone, nor Lynch, nor the law firm.

"In case of emergency," the envelope on my desk read. I tore it open. It was from Littlefield.

"Friend," it read,

Do not desert Lynch in his hour of need. I had hoped we would be working together, mutually enjoying the thrill of entering the Court of Appeals. Since you are reading this, that is obviously not to be. Do not worry about me. I will reappear soon. (I hope my other calculations prove better than the one I made with Lynch.) Worry about yourself. You must now, partially because of me, complete the work of two associates. I have therefore provided you with the enclosed capsules. Please follow my instructions: Pop one now. It's enough to get you off, but not enough to ruin your work. I have taken into account your weight and metabolism. After three days, however, you must go immediately to sleep. Sleep long and well, dear friend. I will be thinking of you.

Cicero

"Are you deserting me, too?" Lynch yelled at me from the door. "My God — we've got to work. No time left."

"No, I'm here," I said.

"Are you?" he screamed. "Then why did you leave my office?"

"I've got to go to the bathroom," I said calmly.

"So that was it," Lynch said, calming down, "good. We can do it. For Christ sake, get in there and piss."

I let him live with his own conception of the world and popped the speed. Just in case he was listening outside, I also flushed the toilet.

39

The clean water in the toilet bowl went rushing out into the pipes of the big building. It would end up with the Hudson River and the clams, where my mind had started. I hated taking drugs. The only thing I'd ever done was smoke some dope. Now I was on speed. Maybe I was on speed: perhaps Littlefield had given me a placebo. No, I was on something all right. I felt a power surge welling up inside me. There was definitely something going on. I hoped Littlefield had accurately guessed my weight.

The main problem was Littlefield's section of the brief: first to get the cases together, then to write it. Typing was no problem. We could muster a hundred secretaries if we had to.

It was now three-thirty in the morning. We were supposed to be in court at eleven-thirty, brief in hand, oral argument prepared. Obviously, Lynch would have to work on the oral argument. That left me with sole responsibility for Littlefield's section. I began to realize that we could actually lose the case. Sure, we had an intrinsic advantage because the Government was attacking the judge. We also had an advantage because a judge's discretionary power to move a case is very broad. Moreover, the scope of a *mandamus* appeal is limited. But if we appeared in court as total incompetents, it would reinforce the Government's argument. How could any court reach a decision that had been advanced by morons? What kind of court would listen to morons? A moron court. Bang, we'd lose.

It was three-thirty in the morning. If I got the brief to the secretaries by ten, it would still be all right. Plenty of time to type, even time to proofread. I had at least six and a half hours, maybe more. Plenty of time, I thought. Jesus, I really was on speed. Plenty of time? This was not a case for careful research in the library.

"I'll be back," I said.

"What?" Lynch said. He was locked into his oral argument. I don't think he even realized I was in his office.

"The plan is that I do Littlefield's section of the brief. I'm going to do it. But I'll be out of touch. We can combine all three sections in the morning."

Now his eyes snapped on. He gave up his romance with his pencil and yellow legal pad.

"That's the plan, is it?" he said. "Of course, you've got to do Littlefield's section. But who's going to run to the library and get me cases?"

In fact, it was a reasonable question. I might have felt the same way if I had to write an oral argument for the big court in six hours.

"Who's around?" he said. "Isn't anyone else working in the damn office tonight?"

"The Xerox crew," I said. "It's kind of quiet. The three secretaries we've got on hold outside."

"No goddamned lawyers?"

"I didn't see any."

"No lawyers," he said, "No bodies. No paralegals?"

"I don't think so," I told him.

"Where is the goddamned list?" he said. It was right next to his telephone. "The secretaries aren't doing anything. Tell them to go through the list of the parapersons, I mean paralegals. From the bottom. Working up. I want them called, and I want one of them in here now. Tell the secretaries that if they get anyone on the line, to switch the call to me. If they can't wake up a para, tell them to start with the associate lawyers, working from the bottom. If they can't wake up an associate, tell them to start with the partners. All the way up the list."

"All the way up?" I asked.

"No goddamn it, not to Bass. Do I have to explain everything?"

"I wanted to make sure."

The intensity of the work was good therapy for him. He'd given up on Dad and Gramps. We weren't dealing with metaphysics. He was actually making sense.

"I'm going to do my section in my own way," I told him. "I just wanted you to know. You might not be able to get me on the telephone."

"Your own way," he snapped. "What the hell does that mean? Are you going to give me cases or not? Will there be cases in your brief?"

"A lot of cases," I promised.

He looked at me hard. "Is Littlefield still here?" he said. "Maybe I went too far. Christ. It's the pressure. Is he here?"

"He's gone, definitely gone," I said.

"I just expected a goddamned brief," Lynch said, "I mean, all I wanted were a couple of relevant court decisions. I can't go to the Second Circuit citing . . ." He stopped. "Who the hell was he quoting?"

"Plato," I said. "Rawls. Kant. He's fond of Cicero, too."

"If it wasn't three o'clock in the morning. If we didn't have to be in court at eleven-thirty."

"It's three forty-five," I said. Frankly, this wasn't the time to discuss the Cicero memorandum.

"Is he dumb or brilliant?" Lynch said. "What is it? What the hell kind of brains does he have? What the hell goes on at Yale Law School?"

"He's dumb and brilliant," I said. "They go hand in hand. I've got to move. It will be done by ten. You'll get a lot of cases. But I've got to move."

"If it's in by ten, and if it's any good, we might make it," he said. "Out of touch? Christ, listen, I'm relying on you. I need you."

"I know you do," I said. It was the truth.

The secretaries woke up the first paralegal they tried. The poor slob got to hear Lynch scream at him. Just to make sure the first para took him seriously, Lynch had the secretaries wake up another. They were both told to get down on the curb. Then the secretaries called the firm taxi service, and Lynch began to feel better. I was glad he had company, but I didn't want any. To get my quiet, I had to get the relevant cases Xeroxed. I grabbed two of the boys from the copying room, and took them into the library with me. This was a breach of the "rules" but what the hell. When I found a relevant case, I gave it to one of the boys, and he ran to the copying room to Xerox it. Using them both, working them in relays, I had forty good cases, and certainly the key Supreme Court decisions in a neat bundle by five. Then I cabbed back to my apartment.

*   *   *

As soon as I got home, I felt better. I put on a record, threw out the two remaining pills Littlefield had left me, and ran a bath. I got into the good hot water and began to read the cases, marking good quotes with a yellow soft-tip pen. When I'd gone through them once, I got out of the bath, had more coffee, and went through them once more, disregarding some, arranging them into a rational order, using the key Supreme Court decisions as my starting points, then adding the Second Circuit decisions to show how the rules laid down by the big court had been interpreted in our favor. Naturally, any decision that didn't favor us was shown to be distinguishable on the merits.

With the cases arranged, I sat down at my own small typewriter, and began pounding out an argument. When it came time to cite a case, I scissored out the quote from the Xeroxed copy and cut out the citation, too, so there was no chance of misciting, and any error had to be the secretary's. The light began to come through the window. It got brighter and brighter as I scissored and typed and Scotch taped together a brief. Maybe it was the dopey morning feeling, but I began to believe that what I'd put together wasn't bad. Moreover, it fitted in with the other section of the brief I'd already prepared. I began to think it was conceivable that we might win, if Lynch didn't blow it in court. If I could finish in time.

Because I was having these slightly idiotic feelings about our possible success, I stopped work and made some breakfast. I had more coffee and finished up. I dressed carefully and neatly because we were going to court, and read over the whole thing again, making some minor changes. At nine-thirty, I took a cab to the firm.

*   *   *

"This is good," Lynch said, reading quickly. "Get it typed in final." I took it down the hall to our battery of secretaries. Because the brief was divided into three sections, we could save some time. Each of the three sections went to a different secretary. I proofread pages with two other associates as they came off the machines. Since it's not good to proof your own stuff, I did Lynch's section. His was all right, too. All this took about forty-five minutes. When the stuff was typed and Xeroxed the two other associates took over the job of getting the briefs bound up in their nice blue covers. I went back to Lynch's office to see if I could help with the oral argument.

It turned out I couldn't help, because he was dictating some last-minute thoughts to his secretary. He was nervous and tight and had not had any sleep and looked like hell. It is a big thing to argue in the Court of Appeals, when you know reporters will be there and the case will probably land in the newspapers. Finally, he looked up and said: "Get the Xeroxes of every important case and put them in my attaché case. Get one of the big firm suitcases and load our briefs into it. Got it?"

"Sure," I said. I already had extra copies of every case I'd cited, so it only took a few minutes work, using the copying room boys again, to get copies of Lynch's cases. I put them into his attaché case and checked with the other two associates. They had the jacketed briefs in a big stack. There were so many they filled the entire suitcase. It was now eleven-fifteen. Lynch came running out of his office, holding a manila envelope and wearing his overcoat.

"Got the cases?"

"I've got the briefs," I said.

"Ready."

"I'm ready," I said.

"Well for Christ sake, did you call a cab?" Surprisingly, I had.

40

On the seventeenth floor of the Federal Courthouse, the Second Circuit Court of Appeals holds sessions in a big teak room. Since this was a case involving a judge, the room was packed. Lynch's wife was there, and one of his children. There were other judges sitting in with the spectators. We had to push our way through to the little fence that separates the onlookers from the attorneys arguing the case. We finally got through the gate, and sat down at a big oak table. Lynch and I were on one side. Three lawyers sat on the other facing us. Finally the judges came in and asked who was presenting the oral arguments. They looked dismayed at the fact that there were five attorneys. Two against three, I thought, that looks good. And all three of the other attorneys got up and argued. It was going to be three against one.

While they talked, Lynch muttered "no, no," whenever they mentioned a case. Luckily, he did it in a low voice. His hands were shaking, his face chalky. One of the judges asked to see a case. Did anyone have a copy of it? Or should they send their clerks out to the library?

"Give me the batch of Xeroxed cases," Lynch said.

"They're in your attaché case."

"What attaché case?"

"Yours," I said. The one you left in the office. Christ. I wanted to say it wasn't my fault. I felt like hell. I felt as if

I was the worst lawyer in the world because Lynch had forgotten his own attaché case.

"Do you have the oral argument?" I whispered. I could run back to the office for it. The three lawyers against us were running on and on. Maybe I could get back in time.

"Goddamn, Christ, what the hell do you think is in this envelope?" he said, picking up the envelope, tearing it open in a ragged slice because he could not control his hands. If he would stop looking at the tall bench filled with judges, he might get under control, I thought. Should I tell him that?

I didn't have time to tell him anything. The third lawyer stopped talking. The judges began muttering to each other, as if the case was over. Lynch immediately jumped up, clutching his oral argument. He careened over to the lectern, the upper part of his body swaying. He was tall and that was a lot of swaying. Here we were, representatives of Bass and Marshall, the prestigious Wall Street firm, sending a semicomatose, swaying, frayed man, who had not slept for three days, up to the lectern in the giant teak hall, before maybe one hundred spectators, before black-robed judges staring down from the high bench. Not only was I embarrassed for Lynch, I was scared. I was now the only attorney left on our side of the table. If Lynch collapsed, I might have to argue. Lynch was trying to get control of his papers. Christ, he was having trouble just getting them to lie down on the lectern.

He managed to get the papers flat. And began whispering. He was, after all, the descendant of two of the most famous judges in United States history, so the court allowed him to whisper for quite a long time. We were apparently going to be allowed to deliver a silent oral argument. My God, I thought, we will lose the case.

And after all that goddamned work. He whispered so softly that the only reason I was sure he was actually talking at all was that when he swayed, his body half turned, and I could see his face. He was trying, all right, the lips were moving.

The spectators began to shuffle in back, making matters worse. I glanced briefly at the three spiffy attorneys sitting across from me. Their faces were like Hallowe'en pumpkins — gigantic spreading smiles that reached their ears. Clearly Lynch was a moron. *Res ipsa loquitur,* "The thing speaks for itself." A fundamental legal doctrine. Only in our case, the thing did not speak. Thus, proving himself a moron, and by implication, the judge who had ruled in our favor. This could not go on indefinitely. Either the court had to commit Lynch or ask that he talk. Respect for his forebears was certainly in order, but could they allow the man to present a silent argument before one hundred people?

"The Court finds it difficult to hear you," one of the judges said politely.

"The Court finds it difficult to hear me?" I almost jumped out of my chair, because Lynch yelled out the statement. His voice seemed to knock the judges back against the teak walls.

"I will therefore begin again," Lynch screamed. "I do not wish any of the erroneous statements of opposing counsel to go unanswered."

God, calm down, calm down. Calm him down, God, please, I prayed. I was white, too, now as white as Lynch. He was trying his best, I knew that, I felt for him. And wanted to strangle him, or at least muffle him. The teak courtroom was apparently acoustically perfect, because Lynch's screaming argument was louder than Eric Clapton.

Finally, possibly through divine intervention, Lynch

calmed down. He did not reach normality, but he stopped screaming. His hands shook and sometimes his voice boomed, but he communicated a real feeling that he cared about the case. His arms waved, and his tie went back over his shoulder. But he looked honest and nervous and as if he cared, really cared. He looked different from the slick attorneys sitting across the table from me. They had just a touch of gray at the temples, dark wool suits, blue ties striped with white. Gray at the temples. Lynch did not have any hair on the side of his head. He looked Indian, American, scared, cornered, caring, wanting, suffering, real. And honest. My God, the total effect actually made me feel we were completely right, and the other side was a bunch of bastards who never should have dared bring the case into court. It was a remarkable display. The judges asked no questions, but they all leaned forward as Lynch went on. And he did for a good long time. They made no attempt to stop him. He finally finished with a boom.

"The Court thanks Counsel," a judge said.

"And Counsel expresses his appreciation for the Court's patience," Lynch replied.

Everyone stood up as the judges filed out. As soon as they were gone, Lynch staggered back to the big table. He had some energy left all right; supporting himself with both arms on the table, he yelled at the opposing attorneys. "You cited your cases all wrong." The attorneys got up, backed away. "If I had my Xeroxes, I'd prove it to you," Lynch shouted. "You didn't cite your cases honestly."

*   *   *

We went home, that is, to the firm, together in a taxi. All in all I was proud of him. It had been exciting and crazy in the Court of Appeals, but when he'd stood up there and talked, he had looked honest. He was never going to be an academic genius. He was just a partner in a big law firm. I could not make him calm and sane. I could not give him psychotherapy so that he could argue a case without the ghosts of his ancestors hovering at his shoulder. But he'd been scared, I knew that, and he'd stood up there and talked. Damn well, in fact.

"I want to tell you one thing," he said, "when you're arguing in court, you can't keep your mind clear and you've got to rely on your people to do things for you like making sure you've got your attaché case."

"It won't happen again," I said.

"You filed the briefs though?"

"Yes."

"You did a good job on the briefs."

"Thanks," I said. "I thought your argument was a tremendous success."

That set him off. He bounced in the seat.

"I believe my argument was the turning point," he said.

"You did a great job."

"It went tremendously. I did do a good job. A tremendous job."

"It went pretty well," I said.

"Damn well."

What the hell, I gave him what he needed: "You made the best argument I've ever heard," I said. "It was beyond praise. It was absolutely perfect. It was a masterpiece."

"Thanks," he said. "Thank you. Thanks a lot."

* * *

Back at the firm, Lynch visited with partners, blowing off steam, getting congratulations. I wanted to blow off steam, too, tell someone the whole thing, so I went to

Littlefield's office. His name was still on the door and I almost began talking before I came to and realized he was really gone. I sat down at his desk. Wellington Rolls was gone. Littlefield was gone. I wondered who was next. Cosmo Bass? No. Not the deity. Lynch? If he'd survived this, he could survive anything. Lawrence? Camilla? Me?

41

It was not a perfect day for eating in Battery Park. The strong summer wind blew towering clouds past the sun, so I got its rays in bursts, a sun squall. I had to hold on to the wrapping of my sandwich. Papers blew by me with the pigeons. I was alone on my bench and wanted to stay that way. The wind helped keep down the park population, but there were still some strollers, and a few of the usual nuts. One of them was an old man bent over double, chasing pigeons with birdseed. He hopped like a squirrel after the pigeons, throwing birdseed at them.

I wondered what to do in the afternoon. Lynch and I had done too good a job. We'd received a verdict in our favor within three days from the Court of Appeals. Our case was now out in California, being handled by another firm. Now and then, Lynch jetted out to give them advice; he had, after all, had his picture in the *Times*. I wondered if there would be a third big portrait. Maybe Lynch would be elevated to a judgeship. I did not think he would sit on the Supreme Court of the United States like his grandfather, but he might get something. He was being very nice to me, and had even offered to let me fly to California with him. I couldn't do it because I was too busy.

I had a small reputation in the firm now as the guy who'd done two people's work in one night. After Lynch got his dose of praise, sometimes he actually told people about my part in it. Word spreads in a firm. If I could do two associates' work, why not let me? I was obviously on the rise, striving for partnership. Assignments came in from all over. I could nibble on the Proctor estate this afternoon if I wanted to. It was a sort of endless assignment, given to me, I think, because the estate department wanted to get a hold on me. Maybe today I'd arrange to send out Mrs. Proctor's collection of personally painted water colors. Mrs. Proctor had had three sons, and it was our job, as executors, to make sure that everything got evenly distributed. I thought I'd probably let one of the mail room boys go through the water colors at her big apartment. That would certainly be fair, random selection. We hired expensive appraisers for the Monets and Sargents. As executors, the firm wanted to be fair. But the old lady's water colors? Wouldn't we be squandering the estate's funds in having them appraised? I'd ask if my idea about letting a mail room boy choose made any sense. People sometimes listened to me now. Even partners.

This was a good sandwich, but the pigeon man kept interrupting my thoughts. He ran by, just missed catching a pigeon by the tail. He was probably into force-feeding. He was probably confused and a nut. He wanted to help the birds and kill them at the same time. So he tried to catch them, and when he couldn't, he threw birdseed at them as if he were a machine-gunner.

Maybe I wouldn't work on the Proctor estate. I could do that anytime. I would only do that if I needed an excuse not to work on the Ligon Corporation. I was not in the mood to research the Federal bankruptcy laws. If the partner in charge told me I had to do it this afternoon, then I'd say I had a crisis with the Proctor estate. He might believe me. As I say, now they sometimes listened to me.

My problem was having someone to talk to. I'd tried Littlefield's apartment every day. Every day, the phone just rang and rang. I would have felt better if he'd at least told me his plan. Finally, after a week, I got an answer of sorts. The telephone had been disconnected. No new number was supplied. I tried information, then, but there were no new Littlefields.

There was no reasonable substitute. I let Newman come to me when she wanted to. I let her talk. I was available for consultation on all matters except her affair with Lawrence. I was there if she wanted to cry. But I was not going to go to bed with her. Maybe she wouldn't have done that, even in her weakest moments, but I wasn't even going to try to get her back. She and Lawrence were working very closely together now that Rolls was out of the way. Lawrence had picked up a hell of a lot of work that Rolls would have done, so they were working late together, almost every night. I didn't want to know what else they were doing. I guess I knew, but I didn't want to commit mental suicide. Goddamn it, I was still in love with the bitch. All right, she wasn't a bitch. She could run her own life. She'd had a bad divorce. Maybe she needed the thing with Lawrence to wipe it out. I don't know. I wondered how long they could get away with it. That would lead me into thinking about what they were actually doing. Mental suicide.

I was about to commit it when the pigeon man sprinted behind my bench. He was certainly an avid ornithologist. I might have believed he was a professor of pigeonology, if he'd had his fly zipped, and wore a belt instead of a string. Now he was crouched behind my bench. That was even worse that having him sitting next to me. I turned around and stared at him, and he jumped and sprinted for a garbage can. He didn't get in it. I saw his plan clearly: He was hiding, waiting for a pigeon to come strolling along the path. He had his bag of birdseed ready to dump on the pigeon's head. There are court buffs who spend all their time sitting in courts. They have their favorite judges, and sometimes applaud when a favorite makes a startling remark. They just get off on courts. This man got off on pigeons. Now you know why there are so many pigeons in New York.

I decided I would work on the tax deductibility of the Keel Corporation's sailboat. Was it deductible? If so, how deductible? Could one hold business conversations on a boat designed for ocean racing? If not, could they paint the name of the Keel Corporation on its side and pretend it was an advertisement? If they painted the name of the corporation on the boat, would the Yacht Racing Association allow the president of Keel Corporation to race? It might be fun researching the rules of the Association. I might even get to see the inside of the New York Yacht Club. The Keel Corporation made tractors, not keels. If they'd made keels, the job would have been much simpler. We could have argued that the boat was used for testing purposes.

Birdseed landed on my head. For a second, I thought it was rain because the clouds looked ominous. They were tall, thick columns, stretching way up. But they were not compacted yet, so it wasn't rain, but birdseed. I was obviously going to lose this battle with the pigeon nut. He was just too damn shrewd. I looked around, trying to find him, couldn't, and birdseed still landed on my head. He must have known every inch of the park. There must have been secret hiding places I would never discover. Maybe he had climbed into the garbage can when my back was turned. What the hell, I thought, it means more to him than to me. I'm probably sitting in prime pigeon territory. I'll give it back to him, I thought. He can sit here and throw seed at pigeons in the rain.

42

That day, for unknown reasons, I became fascinated with the deductibility of the ocean-racing sailboat. I sort of hate to admit it, but I really wanted to find a sensible way to let the president of a huge corporation write off his expensive plaything. Maybe the reason had something to do with Wellington Rolls — perhaps he'd deeply implanted sailboats in my brain. I ended up, nine-thirty at night, with piles of the black C.C.H. tax reporters on my desk, many case reporters, and even law review articles. I was going all the way on this one. The president would get to deduct his boat, no matter how much money he made or we'd take it to the Supreme Court.

The reason I stayed around, worked late, might also have had to do with the rain. Those afternoon clouds had worked up a beautiful storm. The lightning slashed at the tops of buildings and a red haze hung over the Hudson River. There was a power reduction, and the lights in my office dimmed slightly. This was a rain good enough to rob the whole city system of electricity. Anything could happen in this rain. And it was better to watch it from my office than from my studio apartment where I just got to look at the next studio apartment across the street from me.

My light dimmed again, brightened, dimmed. There

was a human network at the firm, too, a sort of power grid. And when you joined the firm you were plugged into it. The long gray line of partners got the system spinning. The system built up power. The power surged through all the offices and gave you the psychic energy that kept you rotating, spinning, working through the night. Electric adrenalin. But someone had thrown the wrong switch, sent an extra burst into Rolls, blown him out. There had been a faulty connection there. The latest memo said he was doing well. I hoped so. But when he came back, I hoped they plugged him into the psychic grid carefully.

My lights were flickering. This rain was leaking down into the gut of the city and sinking it. It was sending the current back down to the earth, away from our buildings. Down in the subway, I fantasized pools of water, red with a thousand volts, frying subway rats. Now the lightning moved out into the river, suspended from black night clouds. The lightning attacked the river's black back, stinging it again and again. The river kept flowing. The thunder blew across it like invisible cavalry. The Hudson didn't give a damn.

"Can I come in?" my friend Miss Newman asked. She was always polite to me now.

"Sure," I said. "Scared of the storm?"

"Some storm," she said. She sat down. She began to light a cigarette.

"Don't do it," I said. "You're not the type. You can't play the part."

She stood up on that, though I hadn't thought it was really a nasty thing to say. But all the corporate securities people smoked, and she was trying to be one of the boys. Maybe I was nastier than I thought.

"Smoke," I said. "Smoke. Sorry."

Now of course she refused. And I loved her. I really

can't explain it. She always did exactly the opposite of what I asked, and I loved her. She put her cigarettes neatly away in a silver box, and put the box neatly into her purse.

"Are you nasty tonight?" she said.

"Lightning brings out my worst qualities," I told her. "But I'll try to calm down. Don't leave."

She was facing my desk and the window. I'd turned away from the window so that I could look at her. I only saw the lightning when it blazed across her face. She was random neon, facing the window.

"How are you doing, Sam?" she asked. "What are you working on?"

"Boats," I said. "It's a lot of fun. I'm really getting into boats." I didn't ask her what she was working on. That would lead into the issue of who she was working with. "The tax deductibility of ocean racers."

"Listen, I want to talk to you for a second about Lawrence."

"Forget it," I said. "Now you can leave. Talk about something else though, because I want you to stay. The truth is that I'm scared of storms. I need company."

"I guess I'll go then," she said. "You're impossible."

I thought about it. Maybe I could take a little Lawrence. I could try.

"Give me a little Lawrence," I said. "In small doses. You're getting married. He's divorcing his wife."

"Stop it," she said, lighting up with the sparks outside my window. Blond hair looks good in lightning.

"I'll stop," I said. "Is something wrong?"

"Nothing," she said. "Except that he goes to see Bass tomorrow."

"What does that mean, he goes to see Bass?"

"He's been at the firm eight years," she said. "He's doing a lot of Rolls' work. Someone has to take charge of it. Either they bring in someone from the outside, or they give him a partnership."

"I just can't get excited about it," I said. "I mean, I hope he doesn't make it, of course. I hope he gets a job in Alaska. But I don't think it will kill me if he doesn't get fired, if he gets a partnership. I won't die. Why don't we talk about Littlefield? There was a second there when all three of us were good friends. Remember his apartment?"

"I'm worried about this Lawrence thing," she said.

"Yes," I said. "If he doesn't make it, you two won't be able to work late together. Fine. You don't give a damn about Littlefield, although he's disappeared to Istanbul or someplace. But you're worried about whether Lawrence makes partner."

When I talked, there was usually a power reduction. When Camilla talked, she got the lightning. There was something unfair about the way nature was treating me. And there was something unfair about the way Camilla was acting.

"I think I really have had it," I said. "I hope Bass fires the bastard. I hope Lawrence is fired on the basis of moral turpitude. A spanking would be in order. Maybe I'll give him one myself." This time I got the lightning.

"You don't understand."

All the lightning was running my way. It was like winning at cards.

"Do I understand correctly or not?" I asked. "Are you fucking Lawrence or aren't you? Is my understanding correct? A simple yes or no answer will do. Have I been wrong for months? Make me understand. If I'm wrong you've got a chance to straighten me out. Just give me a simple, direct, yes or no answer."

"Why do you concentrate on fucking, for Christ sake. The rest of the world doesn't have your fixation. Does it make one hell of a lot of difference if I fuck Lawrence. Or if I fuck you."

"The rest of the world didn't want to marry you," I said. "Was that an admission of guilt? Is that your yes?"

"I can't talk to you," she said, and stood up.

"You can't say yes or no, because it's yes," I snapped back. "You don't want to talk about Lawrence. You want to fuck him, and then, worried about his future, you want to get consolation from me. But you don't seem to understand: I happen to be very fond of you." What the hell; I let go. "You don't understand, I happen to probably love you. At least, you interfere with my work. I'm in love with a goddamned bitch. But I am going to get over it." I was rolling now and couldn't stop. "I'm going to get over you. I'm working on it. People do get over other people. They are supposed to be able to do it with time."

"You don't understand."

"Yes or no," I said. "Do you fuck Lawrence? Did you fuck him yesterday? This morning? How was it?"

She went to the door, but had a second thought. She turned around and screamed. *"You broke our contract, you bastard."*

She got the lightning for her scream. There seemed to be some rationale to the lightning. Maybe nature did have a purpose. Maybe natural law actually did exist. Maybe Cicero was right when he argued that we were all born with a God-given small set of laws in our brains. When the flash went by, Camilla was gone.

I turned back to the window. I was definitely not into boats anymore. Maybe the president would not get to deduct his ocean racer. Maybe I would toss a coin to decide if he could. Maybe I'd write a Cicero memorandum in memory of Littlefield.

I said several words out loud. Shit, fuck, you know the

words. I stopped looking at the storm, and let my head slump down. More lightning. It lit up the white stripes on my tie as if I'd bought it at one of those novelty shops where they give you a tie and a battery pack. The stripes turned on, as if I'd pressed a hidden button, and seemed to twirl. A snake reaching up to my neck. I couldn't see the top of the tie, the snake's head, I didn't know how far the snake had gotten. Somewhere under my electric tie was a body. The body had an irrepressible desire to strangle Lawrence.

43

I went home, and had a hard time because of the storm
— the one in my office, not the one outside. I couldn't
get to sleep, and in the morning I rolled into the office
blurry-eyed but at exactly nine-thirty. I suppose I did
care whether Lawrence made it. I was hoping that he
would take a long walk — like the ones in the old
Cagney movies — to Cosmo's office. Because Cosmo
Bass looked like Cagney, there was at least some tiny
basis for my silly fantasy. I wanted Lawrence in the
electric chair. But I didn't want him to do it manfully,
the way Cagney wanted to, and usually did, unless a
priest had convinced him to scream in order to provide
proof for juvenile delinquents that crime did not pay. I
wanted Lawrence to crawl out of Bass's office weeping.

Lawrence wept, but he kept the tears in check until
he'd had his second glass of champagne. When you're
elevated to the partnership the secretaries bring out
champagne, and secret little cakes and cookies. They
must know ahead of time what's going to happen.
Probably Cosmo Bass's secretary alerts them. So there is
a sudden surprise party at the firm for the new partner.
New partner Lawrence.

I never got to see him on his way to Bass's office, and
didn't know he'd made it until I heard the party. The
sounds of a party in a Wall Street law firm suddenly

replacing the sound of typewriters is strange and eerie, and naturally attracts you.

Lawrence was pouring champagne into paper cups forced at him by the hands of partners, associates and secretaries. I guess he had a right to smile; eight long years of work, and he'd made it. He could go to the Wednesday partnership lunches, and talk about associates' futures instead of worrying what the partners had planned for him. He was suddenly released from a gigantic burden of doubt. So he poured champagne, shook hands and wept. I noticed that Cosmo Bass did not attend the party, but Lawrence was happy anyway, riding high even though his elevation to partnership had something to do with the heart attack of his mentor, Wellington Rolls. Maybe if I'd gotten to Rolls faster, maybe he would have been in better condition now, able to return to the firm. I'll never know, but I do not think Captain Rolls would have made Lawrence a partner. The Captain was capable of anything, of course, but there were certain standards he maintained for his officers and men.

Lawrence saw me through his tears.

"Get some champagne," he screamed.

I nodded. It was a big group of people, which was nice, because the crowd made it impossible for me to get anywhere near Lawrence and congratulate him. Hell, would I have congratulated him? Or punched him? I'm glad I didn't have to make a decision. The crowd had pushed Camilla Newman off to the side, too. She saw me and brought a cup over.

"Thanks," I said. "Sorry about last night."

"What?"

It was hard to hear with all the fuss everyone was making about Lawrence.

"I'm sorry."

"Will you talk to me?"

"Sure," I said.

"When?"

"Anytime," I told her. At least that's what I tried to say. And hoped she heard. There was a lot of noise, increasing with the amount of champagne. She said something back to me. I really didn't hear it. But I decided she'd just come to me. She vaporized in the crowd.

I was proud of myself. I hadn't said anything nasty to her. I hadn't asked if she was happy now, if her dreams were all fulfilled.

Lawrence got up on top of a desk and told everyone how much he appreciated the surprise party, and how much he liked us all. I measured him as he talked. He was about my size, but fatter around the stomach. I was pretty sure I could take him. Especially if I hit him first, before he realized what was happening.

Sure, I could take him by surprise. He was a partner now. How could an associate hit a partner? Maybe I could hit him twice before he understood.

I would aim for his neck, the windpipe. If I connected well, he would go down on the floor gurgling, his hands at his collar. I'd grab his tie, bring him up for the second punch. This one would go directly into his face. I would want him to have some marks he'd see in the morning.

I would probably only have to hit him twice, I decided. Any more than that might be murder. I would have to remember to control myself. But it would be sad not to be able to give him at least one good punch in that stomach. It needed toning up.

44

The telephone rang in my office. I thought it was Newman calling to make an appointment for our talk. I was beginning to understand that I ought to talk to her, and control myself. If she still needed to talk to me after our thunderstorm conference, there was something important on her mind. Maybe I didn't understand. I probably didn't, given my track record with Camilla Newman. Maybe she'd even tell me something that would make me stop wanting to kill Lawrence. It is not productive to walk around wanting to kill someone.

I answered.

"Can you talk?" Littlefield asked.

"Christ," I said. "Littlefield. Where the hell are you?"

"Can you talk?"

"Jesus," I said. "Littlefield."

"Appropriate," he answered. "Littlefield has been resurrected."

"You bastard. Where have you been? Yes, I can talk. For Christ sake. Hold on."

I told Mrs. Moultrie to hold all my calls. I told her to stop anyone from approaching my office. Anyone, I thought, even Camilla Newman. It's very dramatic to ask your secretary to hold all your calls. Especially when you're an associate, and hardly ever have important ones.

"Where are you?" I said.

"Physically?"

He was not in New York. The phone connection had the slight hum of long distance fatigue.

"Yes," I said. "Where the hell are you?"

"I am in New Haven. Calling you from the offices of the *Yale Law Journal*. The quarters are rather cramped here. You realize of course that the *Yale Law Journal* is in an atticlike dwelling. We have nothing comparable to the setup at Harvard. Your small white *Law Review* building that stands by itself, aloof from the rest of the school. We are not so exclusive."

"Listen," I said, "I wasn't on the *Law Review*. Will you come up with some facts? What are you doing in New Haven? You had a plan. Is this part of it?"

"Of course," he said. "May I congratulate myself?"

"Congratulations," I added, redundantly.

"Thank you," he said. "I am proofreading the galleys of my masterpiece, the interconnected chain of Cicero memoranda, which are the featured articles in this month's *Yale Law Journal*. May I add that the especially fine piece I did for Lynch will be on view in the following issue? I do, sincerely, believe it was my masterpiece. At least it was the only memorandum I have ever written under conditions of complete abstinence."

"I don't understand," I said. "Slow down."

"What's your problem?" he said.

"Start with the interconnected chain of Cicero memoranda," I said.

"You will recall that I became so bored with my work at the firm, that I wrote a series of memoranda for the tax department that analyzed current decisions of the Internal Revenue Service in terms of the great legal philosophers."

"I remember all that," I said. "What the hell do you think got you fired?"

"Now, remember that I disguised my citations of the great legal scholars by . . ." He paused. "What the hell," he said. "Look, I made up case names."

"I know all that," I said. "But how does it tie in? What was the plan?"

"Simply put," Littlefield said, and, of course it was impossible for him to put anything simply, but I let him talk anyway. "I have taken out the fictitious case names, and replaced them with the proper citations. I have also deleted the names of our clients, et cetera, so that the papers are not connected with the firm. It is, of course, against the canon of ethics to speak about clients. Cleaned up, in the manner I have just mentioned, the tax memoranda become, suddenly, the most brilliant tax study that has appeared in recent years. You ask: interconnected? Yes. I have linked all of the cleaned-up, polished Cicero memoranda into one gigantic paper analyzing the Internal Revenue Code in terms of fundamental principles. By the way, you are speaking to Assistant Professor Littlefield. I argued for the title of Associate Professor, but they were not prepared to go that far. I even tried to bluff them by suggesting that I would take my work elsewhere, possibly to the *Harvard Law Review*. Unfortunately, my bluff did not work, so it is only Assistant Professor Littlefield. Yet, I am on salary. And I believe within a year's time it will be Associate Professor. Once the jealousy of my colleagues has abated. Perhaps even full Professor."

"What the hell does it mean, Assistant Professor Littlefield?"

"I am on the faculty of the Yale Law School. I have returned."

"You're too young to get on the faculty."

"Too young?" he said. "Perhaps. It is possible I may have to grow a beard. I do not want my students to treat me with disrespect. Yes. I am too young to be on the faculty, but too brilliant not to be. Moreover, I am hogging the *Yale Law Journal's* pages, and some professors whose work is not as good as mine are complaining. I suppose that has something to do with why it is Assistant Professor Littlefield and not Associate Professor Littlefield. Are you well?"

"Moderately," I said. "Better, now that I know what happened to you, Assistant Professor."

"I can't wait for the publication of these articles," he said. "I would really like a report on the reaction in the tax department. And of course, a report on Lynch when he sees the Cicero memorandum appear in print. By the way, I see that the two of you came through. I read of your victory in the *New York Times.* How did Lynch acquit himself?"

"He yelled a bit," I said. "But he did all right. And I think he's sad he fired you."

"I regarded it as an honor," Littlefield said. "Please, give him my warmest regards. I will always believe in my heart that if he had had more time to study the Cicero memorandum, he would have handed it in to the Court. Possibly, the only problem was that he reviewed it at three o'clock in the morning. Of course, possibly, he is an idiot."

"You took him by surprise. I mean, no cases."

"Cases, research. The law is too complicated. That is why I took it upon myself to uncomplicate the Internal Revenue Code. The taxpayers of the nation will be grateful. Once you return to fundamental principles, the entire code can be simplified. I believe that after the publication of my papers, the code may be reduced in bulk. It will no longer be a three-volume tome. Perhaps one volume, with my papers as an appendix."

"I wouldn't bet on it," I said.

"It does not matter in any case. It was not a part of my plan. How goes it at the firm? What news?"

"Goddamn it." I exploded. "Congratulations. You goddamned made it on to the faculty at Yale."

"The youngest member, as you say. Yes, I am happy with the results of my plan. Yes, it is splendid to be once again within the quadrangle. And it feels so much better here than it would have on the way down, had I jumped from my window. That was, of course, my only other option. Frankly, the firm was driving me nuts. And my Cicero work was bound to be discovered sooner or later. Luckily, it was later. Luckily, I had enough time to build up a substantial body of scholarly theory. But I ask, what news? Rolls' condition for example."

"Improving, I hear. They don't tell us much."

"Cosmo Bass?"

"At the last firm outing, he gave a short speech," I said. "He said, 'Rumors to the contrary notwithstanding, I shall never retire.' I think those were his exact words."

"And *In re Newman*?"

"Bad," I said. "And her friend Lawrence made partner."

"I suspected as much. Partner Lawrence. I can see that I retired from the firm at the right time. I also suspect there will be hidden repercussions. They may work in your favor. They may work against you."

"What repercussions?"

"Let's not dwell on the future," he said. "Why should we, when I am probably wrong? I have been wrong about a great many things concerning Bass and Marshall. I refuse to be the bearer of bad tidings. After all, I am your friend. However, if you run into trouble, feel free to consult me. By the way, I hear that the consulting fees one can earn in tax law are enormous. I expect that Assistant Professor Littlefield will soon be a rich man. For you, of course, no charge."

"What repercussions?"

"Forget it," Littlefield said. "I have been wrong about too many things at the firm to serve as your fortuneteller. I used to regard the firm as a gray line of lawyers marching steadily and stupidly toward the final precipice of death — servicing the clients of Cosmo Bass and leaving behind children and paper. Leaving school boards better than they found them, making baldness respectable. Providing the deep guttural voices booming behind the ministers in Connecticut and Westchester: 'I shall not want . . .' I pictured them as a great gray engine, all lined up like pistons, metal-gray faces and suits. The pistons pumping, lights blinking, typewriters pounding, bells ringing, secretaries huddled around these piston men, oiling. I was wrong. My God, consider the strange individual abnormality of our friends Lynch and Rolls. Consider even the strange sayings of the benefactor, Bass. Who can tell what will happen with men like these?"

I decided to pin him down when I saw him. I wanted to see him soon.

"Get down here to New York," I said. "I need friends."

"If possible I shall never again visit New York. Come to New Haven. Come this weekend. I shall introduce you to editors at the *Journal* who may assist in curing your problem with Miss Newman. There is one particular diminutive blonde. And others."

"I'll come this weekend," I said. "I'll forget the work."

"Wonderful," he answered, "I shall prepare proper festivities. I believe that as an assistant professor, I am entitled to charge almost anything to the school. You shall find me at the *Journal* offices. I will work until the time you arrive, making sure, therefore, that I will be able to take off the entire weekend. Yes, I will prepare a proper feast. Acapulco Gold."

"Just get some booze," I said.

"Anything you say. Your morals are peculiarly silly."

"Camilla Newman told me that, too."

"I can see it is certainly time for a visit. I waited far too long before getting in touch with you. I apologize. I was extremely busy getting my plan moving. But that is no excuse. It was selfish of me not to have called. The mitigating circumstances were that I was desperate. Can you hold out until the weekend? Perhaps I could train in to New York. It would be horrible, but . . ."

"I can hold out," I said, cutting him off. "You've made me feel better, just talking to you."

"It works both ways," he said. "Reciprocity. A fundamental natural-law axiom. And one violated, of course, at the firm."

*　　*　　*

When we'd finished talking, I felt a lot better and had no desire to work.

I strolled out of my office. There had been no calls, Mrs. Moultrie said. And only one visitor. Camilla Newman. She had left no message, but my secretary told me that she'd been on her way out, apparently leaving for the day.

45

No one knew where Camilla was, but I knew she was not with Lawrence, because the new partner with his new responsibilities was working late. I kept trying her apartment, but there was no answer until exactly eleven at night.

"Now you're available," she yelled into the phone. "Bastard."

"Calm down," I said. "Don't hang up."

"Bastard," she yelled. "You don't care about people."

"I care about you," I said. "I love you. What's wrong?"

She hung up on me. I called her right back. The phone rang about twenty times before she answered.

"I needed you," she screamed. "You wouldn't let me explain." Now she was sobbing.

"Explain it all to me," I said. "Stay where you are. I'm coming over."

"I knew something was going to happen. I needed help. Bastard."

"I'll be there as fast as I can," I said.

"I won't."

"Stay there."

"I'm not going to stay in this asshole, goddamned, one-room shithouse any longer. I just came to get some money. I'm going."

"Wait for me."

"Fuck yourself."

"Wait five minutes. What's wrong?"

"I'm going."

"For Christ sake, where?"

"Out. Walking. I don't know. Maybe to Central Park. I need air."

"Will you wait five minutes?" Central Park at eleven at night? She was clearly out of her mind. How long would it take me to get there? If I couldn't catch her at her apartment, I was going to have to plunge around in the bushes of Central Park like a rapist.

"Camilla," I said, "what's wrong? Tell me?" Keep her talking, I thought.

"You bastard. What's *wrong*? What the hell do you think is wrong? Everyone is a bastard. Everyone."

"You're not," I said. "Don't go out. Let me talk to you. Let me come over."

"Every one of them is a bastard," she screamed.

I asked her again what was wrong. Maybe if I could get her to say it, she'd calm down.

"I'm a better fucking lawyer than any of them," she said, "including Cosmo Bass."

"You're right," I said. "You're a great lawyer."

"You're goddamned right I am."

"Camilla," I said, "listen. What happened? Did you get screamed at? Did someone hate your work?"

"You asshole," she said. "You stupid, stupid idiot, moron. How many times have I been screamed at by Wellington Rolls?"

"Tell me," I said. "Just tell me."

"I've been fired," she shouted, and hung up.

*   *   *

My cab driver hit the East Side Highway. Every time I promised him more money, I got an extra ten miles on the speedometer. Luckily, he was young and could drive.

"Are you paying if there's a ticket?" he asked.

"Sure I'm paying. And give me ten more miles. How does a thirty-dollar fare sound to you?"

"Reasonable," he said. "I'd like forty, but this doesn't go any faster. I got forty once."

I told him to stop talking, and keep driving. He'd almost sideswiped a limousine, but then he buckled down and concentrated. Running a series of lights, we got to Camilla's apartment building in just inside of ten minutes. She was coming out the door.

"Don't touch me," she said. I kept a hold on her arm anyway.

"Where're the bucks?" the cab driver yelled.

"I said don't touch me. I'll scream."

"Do it," I said.

"Oh fuck it," she said quietly. I led her over to the cab, pushed her in. I told the driver to take us to my apartment.

"No," she said loudly, "Central Park."

"You want a drive through the park?" the cab driver said.

"Just drop me at the park. This clown can go to his apartment. Maybe you can drop him first. It's on the way."

"Go to the park," I told him. "And don't drop me."

"A wise decision," he said. "You don't want to go walking alone by yourself this time of night, not in the park."

"Eat it," Miss Newman told him.

*   *   *

"We'll probably get mugged and killed here," I said. When the wind rattled a bush, I jumped. I saw shadows on the other side of the knoll. Maybe they were little kids. Maybe they were bigger. "Talk to me," I said. "Talk it out."

"Maybe he knew beforehand that he was going to make it," she said. "I don't know. He started suggesting it might be easier if I moved to another law firm. It might look better. I told him to get fucked. Why the hell should I move to another firm? He said because he couldn't move when he was coming up for partnership. He said it wouldn't make any difference to me. I'd only put in a year at the firm. Bastard. I told him to eat it. Maybe I'd only put in a year, but it was my year. I actually liked working for Wellington Rolls."

"I can see how you could," I said. "At one point I kind of got off on it, too."

Someone was laughing down in a bush-filled gully. It was probably a rape. I was beginning to think I saw people in trees.

"Then he makes it. I could see it in his eyes right there at the party. He tells me now I've got to go to another firm, because how can you cross partnership-associate lines. I mean, he says there might be a messy divorce and everything, but it will all be fine if I'm at another firm. This happened just three hours after he had made partner. He was partner-mad. I don't know who the hell he thinks I am. I told him to get fucked. If he was a big partner, then he could fire me. He said people were beginning to know what was going on. I told him I didn't give a damn. I think he was upset that I didn't fit into his neat little partner plans. I also told him that I wasn't going to hang out with him anymore, so what the hell was the problem? I told him he was a bastard, coward, and I didn't sleep with mules. What was the problem? Was it just that it bothered him to have me around?"

"Let's get out of the park," I said. "Did you hear that scream? If they weren't laughing too, I'd call the cops."

"Are you going to let me talk? This is my park, it's mine as much as anyone's. Fuck them."

"Talk," I said. Fast, I hoped.

" 'You are definitely not going to follow my suggestions?' Lawrence said. At that point I gave him the bird. He was coming off like a partner. Words weren't adequate. If he'd said anything else, I'd have slapped him silly."

"Maybe I will," I said.

"He's not worth it. Let me explain how the process works. I'm called in by the managing partner, not by Cosmo Bass, not by Lawrence. And this little man says, 'We've been reviewing your work, Miss Newman, and we suggest you might find it more suitable working where your true talents, and you do have them, might be better appreciated.' If Rolls were there, I'd have gone to him. He's not stupid. All he cares about is the work. The hell with everything, everyone else. I did the damn work. He knew it. But Rolls isn't here, and I'm talking with some slimy little man I've just passed in the halls, maybe twice. I mean, the managing partner just handles administrative details. I said, 'Are you firing me? Where is the proof? What is wrong with my work?' He kept saying 'I suggest you seek employment elsewhere. Where your talents . . .' You know what the hell he said.

"We sat there for maybe twenty minutes. Every time he suggested I said, 'Am I fired?' And asked for proof about my incompetence as a lawyer. I just wanted him to say *fired*. Do it right, the way you said Lynch did with Littlefield. Christ, maybe he wanted to preserve my reputation, you know, I would resign. Therefore, I had not been fired. Therefore, I could get another job. Great."

She was talking loudly, forcefully, and I was sure her voice was drawing every mugger in the city to us. I saw them approaching in a circle. Our only hope was that there would be so much competition the muggers would end up killing each other over the issue of who would get to do the actual mugging.

"I got so damn angry," she said, "so damn angry, that finally I stood up and slapped him across the face. He should have been Lawrence."

"I'll take care of that," I said.

"No you won't," she said. "I don't want you to. Tell me you won't. They'll just fire you."

"All right," I said, "I won't."

"I slapped a little man I didn't know, who probably hated doing what he had been told to do. Then I said, 'Am I fired?' 'Yes, Miss Newman,' he said, 'you're fired. I'm sorry.' He said he was sorry. I came running to your office. Where were you? On the telephone. Your secretary goddamned barred your door. That ended it for me. I left. I've just been walking ever since. Goddamned fired."

"You could take it all to Cosmo Bass," I said. "He'd kill Lawrence. And whoever else was involved."

"I don't know," she said. "I need time to think."

She was winding down.

"Let's think at my place. This weekend, we'll go to New Haven. A big party. It's going to be for you." I told her about Littlefield.

"Let me think here for a minute," she said. "You go. I'll sit and think."

"Listen," I said, "we'll probably get killed here. Think about that too." It couldn't be joggers doing all that running through the bushes.

"You're nice," she said. "Thanks."

"Thanks," I answered.

"Lawrence is fucked up."

"Right," I said, "he's certainly fucked up."

"I'm going to begin to feel better," she said, "I will feel better."

"That's right," I said.

"I will feel better," she said loudly.

"Sure you will."

"I'll make myself feel better."

"Right," I said. "Sure."

"And I thought I had things under control. Do you still love me?"

"I don't know what I think," I said. "I feel blown away. I don't have it straight. I love you when I'm mad at you. But you've blown me away." I put my arm around her anyway. "I'm not going to lie to make you feel better," I said. "I don't know what I think."

"So you don't love me?"

"Does it make any goddamned difference right now?" I said.

"Sure it makes a difference." She cuddled against me. "Sure. I want people to love me."

"You don't love me," I said. Cold pure logic. Also the sign of a sucker being born.

"I could love you."

"Great," I said.

"So we'll still not sleep together," she said. "Right?"

"Right," I said.

"That's too bad. You were the only person I actually liked sleeping with."

"Right," I said. "Sure." I was going under like a sleepwalking sucker.

"You were the only one I liked sleeping with. For Christ sake, it's the truth. Lawrence was a jerk." Sure, I thought, sure. And, of course, I began to believe it. "Actually we barely slept together."

"If you like me so much let's get the hell out of the park," I said. "If you care about who you sleep with so much let's run before you get raped."

"I do like you that much," she said. "I think I love you."

* * *

We ran for the subway, nothing chasing us except the day she'd had. After twenty minutes, we got a train. It was late at night, but the train was crowded. We squeezed into two seats. The man next to Camilla looked like a tired lawyer. The *Wall Street Journal* lay on top of an attaché case held up by his knees.

"How are you?" Camilla asked him. I'd certainly put her in a better mood.

The tired lawyer gave Camilla one of those sidelong, subway stares. She doesn't look like a freak, he was thinking, so why does she talk like one?

"This young man next to me is the only one I like sleeping with," Camilla said to the lawyer. "Now do you believe me?" she asked me. She turned back to the lawyer and gave him a pretty smile.

The tired lawyer started to get up. You knew he'd ridden this subway a million times, knew he'd been forced to move by muggers, winos, sickies, panhandlers, and people who'd thrown up on him. Now pretty young girls who looked like his daughter were forcing him to move. Camilla seemed to have pushed him to some ultimate turning point. He sat down. He unfolded his paper again, began to read.

"Actually, I've never slept with her," I said. "Actually I don't even know her."

"Can I read in peace?" the middle-aged lawyer said. "Will both of you shut up?"

"Actually, he's lying," Camilla said. "Actually, he's

fucked me a few thousand times. Most recently on the desk of Cosmo Bass, founder of Bass and Marshall. You've heard of Mr. Bass? A great lawyer. A gentleman. A great place to fuck."

He got up again. He got up slowly, aching all over, tired, middle-aged, shaking his head. He got off at the next stop. I figured he'd reached the point where he'd begin taking taxis. I hope he found one. It was hard to rationalize what we'd done to him. But now Camilla was fighting back. Maybe that was the rationalization. Now all we needed was a plan. Which we could get from Littlefield.

The hell with it, I thought, you only have one girl. I began kissing Camilla in the subway car. If there is only one, the rest of it doesn't matter.

46

I'd learned by now that it helped to swivel my chair and take regular peeks at the view from my window. It disconnected me from the firm, connecting me with a four-by-six square of the outside world. It was a bright, sunny day. The street looked good. Its narrow twists and huge buildings reminded me of a cowpath gone mad. There was no logical order to the location of these huge buildings. Someone, probably an Indian, had taken a shortcut, dodging trees. The path got worn down, used by others. Then a bunch of whites came and paved it over after it had been widened by their cows galumping along it. Then the huge buildings went up. That was the only explanation I could think of. No one in his right mind would have put the heart of the business world, and the heart of its legal machine, on a street this small and silly looking.

"Mr. Lawrence would like to see you," Mrs. Moultrie said.

"When?"

"He asked to see you now."

"He did, did he?"

You could say that if you were a partner: "Now."

"Tell him I'll be along in a while," I said.

"With him shortly?"

"Quote," I told her, "tell him I'll be along in a while. I'm busy looking at the street."

"It's your life," she said. She meant my death. Lawrence the partner. I had a good secretary. She cared what happened to me. In fact, I did too. As Littlefield repeated on our memorable weekend in New Haven, there are "options within options." I went back to my desk. On it was a letter from Wellington Rolls. Captain Rolls indeed appreciated the role I'd played in saving his life. He wished there was some way he could "amply" reward me. But could one amply reward such an act? If we were on shipboard, I thought, he could order the whole crew out. I could march down and receive a medal, while Rolls signaled the gunners to fire the cannons. It was a damn nice letter. He would be back on the quarterdeck soon, he said, signing his letter "affectionately." If I wanted to be a partner, I was actually in a pretty good position. Two of the most iconoclastic, irrational, yet strangely appealing partners were definitely on my side, Lynch and Rolls. I believe that even Cosmo Bass had some sort of affection for me, although even if it were true, it would never alter a decision he made concerning the firm.

"I delivered your quote," she said, returning. "He didn't sound pleased with it."

"If he wants me, he can come here," I told her.

"Would you like me to convey that message?"

"No," I said, "I'll go shortly."

Of course, if I wanted to become a partner, I'd have to choose a specialty. Maybe I'd go into litigation, working with Lynch. We had won a case. It was conceivable we might win another. Then it would be a long wait. At least another six years. Rolls might die of a heart attack. Lynch might be made a judge. Cosmo Bass might begin to receive reports from Lawrence concerning the quality of my work. In the end, I might take the long walk to Bass's office and get fired. Of course, I could become friends with Lawrence. Six years is a long time, and anything is conceivable. Or I could follow Littlefield's advice and become a partner immediately. There were, as he said, options within options.

"He's angry," she said. "And wants to know what's holding you up."

"You didn't make up any excuses?"

She looked sheepish. "I did tell him you were very busy," she admitted. "Was that wrong?"

"No," I said, "it's fine."

I loved the way Lawrence was trying to get me. Here we were maybe forty yards away from each other. He told his secretary to get me. She called my secretary, who talked to me. He was certainly playing big partner. I decided it was time to pay him a visit.

*   *   *

"You wanted to see me?" I said from the door.

"What the hell did you think? Didn't you get the message, or is my secretary nonfunctional? Maybe I'll have to straighten her out."

"I got all the messages," I said. "Don't blame her."

"Then what the hell were you doing?"

"Environmental research," I said.

"For Christ sake," he snapped.

He was trying to play Captain Rolls, but he didn't have the brains for it. Or the office. It was too small. Papers were piled on the floor. Various parts of Hudson Street deals, in various stages of completion. I had to admit that at least he seemed to be doing a lot of work.

"You know what happens when you get to be a partner?" he said.

"What happens?" I said.

"You think there is going to be less work, but there's more. When you make it, you'll find out. And the pressure is greater. You're in charge. You've got to live with the pressure. You think the strain will be off, but it isn't. You get a few seconds of glory, then it's back to the work and there's more of it."

"You do look busy," I said. And messy, I thought, not spiffy, the way Rolls would have liked. The top button of his shirt was undone, and he'd slipped the knot of his tie down. Captain Rolls would have straightened out this seaman, even though Lawrence was a partner.

"For Christ sake," he snapped, "I look busy? There are hundreds of deals going on. I need some bodies. You're going down to Hudson Street this evening."

"Awfully sorry," I said. "I've got other plans." I would not normally have said something like "awfully sorry," but I'd spent the weekend with Littlefield.

"What plans?"

"I prefer not to reveal them." I wondered if that was a line out of "Bartleby." I'd read the story because Cosmo Bass asked me to. It was O.K. But I liked *The Honorable Peter Sterling* better. That was one hell of a book, and older than Cosmo.

"Are you giving me some kind of shit?" Lawrence said. "Don't you understand? This is priority. It has to go out. I've got to have mules."

At least Rolls used the term huskies. I preferred the image of mushing along some snowy trail. Moreover, mules reminded me of Camilla Newman. Mule was what she'd called Lawrence.

"What was the question?" I said. "There was a question."

"What's the matter with you?"

"Lawrence, that wasn't your question. You asked if I was giving you shit, didn't you?"

The socketlike eyes gave me a binocular look. He was snapping out of the work syndrome and beginning to recognize me.

"What?" he yelled.

"You asked if I was giving you shit. I am. Question. Answer. Don't you understand English?"

The binoculars that someone had managed to implant deeply into his skull wobbled around. He reddened. Now that was more like Wellington Rolls.

"I can fire you," he yelled. "One more word and maybe I will." Good. This was partner Lawrence talking. New partner. Power partner. Deal-maker. Mule skinner.

"And I can beat the shit out of you," I said. "You don't have the guts to fire me. I don't go out like Newman. I go to Bass first. You don't have the damned guts. I don't know what the partnership agreement states, but Bass will kick your butt over the Newman thing. If he can't fire you, he'll put you in the mail room. So, it's like this, one more word and I beat the shit out of you. Am I getting through? Do you understand? I'm not supposed to hurt you. At least I've been asked not to. I do try to keep my promises. So I'm going this far: I'll give you the chance. Not one more word."

There was a small streak of Rolls in him. Either that or he was an idiot: "You little bastard," he snapped. He leaned forward as if he were going to bite me. His head came halfway over the glass top of his desk. The tie came with it.

I grabbed the tie, and yanked it back as hard as I could. The knot went fully tight around his neck as if he'd just been hung. At the same time, I jerked down on the tie fast and hard. His head wacked on the glass top.

They make good ties at Brooks Brothers. It would be

easy to hang people with them. Someone also makes good strong glass tops. The glass held. His head hit as if he'd fallen on concrete. I gave his forehead a good push back. Like a rag doll, he flopped back into his chair, slowly recovering, his head swinging from side to side. If he didn't get it together in time, I decided I'd loosen his tie for him. I didn't want to kill him. He came to in a minute and a half, not completely conscious, but enough so that his hands went to the neck, clawing at the tie.

"I suggest you slide the knot down," I said.

He was moaning, didn't hear me. But he finally got it loosened enough to breathe. Then he fell forward. I thought maybe he was going to throw up.

"Try breathing," I told him. Actually he was trying. It just didn't sound that way. It was moan-breathing. I guess he was in pretty bad shape. When I flipped him back up into a more or less sitting position, his binoculars were red.

"Are we going around again?" I asked.

"What?" he moaned. It was a horrible, choked loud moan, and I suddenly remembered that his door was open. Yelling was normal. But dying gasps might bring his secretary. I shut his door, punched the intercom, told her that Mr. Lawrence requested no further calls, or interruptions. We were deeply involved in one of his major deals. No interruptions, even from bank presidents.

"You bastard," he gasped. Maybe I had a secret streak of Rolls in me. Training was enjoyable. I wanted him to perform: I wanted to teach Lawrence not to say bastard. That seemed reasonable. And possible.

"Don't say bastard," I told him. "Can you hear me?"

"Bastard," he moaned. Maybe I wasn't being fair. He'd gotten a good dose of the glass. Maybe he couldn't hear me. Maybe he was talking in his sleep. But there was also Camilla Newman.

"Don't do it," I told him.

"Little fucking bastard." He choked it out.

Suddenly, I really wanted to kill him. But hell, Lawrence was in no position even to pinch my arm. He was bleeding from his mouth and nose. And I was not Wellington Rolls.

I arranged him as best I could, and went out to see his secretary, closing the door of partner Lawrence behind me.

"I'm afraid there has been an accident," I told her.

"What? What kind?" She stood up.

"Everything is perfectly all right, but Mr. Lawrence became so excited while putting together one of his important deals that he managed to smash his head on his desk."

"He slipped?"

"That is exactly right," I said. "He slipped." A slip of the tongue. "We don't want to get anyone excited, but the building people have to be called. I believe that Mr. Lawrence will be able to walk, but I think that he will need assistance to do so."

"Right," she said. She seemed to have a cool head. And no desire to plunge into Lawrence's office. I left the rest of the job to her, and started for Cosmo Bass's office. I had decided to follow Littlefield's advice and become a partner immediately.

Epilogue

I've been typing this out at the offices of *Newman and Weston*. Littlefield was right: Newman did agree that I could be a partner, too, although I think she liked the idea of having at least one associate. I argued that a law firm called *Newman* sounded stupid. I think *Newman and Weston* sounds as good as *Bass and Marshall*.

It's taken me quite a long time to write all this down, but at the beginning I had to do something. Sitting in a two-person office begins to depress you after a while, when there isn't any work to do. For a while, I thought we might have to sit here as long as Cosmo Bass did. That worried me, because we didn't have enough money to last two years. We conserved our funds by moving into the same apartment, and got a little more money from my family, but it still wasn't much. I doubt we'd have made it if Rolls hadn't gotten back on his feet.

The captain has expressed his appreciation by sending us legal work. No big deals, but we've been down to Hudson Street twice. Since we've started to get some business, I actually have to do some work, and can't keep typing. Cosmo Bass has even sent a small matter to us, a piece of estate work. He shook my hand when I resigned from the firm. I like to think he was sorry to see me go. If Lynch remembers me, and sends a client, we may actually hire an associate. So I'm stopping here, and giving the damn thing to our part-time secretary to type up.

I just hope I'm not conveying the wrong impression. It's not that we're flooded with work. If it were not against the rules of the Bar Association, I'd ask you to send us anything you can. We might even do it for free, if you've got a good idea and we think you might develop into a wealthy client. Hell, we might do it for free anyway. But I can't ask you to send us work. It is against the rules to solicit. On the other hand, Newman is an excellent lawyer, and what other two-man firm lists a Yale law professor as "of counsel"? I think I'm allowed to tell you that much. Take it from there.

By the way, it's probably against the rules of the Bar Association to write about law firms. So I may be in trouble already.